PRAISE FOR WILLIAM BERNH
NOV

"*Twisted Justice* has the most mind-blowing twists of any thriller I've ever read. And everything works."

— RICK LUDWIG, AUTHOR OF *PELE'S FIRE*

"I could not put *Trial by Blood* down. The plot is riveting —with a surprise after the ending, when I thought it was all over....This book is special."

— NIKKI HANNA, AUTHOR OF *CAPTURE LIFE*

"*Court of Killers* is a wonderful second book in the Daniel Pike legal thriller series....[A] top-notch, suspenseful crime thriller."

— TIMOTHY HOOVER

"Once started, it is hard to let [*The Last Chance Lawyer*] go, since the characters are inviting, engaging and complicated....You will enjoy it."

— *CHICAGO DAILY LAW BULLETIN*

"Bernhardt is the undisputed master of the courtroom drama."

— *LIBRARY JOURNAL*

TWISTED JUSTICE

A Daniel Pike Novel

WILLIAM BERNHARDT

BABYLON BOOKS

For my WriterCon partners:
Rene, Melanie, Laurel, Chris, Cheri, and Christy

Things fall apart; the centre cannot hold;
    Mere anarchy is loosed upon the world,
    The blood-dimmed tide is loosed, and everywhere
    The ceremony of innocence is drowned...

— "THE SECOND COMING," W. B. YEATS

FOREWORD

Chapter 1 is a flash-forward. Chapter 2 takes place several weeks earlier, and from that point on the story is told in chronological order. If Chapter 1 appeared in chronological order, it would come between chapters 35 and 36.

For the benefit of those who have not read *Trial by Blood*, a small portion of the Epilogue from that novel is repeated here in Chapter 2.

THE LOGIC OF SACRIFICE

CHAPTER ONE

ELENA EMERGED FROM THE WATER AN INCH AT A TIME, FIRST THE top of her head, then her forehead, her face, her neck. She moved slowly, clinging to the ocean bed as if walking underwater came naturally, as if she were a mermaid who had suddenly discovered her legs. Her shoulders rose above the water line, then her arms, her breasts. She imagined herself as Botticelli's Venus emerging from a watery half-shell, hair slicked back, body on display for all to see.

"Mama, look! That lady isn't wearing anything!"

"Where did she come from?" another voice asked. "I've been on this beach all day."

"She's hurt! Someone do something!"

Elena heard the cries echo in the clouded reaches of her mind, but the meaning of the words did not register. She had been damaged and she had traveled so far, so fast. Each step was a struggle. She moved like a relentless sea nymph with nothing to hide, no cause for shame, each step a triumph only she understood. The sand oozed between her toes, slowing her, but the sun felt so warm on her body that she almost wanted to cry.

"Hey, kid! You need some help?"

For the briefest of moments, she allowed her gaze to drift. She was bruised and blood-blemished, on her arms, on her left thigh, on the side of her face. Venus should be immaculate, not battered and beaten. Barely alive. How much had she lost? How much more could she lose?

Someone ran beside her, a young man, a little older than she was. Bearded, bloated, hardly Michelangelo's David, but bearing a concerned expression. "You want my towel?"

She tilted her head slightly. Why would she want his towel? The sunshine was a delightful change, after so many days of darkness.

"You know. To cover yourself."

Her gaze intensified. A small crease formed between her eyebrows.

"Um, maybe you don't know, but...you lost your suit. And I think someone already called the cops."

Her suit? Did he mean her rags? Her slave clothes? She was glad to be rid of them.

"You should probably see a doctor, too. You're banged up pretty bad."

A doctor. A doctor. She thought she knew what he meant. Her brain was still muddy, like the sand beneath her feet. But she couldn't allow that. She couldn't bear to be trapped, confined, not again. She fought so hard to be free. Better to bleed to death than be a prisoner.

"Look, I don't mean to be pushy, but I know a guy. I could get you in to see him. And then maybe we could get you some clothes and a hot cup of coffee. You'll feel better in—"

She ran. Bolted away with all the speed she could muster.

She kept running until she reached a brown dirty strip surrounded by tall trees. Two more seconds and she found a sidewalk. A second after that, a street.

Cars zigzagged across her field of vision. She barely recognized them. It had been so long. But she had to make it across. She had to flee.

She darted into the street. Horns blared. Brakes squealed. She heard shouting in a tongue she did not understand. Keep moving, she told herself. Don't let them capture you.

Water flew off her hair and skin as she increased her speed. She heard a whistle somewhere behind her. "Stop! Hey, stop!"

No, no, no, no, no. She could not let it happen to her, not again. She would not be someone else's tool. She had to be free.

"Please stop! You're hurt!"

She knew she was injured, but she also knew she would get better. If only they would leave her alone. She looked around desperately, trying to find someplace to hide. Shops, restaurants, bicycles, boats. She didn't know where she was. She didn't know where she would be safe.

She heard rapid footsteps gaining on her. She crashed into people, trying to move faster. She hit a large woman full on, knocking her to the pavement. The woman shouted. Suddenly everyone was looking at her. Suddenly there was nowhere to run.

Someone tackled her from behind. She fell hard. Her bare knees scraped against the concrete. Blood rose to the surface.

"Miss, I'm taking you into custody for your own safety. Do you know where you are?"

He whipped her body around to face him. He wore a uniform. Glittering pieces of metal. She tried to struggle. He grabbed her fists and forced them down, pinning them between her breasts.

"I'm sorry, miss. You're not leaving me any choice."

A second later, he snapped cuffs around her wrists.

She screamed. It was a loud, keening scream, like something a banshee might release. Piercing and penetrating, sharing her pain with everyone who heard it.

A large crowd gathered around them. "Kid, please. I'm trying to help you. Are your parents around here?"

She did not answer. She did not know what to say.

"Do you have anyone? Anyone we could call?"

She tried to remember, tried to bring back the shattered remnants of what came before. But it was so hard. And part of her didn't want to remember.

"Can you at least tell me who you are?"

Something triggered inside her head. "I am the wave that aches for the shore. I am the fire that never burns cold. I am the lover who can never be kissed."

Holding her beneath the arms, the man raised her to her feet. Between the gash in her side and the bruises on her knees, she could barely stand. "Sure, whatever. But can you give me a name?"

"Izzy. *Izzy?*" She shrieked, and all the strength went out of her. Her legs buckled. But for the man holding her, she would've crumpled to the pavement. "Please...don't let them take me back." Her eyes closed and she could feel her consciousness fading.

"Save the others," she mumbled, her last words before the sleep came. "Before it's too late."

CHAPTER TWO

Many Weeks Before

DAN ROLLED OVER, BUT THE BED ON HIS BOAT WAS SO SMALL THAT moving even slightly put him halfway on top of Camila. "What's that racket?"

She blew hair out of her face. "Someone is at your front door. If you can call it that."

He immediately tensed.

"Relax, Dan. Murderous thugs don't knock."

Sound point. And they would've come in the dark. The sun was already rising.

Camila touched his shoulder. "Probably a client who needs the city's most famous defense lawyer and can't wait for business hours."

"Maybe. Still weird." He grabbed a robe. "I'll see who it is."

"Right behind you."

"You don't have to—"

"Just in case you need a martial-arts mayor to take them out."

A minute later he was topside. He opened the outer door of the boat. Camila stood behind him, covering herself with a sheet.

Detective Kakazu waited outside.

"Jake? Kind of early. What's going on?"

He glanced at the two officers standing behind Kakazu, Sergeant Enriquez and a cop he didn't know. "I'm surprised you were sleeping," Kakazu said. "We've been awake all night."

"That doesn't explain why you're bothering us. Look, if this is some crap Belasco put you up to, forget it. Leave me alone."

The officers looked at one another.

Kakazu drew in his breath. "It does involve Belasco. In a way. He's dead."

His lips parted. "The district attorney? Dead? When? How?"

"We're only beginning to unpack the details..."

Camila pushed forward. "This is an outrage. I don't know what you're doing, detective, but it should have gone through the mayor's office first."

"That wasn't possible in this case, ma'am."

"And why not?"

"You couldn't be objective about your...paramour. And this involves you, too. Directly."

"Stop talking in riddles and tell me what you're babbling about."

The men glanced at one another. Kakazu shrugged. "You're going to find out soon enough. We received a recorded conversation by anonymous email. We've already checked to make sure it's authentic and hasn't been altered. Our experts say it's legit."

"Get to the point. What is it?"

Kakazu pulled out his phone and played a recording.

It didn't take long before Dan realized he was listening to his own voice. His and Camila's.

"There are ways we could deal with the district attorney."

"What do you mean?"

"We could have him taken care of."

"Just off him?"

"If he's on Sweeney's payroll, he deserves to be offed."

"You don't have to do that."

"For you, I would do anything."

"Likewise."

Kakazu withdrew a folded piece of paper and slapped it into Dan's hand. "This is a warrant. Pursuant to the authority of the St. Petersburg Police Department and Pinellas County, you're both under arrest. For the murder of District Attorney George Belasco."

DAN STARED THROUGH THE PLEXIGLAS SCREEN IN THE VISITATION room, as angry as he had ever been in his entire life. And he had been plenty angry on several occasions. He'd spent years making his rep as one of the best defense lawyers in the city, maybe the state. He'd built a sizeable bank account and a life that, on the whole, was a source of pride. He'd dedicated his life to protecting the innocent, making sure his clients weren't railroaded by the government.

Who was riding that railroad now? He'd acquired few details since his arrest, but he knew one thing for certain. Someone wanted him out of the way. He was on the express train to the death penalty.

He didn't like to admit it—but he was scared. He'd had people out to get him before, but never anything like this. He hadn't slept since they locked him up. His hands trembled and he didn't know what to do about it. The fluttering sensation inside his chest would not stop.

He'd peered through this Plexiglas screen before, but always from the other side. This was a completely different experience. His keen observational powers and his courtroom bag of tricks weren't helping. Normally, he had a gift for noticing what others did not, for making careful observations that later, once he connected the dots, brought unexpected insights. Sometimes those insights broke the case.

But that worked better in the courtroom than behind bars. All he could see at the moment was that, like him, his visitor was extremely angry.

His partner, Maria Morales, sat on the other side of the screen. She'd claimed to be his lawyer so she could get in. Long black hair. Barely any makeup. Earrings that matched the studs on her designer jeans.

He leaned forward on his elbows so she wouldn't detect the trembling. "Go ahead," Dan said into the antiquated phone receiver that allowed them to communicate. "Say it."

Maria pursed her lips. "Orange is not your color."

He smiled thinly. "Any legal advice?"

"You're in a truckload of trouble."

"Thank you, Clarence Darrow." He had another comment, but he suppressed it. He knew this comedy was a mask. Maria was worried about him.

She brushed her hair behind her shoulders. "How many times have I told you to dial it down? How many times have I suggested that you stop pissing off every authority figure you meet?"

"You think this is law enforcement exacting its revenge?"

"I don't know where it started. But when the opportunity arose, they pounced on you like salivating dogs."

"You think this is my fault."

"I don't know enough about it yet to assign fault." She frowned. "But yes."

Maria was younger than he was, but he valued her opinion, even when she was telling him something he didn't want to hear. She was the one who first recruited him into the law firm, an association of four lawyers led by a mysterious figure they knew as Mr. K. He gave them assignments and paid them generously for their services.

He wondered what K would think of this development. A murder warrant could double as his discharge papers from the Last Chance Lawyers.

"What happened to Belasco?"

"I don't know much. I know he was shot. Six times."

"Overkill."

"You'd think. Or a sign that someone seriously did not want him making a miraculous recovery." She glanced at her notes. "His body was found in an alley behind Beachcombers."

"A bar I frequent. Near the boat where I live."

"Exactly."

"It's a frame. Have you heard the recording?"

"Everyone has. Someone leaked it to the internet."

"It's a total misconstruction. We were kidding around."

"Doesn't sound like it."

"Camila was joking. Like, why don't we solve all our problems by eliminating the bad guy? She was being playful. We had just...just..."

"Oh ick. I don't want to hear about it."

"But you know. We were in one of those moods."

"So you said something incredibly stupid that's going to hang you."

"I didn't know we were being recorded."

"Who do you think planted the bug?"

"No idea. But I know who the obvious suspect is."

"Sweeney."

"Bingo." Conrad Sweeney was the richest, most successful, and most prominent man in St. Petersburg. He was a power-hungry power broker who liked to think he controlled the secret machinery that made the town tick. They had crossed paths on numerous occasions. After Dan thwarted Sweeney's plans to derail Camila's political career and uncovered the truth about the Coleman clan, Sweeney went on a rampage. He had expected trouble. But he didn't expect it to come this fast. Or this hard.

"So Sweeney had someone bug the boat, then sent the recording to the cops. It's an illegal wiretap. Can't be use in evidence."

"We both know the prosecution will find a way around that."

"And it's not enough evidence to support a capital murder charge."

"They'll find more. Probably have already."

He tried to stay calm. Maria's answers weren't making him feel better. But he knew she was right. "If Sweeney is behind the recording, did he also off Belasco?"

"Not himself. He'd get someone else to pull the trigger. Someone provided with a strong incentive to never reveal who hired him. And if that's true, the killer is probably miles away by now."

"True."

"Which means our chances of finding him are virtually nil."

"Also true."

"And the chances of tracing the murder back to Sweeney...?"

"Nonexistent. I hear what you're saying. Look, I don't expect you to handle this case. I can represent myself, at least—"

"There is no way in hell that's happening."

He pulled back. "Don't be shy, Maria. Tell me what you really think."

"I'm Latinx, Dan. I don't mince words. You can't represent yourself."

"I can."

"You're stupid sometimes, Dan, but not that stupid. You know the cliché. The lawyer who represents himself has a fool for a client. You can't see the big picture, especially not with an ego the size of the Taj Mahal. I will handle this defense."

"Mr. K might not like that."

"I don't give a damn. I—" Her voice choked. She averted her

eyes. "I—care about you, Dan. I'm not going to let Sweeney and his network of thugs get you executed."

He wasn't sure what to say. "Okay. Thank you."

"Don't make a big deal out of it." She still avoided eye contact. "You'd do the same for me."

"True enough." He knew Maria was doing her best to remain calm, but he was boiling inside. As a boy, he'd stood by helplessly as the cops hauled away his father and locked him up for a murder he didn't commit. He died in prison, long before Dan was old enough to help. Now someone was trying to do the same thing to him. And trapped in this detention center, he couldn't do anything about it. "Okay, your first assignment. Get me out of here."

"Bail on a violent capital offense? That will be tough."

"I'm a solid citizen with no record and plenty of money."

"Yeah. I'll run that up the flagpole and see who salutes."

"I need to get out of here."

"I agree." She paused. "Jimmy won't be able to carry on if you miss the weekly Gloomhaven game."

"You're right. Do it for him."

She almost smiled as she pulled a few documents out of her briefcase. "Do you have any idea what happened? Any at all?"

"None."

"Any alibi witnesses?"

"When did the murder occur?"

"I don't know."

"When the cops arrived, I was with Camila."

"Your girlfriend and alleged co-conspirator. That's not helpful."

"Sorry. We were celebrating my big courtroom win and… you know. It got kind of…intimate and—"

"Would you stop already? Double ick."

"By the way, where is Camila?"

"In the women's detention center."

"Have you talked to her?"

"No."

"Please do. Right after you leave here. She must be devastated. Her Senate campaign was barely getting started. Tell her you're on her case and she shouldn't worry."

"Dan." Maria drew in her breath. "I can't do that."

"Why not?"

"For starters, I can't tell her she shouldn't worry. Of course she should worry. She's facing murder charges. Only a complete imbecile wouldn't worry."

"Then tell her we'll do everything possible to—"

"I can't do that, either."

He tensed. "Why not?"

"Isn't it obvious?"

"No."

"And that's why you can't represent yourself. You've got blinders on. Let me spell it out. You and Camila have conflicting interests."

"What, you think Camila is the murderer?"

"Of course not."

"You think she's going to make a deal with the prosecution? Sell me out for immunity?"

"The truth is, I don't know what she's going to do."

"You never liked her."

"That has nothing to do with this. There's an inherent conflict of interest between co-defendants. You need to be tried separately. And you each need a lawyer who puts their client first."

He flung himself back in his chair. "This is truly frustrating."

"Because you know I'm right?"

"Because—Because—" He exhaled heavily. "Okay, fine. Because I know you're right."

"Camila won't have any trouble finding good representation. But my focus is going to be on you, big boy."

He didn't like it. But it made sense. And reinforced his determination to get out of jail. He'd spent his professional life concocting schemes to benefit clients. Now he needed to concoct something to benefit himself.

Maria checked her watch. "Anything else I can do for you before they boot me out of here?"

"Yes. Could you bring my Air Jordans? These plastic sandals suck."

"You know they won't allow that."

"You're the team sorceress. You can make anything happen."

"Not that."

He sighed. "Could you at least bring some of my sea salt vanilla with caramel ribbons? I just made a batch. Took three days. And I never got to taste it."

She gave him a small smile. "Poor sweet baby. I'll see what I can do."

CHAPTER THREE

DAN WALKED CAUTIOUSLY FROM THE JAILHOUSE SHOWER. HE knew it was a cliché, and he knew this was jail, not prison, but he still made a point of not spending too long in the shower and never bending over. Almost everyone here looked like someone he would skitter away from in a dark alley. Worse, he recognized some of the faces. And he was certain they recognized him.

He'd spent his entire career getting people off the hook, and he had the best win-loss record in the county. So how was it he recognized so many incarcerated faces? Some he had simply seen lurking about the courthouse, perpetually in one kind of trouble or another. Some were notorious jailhouse snitches, to be avoided at all costs. Some were gang members. Even when he didn't know their faces, he knew the look. Hardened criminals. Men who had been behind bars so frequently it didn't bother them anymore.

He thought Maria's chances of getting him out on bail were small. But he hoped that cross she wore around her neck had earned her a miracle. For that matter, his friend Jazlyn Prentice, a top prosecutor in the D.A.'s office, was probably in charge now that Belasco was on a slab. Maybe she could pull some strings. Doubtful, but he needed some source of hope if he was going to get through this day.

He grabbed a towel to dry himself off—when a familiar voice shattered his ruminations.

"Well, lookee who we got here. Goodness gracious how the mighty have fallen."

He turned slowly and saw Jack Crenshaw, former agent with Immigration and Customs Enforcement, a man with a cowboy fetish and a nasty streak that had landed him in prison. Thanks to Dan.

Wonderful. He had taken a serious beating only a few weeks before and he still wasn't anywhere near completely healed.

He wrapped the towel around his waist, searching for a guard. None in sight. "Shouldn't you be in the state pen?"

"I'm on a temporary transfer," Crenshaw explained. Tall and wiry. Not wearing the orange coveralls the other inmates wore. Even without his cowboy hat, he seemed to be wearing a cowboy hat. "Feds need me to testify in an ongoing investigation."

"You're snitching on someone. What did they offer you? Time off?"

"Something like that."

"Do you even know the defendant you're condemning?"

Crenshaw took a step closer. "Are you suggesting that I might perjure myself? Danny boy, I'm a straight-shooter."

"You must be on the go-to list. Whenever the cops need a witness. They know who to call."

"You're barking up the wrong tree, Danny. I reached out to them. And I didn't ask for immunity, money, or anything else." He stepped even closer, till they were practically breathing one another's air. "But I knew that if I was going to appear before a grand jury, they'd have to transfer me to this particular hoosegow. Where you are."

Dan felt his throat go dry. "You offered testimony...to get near me?"

"Word travels fast, Danny boy. Never expected to see you behind bars. And knowing what a tricky little coyote you are, I don't expect you to be here long. So I plan to take advantage while I can."

"Don't be a fool, Crenshaw." He took a step back. He didn't want to show any weakness, but he also knew that, given his current condition, he wouldn't last long in a serious fight. "You'll be caught. Charged. Assault while incarcerated. Three more years behind bars, minimum. Is it really worth it?"

Crenshaw didn't blink. "For me? Yes. It is absolutely worth it. I've taken care of the guards. If you're thinking the cavalry is gonna rush in to save your bacon, think again." His eyes narrowed. "You ruined my life, Danny. We got unfinished business and I intend to wrap it up, right here and now."

"I didn't make you do what you did. You made your own choices. All I did was find out. And for that you're going to kill me?"

Crenshaw chuckled. "Naw. I'm just gonna mess you up. Bad. See how you function without the pretty boy looks. A couple broken legs might end your kitesurfing career. I want you to suffer. Like I've been suffering."

He had to act brave, even if he didn't feel it. "And you think you've got the chops to do it? Only thing you'll get is a prison stay that takes you to the grave."

Crenshaw laughed again, much too loudly. Where were the guards? "Did you think I was gonna do this myself? I'm not an idiot. Let me introduce you to some friends." Two men emerged from the background. Big men. "This here is Willy. He's been charged with grand larceny. And since bail was set at a hundred thousand bucks, he's gonna be here for a while. He needs some kind of hobby to occupy himself."

"Prison assault won't help him pass the time. It will guarantee he gets more time."

Willy was at least a foot taller than him, with big meaty fists and a neck as thick as a cured ham. Broad face. Shaven head. Gold tooth right up front.

"And this other fella is Durant," Crenshaw continued. "Drug offense. Used to be an enforcer. He's what you might call a professional mauler. Not the kind of guy who plays by the Queensbury rules."

Durant smiled. Huge pumped biceps. Screwed-up nose. Tattoos. Bloodlust in his eyes.

"Don't be a patsy. You're being used. Manipulated. Both of you."

Crenshaw whistled. "Look at the Artful Dodger now. Do you think your fancy words and courtroom tricks are gonna save you? Hold him."

The two musclebound men grabbed him, one on each side, pinning his arms behind his back.

"Let me see if I can find the right spot." Crenshaw reared back his fist and plowed into Dan's lower right side.

He cried out. *Damn!* Crenshaw had done his homework. When he was beaten before, they'd cracked two ribs on that side and they still weren't completely healed.

His abdomen exploded. He felt his knees go weak. The pain was so intense he couldn't think straight.

"Did you enjoy that, Danny boy?" Crenshaw grinned, big and broad. "I know I did. Didn't hear a cracking sound, though. Must not have hit you hard enough. Let me try again." Before he'd finished the sentence, Crenshaw landed another blow, hard and fast.

It felt like Crenshaw's fist plowed right through his body. He couldn't seem to catch his breath. He felt his face contort like a squeezed grape.

He had to do something to stop this punishment. Fast.

He gazed up at Willy, the brute on his left, trying to form words with a tongue that barely functioned. "Habeas corpus."

Willy's head tilted. "Whatsat?"

"Ignore him," Crenshaw said. "Punch him in the face till he shuts his trap."

"Habeas corpus. That's how you get out."

Crenshaw ran forward. "I'll kick your teeth out if you don't—"

Willy raised his hand. "One minute." He looked back at Dan. "Talk."

"You're William Martinez, right? I read about you and I have a very good memory. You've been locked up for more than a year due to your inability to make bail. File a writ of habeas corpus. The Eleventh Circuit has released people in your situation before. Some judges believe the whole concept of money bail is an unconstitutional infringement on Fourth Amendment rights."

Willy stared at him. "That takes lawyers."

"Contact Legal Services. I know some people there. Ask for Kimberly. Tell her Dan sent you. They'll take your case. They don't often get one they can actually win. They could get you out in a week. Spend the time before trial with your family, not here."

The other brute, Durant, lowered himself to eye level. "That habeas thing work for me?"

"No. You haven't been here long enough. But you were in a Southside gang, right? I recognize the tattoos. And you had a drug habit. Cocaine, judging from the shape your nose is in. Those are mitigating circumstances."

"That good?"

"You'll have to swear off gangs and commit to drug treatment. But there's a growing feeling that filling prisons with drug addicts is expensive and pointless. Better to get them help.

If you'll commit to three months in rehab, I might be able to get you off with probation."

"I can't afford no rehab."

"There's a fund. We'll get the money."

"You not messin' with me?"

"No. But if you take part in an assault behind bars, you won't get squat from anyone. Courts probably won't even hear your case."

Crenshaw looked as if he were about to explode. "Why are you listenin' to this hogwash? I hired you to hurt him!"

Dan pushed himself to his feet, even though every movement caused pain. "You hired because you thought they were stupid. Turns out they're not." He turned back to the two men holding him down. "I meant what I said, Willy. I'll call my friends at Legal Services, first chance I get. And if I can't get out in time to rep you, Durant, my partners will. That's a promise."

"Don't let him get away with this!"

He ignored Crenshaw's ranting. "So maybe it's in your best interests to make sure I survive my stay behind bars. I'll get on your cases immediately, boys." He thought a moment. "You might even spread the word. I bet you're not the only ones in this hellhole who could use some legal assistance. While I'm stuck here, I might as well be of use."

The two men released him.

"Don't let him do this!" Crenshaw squealed.

Dan laid his hands on Willy and Durant's shoulders. "Spread the word. Daniel Pike and the Last Chance Lawyers are taking clients. From behind bars."

CHAPTER FOUR

DAN EXPECTED TO SEE MARIA SITTING ON THE OTHER SIDE OF THE Plexiglas screen, but to his surprise, he found another of his partners. Maybe the team was rotating visitation duties.

"Oh my God, Dan, how are you?" Jimmy peered through the screen, eyes glistening. "Are you okay?"

Since the man was already on the verge of tears, he decided not to mention the brutal attack in the showers. "I'm fine." Except when I move. "What's happening back at the office?"

"Chaos. Absolute chaos. Maria's doing her best to hold it all together, but it isn't the same. We need our Aquaman. Not Mera." He paused. "Actually, she's more like Harley Quinn."

"Maria is a highly capable attorney."

"But she isn't you. She isn't a leader."

"She can be anything she wants to be."

"That's just it. She doesn't want to be. She wants you home. We all do." He brushed the heel of his palm against his eyes. "I'm sorry I'm being so emotional. Hank says I didn't sleep a wink last night." Hank was Jimmy's husband, an ER doctor. They were both African-American, both a bit portly, and both fonder of cardigans than most people living in sunny Florida. "I never expected anything like this to happen."

He wanted to reach through the Plexiglas and comfort his colleague. "It will all work out in the end. Promise. These charges are garbage. I'm confident they'll be dismissed." A complete lie, but if he didn't say something, he feared the man would break out in a full-on crying jag.

"I'm not. Your case has been assigned to Judge Hembeck."

Oh, the irony. He had appeared before Hembeck on several occasions—as an attorney. She was extremely conservative, always leaning toward the prosecution. Probably the closest thing this county had to a "hanging judge." "That's okay."

"You're all over the papers. And social media."

"Does that surprise you? Don't let it get to you."

"Okay..." Jimmy looked down at his feet. Something was bothering him.

"Out with it."

"Out with what?"

"Come on. We're friends. Better out than in."

Jimmy hesitated. "I—I ate your ice cream."

"The sea salt vanilla with caramel ribbons?" Their office was a Snell Isle mansion Mr. K had converted into a workplace. Among other fabulous features, it had a fully functional kitchen. "Good. I made it for eating."

Jimmy tossed his head from side to side. "I kinda...ate all of it."

"Wow. I made three pints."

"I was binge eating."

"Nothing better for depression than ice cream."

"And in a weird way...it made me feel closer to you."

Now he was going to cry. "Jimmy, I'll get out of this mess. But until I do, please eat all the food you find in the fridge. Might as well clear away the leftovers. Because when I get out of here, I'm going to cook every recipe I know."

Jimmy looked up, eyes wide. "Promise?"

"Promise."

APPARENTLY THE AUTHORITIES WERE ALLOWING ANYONE TO VISIT as long as they claimed to be his attorney. And he knew a lot of attorneys.

Moments after Jimmy left, his remaining partner, Garrett Wainwright, holding an iPad, settled into the chair on the other side of the Plexiglas.

Garrett got right down to business. "Few details about the murder have been released. The crime scene is still locked down. Putting a real dent in Beachcombers' business."

"They'll recover."

"The police are confident they've captured their murderer, so they're not conducting any real investigation. Forensic reports are still under lock and key. Probably not completed. I've been looking into the legal precedents for getting bail in cases like yours."

"And?"

"You already know. Judges tend to play it safe. And it's always safer to leave accused murderers behind bars."

"We got Camila out. She wore an electronic ankle bracelet so they could monitor her movements."

"She was the mayor of the city. Nothing personal, but you don't have the same status. Still, I'm digging up every helpful precedent. Maria will come to court locked and loaded."

"Thank you. I appreciate it." He nodded toward the iPad. "And?"

Garrett unfolded the cover. "Our boss would like to have a few words."

"Can you get Wi-Fi in here?"

"Of course not. I've got a 4G hotspot on the iPad. Top of the line, but reception still may be spotty. We're behind a lot of thick walls.

"You can get cell service in prison. All the best inmates have phones."

"Good point." Garrett started Skype and placed a call. It took longer than usual, but eventually they made a connection. The call was voice-only. They could hear Mr. K, but they had no idea what he looked like. Didn't even know where he was.

Garrett place the phone receiver beside the iPad. The voice was crackly but recognizable. "How are you holding up, Dan?"

"I'm fine, K." He tried to speak as loudly as possible, but he knew guards were watching this operation and he didn't want to attract any more attention than necessary. Don't give them an excuse to shut it down. "No problems."

"Really? I heard you were attacked in the shower. Our old friend Crenshaw tried to cripple you."

Garrett looked up at him, eyes wide. How did K know that? How did he always know everything? "He landed a few lucky punches. I talked my way out of it."

"A few punches is not nothing. Especially for someone recovering from a savage beating. I'm going to see if I can pull a few strings. There must be someone in that detention center who owes me a favor. Maybe we can get you isolated from the general population."

"Don't waste your energy. I'll be fine." He paused. "But I do think you should hire some security. Someone to watch over Maria. And the rest of the firm. Maybe my boat, if you wouldn't mind too much."

He could hear the smile in the voice. "I've already done all that. Don't worry, Dan. I'll take care of the team."

"And Camila, if she gets out."

"She has security of her own." Pause. "But I'll make sure she's safe."

There was an awkward silence. Only a few seconds, but to

Dan, it felt like an eternity. "K, I didn't do this. I didn't kill Belasco."

"You think I don't know that? You don't have to tell me the obvious. Dan, we are behind you one hundred percent. We will beat these charges if it costs everything I have. People before pennies. Do you think Sweeney is behind this?"

"Of course Sweeney is behind this. Sweeney is always behind this."

"He has a strong motive to get you out of the courtroom. But that doesn't prove that he did it."

"Makes him the most likely suspect."

"Perhaps. But still—" He could tell something was troubling Mr. K. "Sweeney has always been vile, but he's also always been...subtler than this." He paused, as if thinking. "I don't know. He had Belasco in his back pocket. And Belasco was running for mayor, which would make him even more useful."

"Are there any other suspects?"

"Not as far as the police are concerned. Which makes it all the more important that we conduct a thorough investigation. I gave some thought to hiring outside counsel."

"No. I trust my team."

"I trust all my teams. And I know many good lawyers. All over the country."

"There's no need. I know my friends have got my back."

He could tell K was not satisfied. "We'll table that idea for now. See how it goes. One thing is for certain. We are not going to lose this case because it's understaffed. Or underfunded."

Garrett spoke up. "The police say they have a rock-solid case. And they're only beginning to assemble evidence, Dan."

He nodded. "Someone wants me out of commission."

"That's about the size of it." Garrett's lips were tight, his expression grim. "I know I should probably say something reassuring, but you're in a bad situation here, Dan. And I'm not sure there's any way to get you out of it."

CHAPTER FIVE

CONRAD SWEENEY GRABBED THE BROWN PAPER AT THE CORNER and ripped it off in a single dramatic swipe. He felt a tingling throughout his body, a incipient adrenaline rush.

The paper fell to the floor. The Miró was revealed.

"Magnificent." The large man beamed with pride. "This will be the jewel of my collection."

"It is brilliant." His chief assistant, Prudence Hancock, stood to the side, hands behind her back, maintaining deference, but always at the ready. "A bit more modern than the rest of your collection, isn't it?"

He did not face her as he spoke. He could not remove his eyes from the artwork. "Funny thing about art. What's considered modern changes as time marches on. Miró is no longer modern. Only modernist. Given the changes in the art world today, soon nothing from the twentieth century will be considered modern."

"Your collection is the finest in the world in private hands. Dr. Sweeney, may I say again what a shame it is that the rest of the world is not allowed to see it?"

"Perhaps in time." He tore his eyes from the art. "But for now, I'm keeping these masterworks for myself. I don't want to fight my way through a crowd of noisy schoolgirls to get a closer look."

"Is that the only reason?"

A small smile played on his lips. "As I believe you know, there are delicate issues of…provenance."

"Coogan is behind bars. The police believe they've recovered everything he ever stole. You're safe."

"Only the passage of time can provide the level of assurance I desire. When my collection is finally revealed to the public, there can be no incriminating aspersions about where it came from. I don't want a repeat of the Getty Museum debacle."

"Understood." Prudence pulled her phone from her pocket. "Ellison is here."

"Show him in. I want to linger with my painting another moment."

"Of course." Prudence left his office, which took some time, given that the office occupied most of the penthouse level of his downtown office building. When she returned, she escorted an older man, graying at the temples. Sweeney had seen Bradley Ellison recently, but the man looked as if he had aged a year since then.

Ellison appeared to have a complaint. He decided to deflect it by seizing the initiative. "Have you found a snitch?"

"Not yet. And that's not what I came to talk about."

"Find a witness before Pike pulls another rabbit out of his hat."

"Pike is not likely to do anything at the moment. Since he's behind bars for the murder of George Belasco. The man I last saw in this office."

"Walk with me." Sweeney knew the gallery outside the elevator lobby was imposing, a long stretch of marble flooring and artwork. Ellison needed a reminder of whom he was addressing. Prudence followed behind them.

"I didn't come here to look at pictures," Ellison said. "We need to talk. Right this minute."

"Take it down a notch," Prudence said, almost growling. "In fact, take it down several notches."

"Don't tell me how to talk, young lady."

Prudence marched toward him. Sweeney raised his hand, halting her. For the moment. "I can see that you're upset, Bradley. That saddens me. I thought we were partners. With a common cause."

"I would never countenance murder. Never."

"Did you like Belasco?"

"I didn't want him dead."

Sweeney repeated himself, this time more slowly, emphasizing each syllable. "Did—you—like—Belasco?"

Ellison's chest rose, then fell. "No. I didn't like him. I feel the same way about a dirty DA that I would about a dirty cop."

"You were on the police force for over twenty years, before you retired and plunged into the world of cold-case investigations. You must have seen more than a few officers on the take."

"Not really. There are more dirty cops on tv shows than in real life."

"'Dirty,' of course, is a point of view. What's dirty to some can be keenly useful to others."

"Did you want Pike this badly?"

Prudence stepped between them, looking fully ready to deck Ellison, but again, Sweeney restrained her. "Yes, I want Pike badly. And this time, his tricks can't save him."

"He'll think of something."

"I'm pretty good at thinking myself. Prudence, do we have our surveillance in place?"

"For the most part. We haven't tapped the camera and

microphone on his computers. He has a firewall we haven't managed to penetrate. And we haven't bugged his office yet."

"Why not?"

"Don't you think the cops will tear that place apart? Looking for evidence? They can't go to trial with nothing but an audio recording."

He nodded slowly. "Of course. Thank you again for reminding me why I hold you in such esteem, Prudence. You are invaluable."

"Working for you is a pleasure, Dr. Sweeney. And an honor."

Ellison pushed himself beside them. "You're behind this whole mess, aren't you? You've got your fingers everywhere, in every pie. I don't want anything—"

Prudence slapped hard against his chest and shoved him into the wall. The paintings rattled. Ellison seemed startled, blinking, as if he didn't know what had hit him.

Sweeney placed a single finger on Ellison's chest. "Stop posturing and moralizing and listen to my words, Bradley. You're already involved. Complicit. In fact, you're on the front lines. I can protect myself. But if anyone gets suspicious, you're the one who goes down."

Ellison slowly found his voice. "This crusade against Pike is your obsession, not mine."

"Are you completely delusional? You're the man whose testimony put Pike's father behind bars."

"I told the truth."

"You think that will get you brownie points in heaven? But for you, Pike might be off in the Keys drinking margaritas and kitesurfing all day. You turned him into St. Pete's dashing crusader, the perpetual thorn in my side. So you will damn well help me pluck this thorn and crush it." His voice deepened. "Or the next body they find in a back alley might be yours."

They stared at one another for several seconds. Prudence

watched for a sign. But Sweeney held back and let the room cool.

Ellison was the one to finally break the silence. "What do you want me to do?"

Sweeney smiled. "I think perhaps this murder prosecution should be...enhanced."

CHAPTER SIX

CAMILA SAT IN THE JAILHOUSE HOLDING AREA, DISGUSTED AND distraught, trying to figure out what to do next.

"Wassa matter, chica?"

The woman speaking to her was dressed in a ridiculously short skirt and a low-cut halter that left little to the imagination. She was obviously a prostitute, as were the two friends sitting on either side.

So this was what it had come to. She was a candidate for the US Senate. And she'd been thrown into a tank with sex workers.

"Just waiting," she replied. "I assume someone wants to speak to me."

"Wish I had someone waitin' to see me, girlfriend. You lucky."

"All depends on who the someone is."

"Why do I know your face? You been in a commercial or something?"

She pondered. It would probably be smarter to hold her tongue. But she couldn't stop herself. "I'm your mayor."

"Sure, girl. And I'm Banksy."

"I intend to be your US senator. But there are men who feel threatened by me."

"Well, we know all about that, don't we, girls?"

One of her friends spoke up. "I intimidate all men. I intimidate them so hard they can't function, half the time. Can you imagine? A body like this, and they can't work it up." She poised her fingers like claws. "I'm the spider queen."

The rattling behind the door told Camila she probably wasn't going to be in here for long. "May I give you ladies a little advice?"

"Long as you don't 'spect us to take it."

"Get off the streets. I know it's hard to find good work. I know your pimp won't like it. Do it anyway. Go to one of the Sweeney shelters. They're all over town. You can stay for thirty days and your pimp won't be able to touch you. That'll give you time to get your life on a different track. Find a better job."

"Who would hire me?" the spider queen asked.

"You're smart, you're funny, and I know a lot of businesses that could use you. The mayor's office has a Job Placement Center."

"I've…thought about makin' a change," the first woman said. "But I feel…trapped."

"I know exactly how you feel. But you've still got time. Trust me on this. It's never too late to change your life. It's not where you start, it's where you finish. You can be anything you want to be."

The woman gave her a long look. "Are we on camera? You with some kind church crusade or somethin'?"

Camila rose to her feet. "No. Trying to make a difference. Any way I can."

MARIA COULD SEE CAMILA WAS SURPRISED TO FIND HER SITTING
on the other side of the Plexiglas screen. Had she thought it
would be Dan? He might be a miracle worker, but there was no
angel in heaven who could get his butt out of jail this quickly.

"To be clear, Camila, this is a courtesy call. I cannot represent you. My firm cannot represent you."

If Camila was experiencing irritation or disappointment, she
hid it well. "You did before."

"Yes, but the circumstances have changed. Dan is also
charged, and the two of you have potentially conflicting
interests."

"We do?" She arched an eyebrow. "We're both innocent. We
both would like to avoid execution."

"I have a list of top-flight attorneys I can recommend."

Camila did not appear placated. "Does Dan know you're
cutting me loose?"

Maria licked her lips. She had always felt there was some…
tension between her and Camila. Did Camila see her as a potential rival? "We are not cutting you loose. We will make sure
you're taken care of. And yes, I have discussed this with Dan
and he understands."

"But it wasn't his idea. Will you be investigating?"

"You know we will. And we will share whatever we discover.
Please don't take this personally. It's a matter of legal ethics."

"I'm not taking it personally. I never take anything personally. I'm an all-business woman." She kept her voice low, obviously trying to avoid attracting attention, though most people
recognized Camila the instant she entered the room. How often
did you see a candidate for the US Senate behind bars? "Have
you heard the recording?"

"Several times. And I have experts working on it, trying to
verify that it's authentic."

"Don't waste your money. It's real. But it was a joke. We
were messing around."

She resisted the instinct to say, ick. "I have to tell you, Camila...it doesn't sound like it."

"That's because you can't see the expressions on our faces. Given the background static, you can barely make out the tone of our voices. You can't see that we were being playful, standing around in his tiny bedroom cabin half-naked."

Double-ick. "You'll have to explain that. Convincingly. On the witness stand."

"You think it will come to that? An actual trial? Over this foolishness?"

"I think that's likely. The cops have staked their claim. It's been in the media. There's no turning back now, not without making themselves look like fools."

"They do look like fools."

"Maybe to you."

"Their whole case is based on one twenty-second illegal audio recording."

"The cops say they have more. Look at it from their standpoint. The District Attorney, the highest, most prominent legal official in the city, has been brutally murdered. In many respects, this is a cop killing. They needed a scapegoat and an anonymous informant gave them one." She brushed her hair back. "I don't think it's a coincidence Dan was targeted. Sweeney, cops, lots of people want him out of the way. He was at the top of the scapegoat list. Why else was he being bugged?"

Camila shook her head slowly, but firmly. "You're wrong."

"About what?"

"That whole rant."

She tried not to be annoyed. "Can you be more specific?"

"Dan was not the target. I was."

"How do you figure?"

"It's obvious. But your affection for Dan blinds you."

"Dan and I are partners. Period."

"Yes, yes, I know. But that does not mean you don't feel stirrings inside when he is near."

"I don't, actually."

"You are correct when you say law enforcement has no affection for Dan, or any other defense attorney. But there is something else they hate even worse. A female boss."

"I'm sure there's a lot of sexism..."

"And what do they hate even worse than a female boss? A Latinx female boss."

"A lot of the men on the force are—"

"The men, yes. That's the key word. And what could possibly make their hatred and resentment even worse? A female Latinx boss who is very pretty. Who they will never get close to."

Maria chose her words carefully. "It's possible you're... personalizing this to an excessive degree. Remember, they didn't bug your home. They bugged Dan's boat."

"Because they knew I would be there. For all we know, they bugged my home as well."

"Sweeney wants Dan eliminated."

"He has also expressed his antipathy toward me. On several occasions."

This was fruitless. And turning into a competition to prove who was most despised. "I suppose it doesn't matter. The bottom line is, you're both in jail now and you're both going up on murder charges."

"Do you know when the murder is believed to have taken place?"

"Not precisely. Why?"

"I was in my office working late that day. I came to your celebration party late, remember? And then I accompanied Dan to his boat. Depending on the timing, I may have an alibi. For that matter, Dan may as well."

Maria hoped that was true. But she also knew that Dan had disappeared for several hours between the courtroom finale and the party. "I'll check it out." She caught herself. "And whatever I learn, I will convey to your attorney, as soon as I know who that will be."

"I will arrange counsel today. I would rather be represented by the best firm in the city...but since you refuse me, I will go elsewhere."

Hoo boy. "We will not leave you dangling in the wind."

Camila gave her a stony glare. "It appears to me that you already have."

CHAPTER SEVEN

JAZLYN TRIED TO KEEP HER HEAD ABOVE THE CHAOS, BUT IT wasn't easy. Since she had been the lead assistant district attorney, and the actual district attorney was dead, everyone assumed she was in charge. She wasn't sure if there was any legal basis for that. She hadn't been elected and there was no precedent for this in Pinellas County. But like it or not, she did appear to be in charge. Her first order of business? A criminal prosecution targeting a man she considered a close friend and the mayor of the city.

As if that weren't enough, she was in the middle of her own campaign for district attorney. Some said that election was now a foregone conclusion, but she wasn't so sure. As soon as someone got a whiff of weakness, maybe someone who thought she wasn't handling this high-profile case properly, they might be eager to take a shot at a regular government paycheck.

Her assistant, Logan Pierce, entered her office. "Are you ready for messages?"

Jazlyn pressed a hand against her forehead. "Are there many?"

"About four thousand and twelve. But I can prioritize."

Logan was a legal assistant and they'd worked together for years, so she tended to trust him. He was smart, skinny, and an excellent dresser, but most importantly, he knew how to get rid of people she didn't want to see. "The press wants to know who will be lead counsel on this case."

Probably Beverly Garfield. But she didn't want to make a public announcement before they'd discussed it. "They can find out as the rest of the world does. When someone shows up at the arraignment."

"Your campaign manager wants you to speak at the local Rotary Club."

"Not this week."

"You are going to have to make some public appearances."

"Tell me something I don't know. Anything else?"

He smiled slightly. "Your daughter wants to know when you'll be home. She wants to make cupcakes."

Thank you for reminding me I have a private life. "I don't know when I'll be home. Frida watches Esperanza after school." Jazlyn adopted ten-year-old Esperanza about a year ago, after a little urging from current murder defendant Daniel Pike. Smartest thing she ever did. "But I'm okay on the cupcakes. Tell her to start without me. She doesn't need my help."

Logan clicked his tongue. "She doesn't need your help. She wants your help."

"I know." She pondered a moment. "Tell her I'll be home as soon as I can. I'll text her. Anything else?"

"Yup. Someone outside to see you."

"Tell them—"

"It's Maria Morales."

Of course it was. Surprising Maria hadn't been by sooner. But she probably had a lot on her plate as well. "Okay. Send her in. Hold the calls."

She flopped down in the chair behind her desk. Why hadn't she become a librarian like her mother suggested?

MARIA ENTERED TENTATIVELY. "JAZLYN?"

The assistant district attorney pushed herself to her feet. "Maria. So good to see you." She reached out her arms.

Maria raised a hand. "Just so you know, I'm definitely representing Dan. The whole firm is behind him."

"Does that mean we can't hug?"

"Only if the cameras aren't rolling." They embraced for a brief moment. "I know this puts you in a difficult situation."

"I'm not handling the case myself."

"Beverly Garfield?"

"She is the senior death-qualified attorney in the office."

Maria winced when she heard "death-qualified" spoken out loud. "I figured as much."

"It's necessary. Dan and I are personal friends. For that matter, it may not be common knowledge, but we actually went out on a date once."

Maria arched an eyebrow. Neither of them had ever mentioned that to her before.

"Don't be alarmed. It didn't go far. Hard as he tried. But my point is, if I handled this case, someone would scream that I'm not objective. Or worse, someone might claim it was a vendetta, since Dan has shellacked me in court so many times. Best I stay out of it this time."

"But you will supervise the case. Oversee it."

"No way around that. Like it or not, I seem to be the head of the office. Earlier than I expected."

"Thank God for that. I know I can trust you to block… anyone trying to manipulate the process for their own ends."

"Of course. Look, Maria, I don't believe for a minute that Dan would murder someone. But there's more than enough evidence to proceed. My hands are tied."

"I get it. So long as the playing field is level, we can beat these charges. I'm confident."

The concern in Jazlyn's eyes was evident. "I hope you're right."

Death-qualified. Death-qualified. She couldn't make that stop ringing in her ears. "What can you tell me about the murder? I don't know much."

"You've heard the audio recording?"

"Of course. Any idea where it came from?"

"Not yet. The sender was careful. Used a burner email account and the message was forwarded repeatedly through accounts and clouds. Even if we manage to trace it back to its source, it will probably be some random library or coffeeshop. Nothing that could be traced back to the actual sender."

"What's the time of death?"

"Haven't heard yet. Medical examiner says the murder took place well before the body was found. After he finishes the autopsy, analyzes the stomach contents, and performs a tox screen, he'll be able to tell us more."

"Can you send me a copy of that when it comes in?"

Jazlyn tilted her head, her mouth stretched in a pained expression. "Eeeeh…"

"Right. No special treatment. I'll make the appropriate disclosure requests."

"Thank you. So much."

"What can you tell me about the murder? Without getting into any trouble?"

Jazlyn shrugged. "Here's what will be in the papers tomorrow. We received an anonymous call from a random cellphone. Probably a burner. Untraceable. The call sent two officers to the alley behind Beachcombers."

"Can you get me in to view the crime scene?"

Jazlyn's lip curled slightly. "If that's what you want. Let me warn you. You won't enjoy it."

"I have no choice. Why was Belasco in that alley?"

"No idea. Mayoral candidates don't normally hang out in sleazy bars. But he had all but retired to run his campaign. He was leaving the office at five most days. Sometimes earlier."

"And Belasco was shot six times?"

Jazlyn drew in her breath, then slowly released it. "And that wasn't the worst of it. His body was…impaled."

Maria felt the blood drain from her face. "With what?"

"Some kind of trident-like stake."

"He was…staked? Like a vampire?"

"Pinioned against the back fence and left hanging. Like a sick scarecrow."

Maria swallowed. "Someone was seriously out to get Belasco."

"Yes."

"But Belasco must've had many enemies. Think of all the lowlifes he put behind bars. This could be retaliation from a Southside gang. Or a drug cartel."

"Hard to imagine."

"What about Sweeney? There's nothing he couldn't make happen."

"But Belasco and Sweeney were pals."

"Sweeney doesn't have pals. Only tools."

"Sweeney contributed to Belasco's campaign in a big way."

"What better way to hone a tool?"

"Then why kill him?"

"To frame someone. Make it look like a calculated, cold-blooded killing by someone who hated Belasco."

"Like Dan? How do you explain away the audio recording?"

"Which was emailed shortly after an anonymous call sent you to the crime scene. The perfect frame."

"The police don't see it as a perfect frame. More like a perfect crime."

"I need to find a way to change their minds." Maria pushed

herself out of her chair. "Thanks for your help, Jazlyn. I appreciate it. Dan will, too."

Jazlyn grabbed her hand. "Tell Dan...I'm thinking about him." She peered into Maria's eyes. "Find the answers, Maria. You're all that stands between Dan and...the worst fate imaginable. I can't help him here. This time around, it all depends on you."

CHAPTER EIGHT

DAN CLUTCHED HIS SIDE AND TRIED NOT TO LET THE PAIN SHOW. Those punches to the gut were getting worse, not better. He needed to see a doctor. And he would. But at the moment, other matters took priority.

He sat on a bench outside the large courtroom on the second floor sporting silver shackles between his wrists and ankles. One of the marshals who escorted him from the jailhouse stood to the side. They had to let him talk to his lawyer privately, but they stayed close enough to grab him if he tried to make a break for it.

Everything about the St. Pete county courthouse needed renovation, but these pews were ridiculously uncomfortable. He supposed he shouldn't complain. It was better than being in the jailhouse, where an old foe was determined to see him dead.

Of course, if he didn't beat these murder charges, he still might end up dead.

Maria scurried around the corner, a briefcase in one hand, papers clutched in the other. "Okay, I got everything filed. I think it might help."

He shrugged. "What have you learned about the judge?"

"Carmen Hembeck. White. Conservative. Well-to-do family in Tampa. U of F grad. Practiced solo for seven years, then ran for the judgeship. Lost the first time but was later appointed. Has been considered for the federal judiciary by the Trump administration, but it hasn't happened yet."

"If she's still in the running, she'll want to demonstrate how conservative she can be. Especially during a high-profile case."

"We can't help that."

"I've seen her name in other crime files…"

"It's time. Are you ready to go in?"

"You can't get them to remove the shackles?"

"Not for this. No jury to prejudice. As far they're concerned, you're a dangerous marauder."

"Wonderful. Let's go."

"One reminder. You are not the lawyer today. So keep your mouth shut, except for the part where you say, 'Not guilty.'"

"Understood. I am a professional."

"Yeah, a professional control freak who thinks any argument would be improved by his input."

"I will be meek as a lamb."

She rose. "Remember that you said that."

"Unless, of course, the situation requires—"

"Be quiet."

THE MOMENT HE ENTERED THE COURTROOM, DAN COULD SEE that this case had attracted an extraordinary amount of interest in a short period of time. Normally, there wouldn't be three people in the gallery for an arraignment docket. Today, half the seats were taken. He spotted people craning their necks, staring at him. He was accustomed to attracting attention, but in an amusing, eccentric way, not in a cold-blooded killer way. In one fell swoop, he'd been transformed from one of the most prominent members of the community to one of the most despised.

Some of the people in the gallery appeared to be reporters, with a few elderly citizens who probably used the courthouse as a substitute for television, increasingly common these days as many retirees couldn't afford or understand the vast panoply of streaming services. A few scruffy sorts were likely homeless, getting out of the heat and enjoying the air conditioning for a little while.

What interested him most was the woman sitting on the front row of the gallery, on the prosecution side. Unless he was mistaken, that was Evelyn Belasco, the wife, now widow, of George Belasco. He'd met her years ago at a bar association function.

He gave her a close inspection. Dressed in black, natch. Sparkly brooch at the neck. Red puffy face. Coach bag. Gucci shoes.

The lanky young man beside her was likely her son. Christopher, if he recalled correctly. Dark blue sneakers. Blue polo. Nick on his left cheek. Face was a little raw, as if he'd recently removed a beard.

The expressions on their faces suggested they wouldn't welcome a word of condolence from the defendant. He averted his gaze. Maria guided him toward their table, as if he actually needed directions.

Two reps from the prosecutor's office sat at the opposite table. They looked nervous, or so he liked to believe. He knew them both. Beverly Garfield and Zachary Blunt. Garfield was a small woman, short and a bit plump. String of pearls. Phi Beta Kappa pin. Dark stain on her right forefinger.

Her partner, Blunt, was known around the office as "the Knife." Dan didn't know exactly why, but it didn't sound promising. He was almost anemically skinny, the kind of guy who made you want to shove a cheeseburger down his throat.

Protruding Adam's apple. Mole beneath his chin. Nice suit. Black alligator briefcase that looked like it came from Thom Browne.

About five minutes later, Judge Hembeck entered the courtroom. Mid-forties. Light brown complexion. A bit too much lipstick, or too dark. Broad shoulders, looked strong. Judge robe fit her like it had been tailored.

The judge's clerk called the docket. As it happened, they were the only case on the agenda. He doubted that was an accident. The judge knew how much attention this case would attract, so she gave it a private setting.

The judge read the style, made sure both sides were represented by counsel, and allowed them to enter their appearances. "Ms. Garfield, do the People wish to press these charges against the defendant at this time?"

Garfield rose. "We do, your honor. And we wish to inform the court that we intend to pursue the death penalty. We are in the process of assembling a grand jury to render a capital indictment."

"Understood." So far, the judge's manner seemed completely neutral, matter-of-fact. "Daniel Douglas Pike. How do you plead?"

Maria rose with him. "Not guilty, your honor. Very much completely one-hundred-and-ten percent not guilty."

CHAPTER NINE

To Dan's disappointment, Judge Hembeck didn't even crack a smile. "Your plea will be so entered. The defendant will be remanded back into custody pending the next hearing."

"About that," Maria said, cutting in. "We request that the defendant be released on bail at this time. We have filed the appropriate motion."

Garfield rose, but did not yet speak.

"A bit premature, isn't it, counsel?" The judge pursed her lips, but he suspected she wasn't all that surprised. She'd seen the motion, presumably. "We usually take this up later. After the dust has settled."

"I know, your honor. But this is not the typical case, as this heavily populated courtroom makes clear."

Judge Hembeck tilted her head. "Proceed."

"In this case, your honor, the defendant is an officer of the court. A well-respected officer of the court."

Hembeck nodded. "I am aware."

"That alone speaks to his unlikeliness to flee. He has a pre-existing relationship with and respect for the court. He's a member of the bar."

Hembeck looked down at her papers. "You want me to offer bail in a murder case because the defendant is a lawyer? That's not going to happen."

"My client is more than happy to submit to monitoring, electronic or otherwise. He will wear an ankle bracelet so the court can track his movements at all times. He will appear in person as often as the court requires. And he will meet any bail the court deems appropriate. Why burden the taxpayer for no reason? He will appear for trial. He looks forward to defending himself against these false charges. There is no reason to make him languish behind bars."

Judge Hembeck turned toward the prosecution table. "Any objections?"

"Dozens," Garfield said.

"I thought as much."

"For starters, this is a murder case, soon to be a capital case, and historically judges have almost never allowed bail in those circumstances. The fact that the defendant is a lawyer is irrelevant. Sadly, we all know respected professionals who have turned to crime. If anything, the bar should be stricter on its own, not more lenient, given the importance of maintaining respect for the judicial system. And I don't agree that Mr. Pike is not a flight risk. He has a history of…eccentric behavior. He is known to be wealthy and well-connected. Who knows what someone facing the death penalty might do? If he decided to flee, he's smart enough to pull it off."

"Would the prosecution be reassured if he wore an electronic monitoring device?"

"Not in the slightest. What good would that do? We would know he was running when he ran, but not in time to stop him. More likely, before he made a break for it, he would rip off the bracelet and disappear. We wouldn't have any advance notice and we wouldn't be able to react in time to stop him."

The judge turned her attention back to Maria. "She does

make some valid points, Ms. Morales. The court might be willing to acknowledge that the defendant is not a likely flight risk. But these are capital charges, and traditionally, courts have preferred to keep accused murderers behind bars until trial."

"Which could be a long time," Maria said.

"Granted."

"Your honor, my client knows many of the people currently behind bars. If the court locks him away with them, his life is in danger. He has already been attacked by people bearing a grudge. We have submitted several petitions for relief."

"I did see that," the judge said. "Extremely disturbing."

"Would the court consider coupling the electronic bracelet requirement with a daily visit with a bail officer?"

Dan looked up at her. *Daily?*

The judge considered. "That would leave him little time to fly to Argentina. Madame Prosecutor?"

Garfield shook her head. "It only takes a few minutes to get to the airport and fly anywhere. Or to drive to Miami and disappear on a cruise ship. Or to walk into the Everglades and never return."

"My client would never do that," Maria said, "and with respect, I think my worthy opponent knows that. Dan is more likely to launch his own private investigation to find the true culprit."

Garfield rolled her eyes. "Yes, as I recall, O.J. also launched an investigation into who *really* committed the murders. Oddly enough, he didn't turn up anything."

Maria fumed. "Are you kidding me? This case is about as far—"

The judge raised her palm. "Counsel. Let's keep this professional."

Maria tucked in her chin. "Yes, your honor."

"You do understand, Ms. Morales, that even if I were inclined to set bail, it would be for an extremely high amount."

"Of course."

"Like, perhaps, a million dollars."

Maria did not blink. "Understood."

"Could your client post that? I don't think you'll find a bondsman willing to help."

"I have talked with the head of our firm, your honor, and he has assured us that he will post the funds. Whatever it takes. And there is precedent for this. If I may remind the court, when Mayor Pérez was charged with murder—"

"The first time," Garfield said dryly.

"—the court allowed her to post bail. She was released and wore an ankle bracelet. And she did indeed appear for trial."

"And will again, no doubt," Garfield murmured in a withering tone. "Your honor, the fact that the defendant consorts with and conspired with someone facing capital charges for the second time only shows what a dangerous idea this is."

"If I may remind the court," Maria said firmly, "the mayor was found not guilty after it became perfectly clear that she had been wrongly accused. The actual culprit has since been convicted and sentenced. That came close to being a hideous miscarriage of justice. And this will be too if we don't—"

"Stop. Right there," the judge said. For the first time, she looked perturbed. "We are not going to try the case during this hearing."

"I'm sorry, your honor." Dan could see the desperation in Maria's eyes. She was losing this hearing and she knew it. "But the test is supposed to be whether the defendant poses a flight risk or a threat to the community. And the answer here is clearly in the negative. Dan will appear for trial. I guarantee it. He poses no threat to anyone. He has been a law-abiding citizen his entire life."

"Until now," Garfield said.

"He has no grudges. No enmity. No—No—"

Dan sprung to his feet. "Your honor. May I be heard?"

Maria's head whipped around. The what-are-you-doing expression was all too easy to read.

"Mr. Pike, you are represented by counsel."

"I know. But as the court is aware, I am an attorney myself."

"And the lawyer who represents himself has—"

"Yes, I know the aphorism. And my lawyer is doing a fine job. But I wanted to expand briefly on one point, with the court's indulgence."

The judge shrugged. "You do have the right to speak on your own behalf. For better or for worse."

"Thank you, your honor. Ms. Morales mentioned that if freed, I would likely investigate the case on my own. She's absolutely right about that. And this wouldn't be a PR ploy. Nothing against the fourth estate, but in my experience, you get more work done and gather more information when you stay out of the papers. I might be able to contribute something."

"Or stir up a lot of dust," Garfield said, her voice more forceful than before. "Your honor, this man has been charged based upon compelling evidence. Any so-called investigation can only be seen as a smokescreen to create doubt in the minds of potential jurors."

"That's simply not true," Dan said.

"This defendant has a history of courtroom trickery and theatrics."

"What I have a history of," Dan said firmly, "is success. Of getting the job done. In many cases, not only exonerating my client but uncovering the true offender. I was the one who solved the Coleman murder."

"I did read about that," the judge said quietly.

"When I represented Gabriella Valdez, I not only proved she had been framed, I identified the murderer."

"Yes." The judge nodded.

"And the case I'm most proud of," Dan added, "was several years ago. I investigated the murder of young Nancy Rockwell, a fifteen-year old girl who was abducted, abused, and killed on her way home from school."

The judge's eyes lifted.

"I don't mean to toot my own horn. But I will say that if I hadn't investigated, it's possible that young girl's parents would never have found the solace they so desperately sought." He looked into the judge's eyes, straight and direct. "This is my promise. I will not flee. I will not threaten anyone. I will investigate this case and I will find out who murdered our district attorney. The cops have stopped investigating. There is no chance they will discover what happened. But I will." He drew in his breath. "If the court gives me a chance."

Judge Hembeck stared back at him, tapping a ballpoint pen against her desk. "You will submit to wearing an electronic ankle bracelet?"

"Gladly."

"And you will check in with your bail officer every weekday?"

"I will."

The judge thought another moment. "Very well. Bail is set in the amount of one million dollars. The defendant will not be released until it is paid in full and the funds are verified. The conditions of his release will be laid out in my written ruling."

Garfield started to speak, but the judge cut her off. "The prosecution's objections are noted for the record." She hammered her gavel. "This hearing is adjourned."

———

BEFORE THE MARSHALS CAME FOR DAN, MARIA SAT HIM DOWN IN a chair and leaned into him. "In the first place, Mr. Defendant, if you ever try anything like that again—"

He held up his hands. "I'm sorry. But it did seem to work."

"I would've gotten us there. You didn't give me a chance."

"I'm used to being the lawyer, not the client."

She exhaled slowly. "This is a difficult change of pace for both of us." She pondered a moment. "And who was Nancy Rockwell? I don't remember that case."

"Several years before we started working together. When I was still with Friedman & Collins. The DA charged some poor loser who was in the wrong place at the wrong time. Had a tendency to hang around schoolyards looking at girls."

"Sounds like a creeper."

"Which is why no one would represent him. But he wasn't a murderer. Which is why I did. Spent months on that case."

"Got him off?"

"And eventually found the killer. Didn't bring Nancy back, of course. But it helped a lot of people sleep better."

Maria squinted. "And you decided to bring this up today because...why?"

He hesitated. "What's the most important thing to know before you enter the courtroom?"

"What is this, *Jeopardy*? Fine, I'll take a guess. Know the law?"

"Know the judge."

"You're lucky she even remembered that Rockwell case."

He lowered his voice. "Nancy Rockwell lived in Tampa. So did the judge, remember?" He paused. "Nancy Rockwell was her niece."

CHAPTER TEN

DAN HAD ALWAYS ADMIRED THE SNELL ISLE MANSION THEY called their office, but never more so than today. Forget the luxurious appointments, the fine-trimmed lawn, the palm trees, the pink adobe finish. Forget the fabulous kitchen and his private office upstairs. This place represented sanctuary. The press could not invade, the enemies could not penetrate. He could be safe, if only for a little while.

This was a place where, he hoped, he could lie down for a moment and try to get his heart to stop pounding like a piston. He had to control his fear.

What he needed was a plan, some line of attack, some angle for restoring his name.

"Glad to be back?" Maria asked as she parked the Jag out front.

"Very much so," he murmured. "But to be fair, any place that doesn't have bars would be a significant improvement."

He stepped inside. He hadn't taken five steps before Jimmy encircled him in a huge bear hug. "I am so glad you're out of there. I was worried."

"No need for that," Dan said, his face a happy mask. "I can handle myself."

"If that were true, you wouldn't've been in there."

A valid point. "Thanks for coming to visit."

"Maria said Crenshaw got in there. Tried to hurt you."

"Tried. Didn't succeed," he replied, lying through his teeth. He'd already made a doctor's appointment.

"Thank God. You were lucky. That man hates your guts."

"There's a lot of that going around these days." He walked toward the kitchen. "Has anyone heard anything about Camila? I'm worried about her."

Garrett sat at his usual spot at the kitchen bar. Today, instead of the keyboards he loved to play, he was hunched over a laptop. "She's still behind bars. I'm sorry, Dan."

The aching inside his heart intensified. "That makes no sense. I get out but my co-defendant doesn't?"

"In the first place," Garrett explained, "she's not your co-defendant anymore. The two actions have been bifurcated."

"Why?"

Maria cleared her throat. "That was done on my motion, actually." She averted her eyes. "Better to split the cases now. We can't assume that you're both in the same situation. Remember, she's a public figure. A politician. She carries a lot of baggage that wouldn't necessarily improve your situation."

"Tell me she's represented by counsel."

"She is," Garrett replied. "Gary Davenport."

"Good. I trust him. Did he raise bail at her arraignment?"

"He did. It was denied."

"Why?"

Garrett pivoted the laptop so Dan could see the screen. "In the first place, she had a different judge. For another, she does not have a spotless record, unlike you. She's been down this road before, remember? The court could not appear to be playing favorites."

"And," Maria added quietly, "Camila never handled a case involving the judge's niece."

"This is completely unacceptable." Dan leaned against the counter, his fingers white. "Garrett, call Mr. K. I'm sure he can pull some strings. There must be some way to get her out."

Maria sighed heavily. "I don't think that's a good idea, Dan."

"Why not?"

"Because K thinks this is for the best. He prefers that Camila remain behind bars, at least for the time being."

"*Why?*" He practically screamed, then regretted it. He was letting his feelings show, the sure sign of the non-professional. "I'm sorry. But can you please explain his train of thought?"

"K feels—and I might say, I agree with him—that there will be enough public outrage about the fact that you're walking the streets. If both of you were free, it would be too much. People would cry foul, suggest some kind of corruption. Too much negative buzz could infect the jury pool."

"So Camila rots in jail?"

"For now. Her lawyers will raise the issue again after the heat dies down. And K was absolutely right about the public reaction to your release from custody."

"I'm wearing a damn ankle bracelet. I'm checking in with that bozo at the courthouse every day."

"They don't care." Garrett punched a few keys, then brought up a new screen. "Not to depress you or anything. But you want to see what people are saying? Here's a subReddit page completely devoted to your case. The Twitter stream is worse."

He glanced over Garrett's shoulder and read. "'Money buys justice.' 'Rules don't apply to lawyers.'" He continued scanning. "Can you use that kind of language on the internet?"

"On Reddit. These people aren't using their real names anyway. If one account is shut down, they'll open another. They don't care. Just so they have an opportunity to share their uninformed opinions."

Dan continued reading. "'Sex-murder cult will continue.' 'Pike drank DA's blood.' Where is this coming from?"

"There's no limit to the lies trolls will post on internet bulletin boards."

He looked away from the screen. "I suppose I should thank them. They're making my life much more interesting."

"Please don't start drinking blood," Jimmy said. "It gives you diarrhea."

"And you know this—how?"

Garrett drew in his breath. "I'm afraid there's yet more bad news. The bar association has filed disciplinary proceedings against you."

"They want my license to practice."

"It's standard procedure when a lawyer faces a serious offense. They have to keep up appearances. Nothing will happen until the jury delivers a verdict."

"But if I lose, the bar will revoke my law license."

"If you lose," Garrett said quietly, "it won't matter if you have a law license."

Good point. "Okay, team. We need to get to work. Jimmy, time to call in all the favors. Contact—"

"Stop right there." Maria strolled to the center of the three men. "Dan, I don't know how else to say this, so I'm going to be blunt. You are not in charge here."

"I was brought onto this team—"

"None of that matters today. You're not the lawyer. You're the defendant."

"I'm the lawyer and the defendant."

"No. You're the sad sack who's been slammed with trumped-up charges. You cannot represent yourself. That stunt you pulled at the bail hearing was the start and finish of you trying to wrest the reins. Like it or not, this time, I'm the team leader."

He tucked in his chin. "Gee, Maria, tell me what you really think."

"I just did."

"And I concur," Garrett said. Jimmy nodded aggressively.

"How quickly the worm turns."

"Oh, stop being melodramatic," Maria said. "We're right and you know it."

"May I offer suggestions?"

"For the moment, no. I know where that leads. I'm perfectly capable of handling this, and I don't want your constant interference. We're both going to have to suck it up and play roles we don't like. You can't be objective about your own defense." She looked at him, blinking rapidly. "I don't want anything to happen to you, Dan."

"Like a lethal booster shot," Jimmy added.

"Thanks for explaining. I wasn't quite sure what she meant."

"I won't let that happen to you." Maria said. "We need you."

"Agreed," Garrett added.

Dan cleared his throat. "I didn't realize you all felt so—"

"I do not want to start a search for a new partner," Garrett said. "Interviews, resumes. It's a drag."

Dan pursed his lips. "Well, I wouldn't want to increase your workload…"

"He's kidding you, Dan," Maria said. "We all care about you."

"I appreciate that. But—"

"There is no but," she said firmly. "Listen. And don't argue."

"Fine." He raised his hands in surrender. "What's the plan, chief?"

She cleared her throat. "Jimmy, time to call in all the favors. Contact—"

"This sounds familiar."

"Shut up. Contact everyone who might have any information about George Belasco. Who are his enemies? Who might have a motive? What has Sweeney been up to lately? Who has he been seen with? Jimmy, don't you have a friend at the court clerk's office?"

"Shawna. She's been helpful in the past."

"Great. If there's been any legal manipulation, any skullduggery in the system, she might know about it."

"I'll get right on it." A tiny smile escaped from the side of his mouth. "Boss."

She continued. "Garrett, I know you've already started researching."

"Haven't found much."

"Keep at it. Get everything that comes out of the medical examiner's office. File for the production of all evidence in police possession, exculpatory or otherwise. Find out what you can about Sweeney and his recent activities. We know he's had some financial setbacks. What's he doing about it? And take a deep dive into Belasco's background. I have a hunch there's a lot there we don't know. That man always gave me the heebie-jeebies."

"I'm on it."

"Excellent. I'm going to draft a motion in limine to suppress that damn audio recording. It was made illegally and produced anonymously. I don't know how the police plan to get it in front of the jury without a sponsoring witness, but I'm sure they have something up their sleeve."

"I can help with the brief," Jimmy said.

"I'm counting on it. You're the best legal writer in the state. I'll map out a strategy for trial. We need to hire someone to handle social media. I'm good, but I don't have time to post everywhere. If we let all this outrage go unanswered, we may have trouble finding an impartial juror."

"That sounds like a good idea," Jimmy said. "I'm sure K will foot the tab."

"He will. I already discussed it with him."

"What about me?" Dan said. "What should I do?"

"Stay out of the way."

"Maybe I could interview some potential witnesses."

"No."

"I know the Belasco family somewhat."

"You really think they want to talk to you right now? No."

"I could call Detective Kakazu."

"No, no, no." Her voice soared. "I will not let you shoot yourself in the foot, Dan. Stay out of the fray."

"That is…not my nature."

"Don't I know it. And by the way, don't go kitesurfing."

"Whaaaaat?"

"You might be seen. And then someone will post about how you're so callous you're amusing yourself, oblivious to the tragedy. Stay out of the limelight for a while."

"May I visit Camila?"

Maria glanced at her associates. "I'm sorry, Dan. I know how worried for her you must be. But it's not a good idea."

"One visit."

"You'll be seen."

"I'll wear a disguise."

"Then everyone will think you're hiding something."

He clenched his teeth together. "I don't like this. Not one bit. I—"

He was interrupted by a pounding at the front door.

"Is the doorbell broken?"

"No," Jimmy said. "Someone is choosing to pound."

The noise continued. "St. Petersburg Police. Open the door or we'll break it down."

CHAPTER ELEVEN

DAN FELT HIS THROAT CLENCH. WHAT NOW? DID THE JUDGE realize she'd made a terrible mistake? Were they here to bring him back? Lock him up and throw away the key?

"Stay calm," Maria said, though her face suggested she was anything but calm. "They probably just want to talk."

"They're going to break down the door for a random convo?" Jimmy said. "I don't think so."

The pounding repeated. "Last chance to salvage the door. We know you're in there."

Dan rose. "I'll go."

Maria shoved him aside. "Your lawyer will handle this." She marched to the door, but he noticed her lovely knees were more than a little wobbly.

She opened the door. He recognized the man standing at the forefront. Two uniforms stood behind him. "What do you want?"

The man flashed his badge. "I'm Detective Jake Kakazu."

"I know who you are. Why are you here? My client is out on bail. You have no right to take him anywhere and I will not allow him to speak to you."

"That's not why we've come." Kakazu pulled a piece of paper out of his jacket. "I have a warrant to search the premises."

"Let me see it." Maria scanned quickly. "Seems to be in order."

Dan appeared behind her. "I'd like to see that."

Maria glared at him. "Dan—"

"Well, it does concern me." He glanced out the door. "Hi, Jake."

Kakazu nodded. "Dan."

"Glad to see you're still involved."

Kakazu's lips twisted. "Wish I could say the same. I'm sorry this had to happen."

"Me too. But if someone has to do this, I'd rather it was someone I know."

"Well, thanks. But I'm still going to search the house."

"I know." He stepped back and let them pass through the door.

THREE HOURS LATER, DAN SAT ON THE SEMI-CIRCULAR SOFA IN the living room with all three of his partners. They were surrounded by spilled debris, trash, fiber, files, and foam torn from cushions. The police even dug up the grounds outside.

This beautiful sanctuary had been destroyed.

None of them had spoken for several minutes.

"I knew this was going to happen," Maria groused.

"Me too," Jimmy said. "But I didn't know it was going to be like this. The whole place smells like fingerprint dust."

"They've destroyed the offices," Dan said. "I get that they had to search the drawers. They did not have to pour the contents out on the floor."

"They say it's the fastest way to search," Maria explained.

"Did you see what they did to Dan's office?" Jimmy replied.

"They punched holes in the walls. They say they received an anonymous tip that he was hiding evidence. Between the sheet rock and the outer wall, apparently."

"Because that's just the sort of thing I would do," Dan groused.

"They would be remiss if they didn't follow all leads," Garrett commented.

"Stop making excuses for them," Maria snapped. "They tore down the drapes. They ripped the stuffing out of the pillows and cushions."

"To make sure nothing was hidden inside."

"Like what? Our cocaine stash? Our secret plans for world conquest?"

"They can't afford to be careless. Whether we like it or not, this has become a prominent case."

"I call BS," Jimmy said. "They're bullies, trying to make this as hard on us as possible. It'll take me a week to get my files back in order. And I have other things I need to do."

"They know this is our place of business," Dan said. "It's hard to imagine they don't understand how far this destruction will set us back."

"That's what they want," Maria said.

"Wait a minute." Garrett shook his head. "They're doing their jobs. Think how they'd be criticized if there was evidence in here and they missed it."

"They're doing far more than their jobs. They're striking back against the defense lawyers they consider opponents. With a vengeance."

They heard a loud thump upstairs.

"Anyone want to guess what that was?" Dan asked.

"No," Maria replied. "Something valuable, probably."

"Oh my God. Oh my God." Jimmy jumped to his feet. A second later he was racing up the stairs.

"This is not going to be good," Maria murmured.

Dan looked at her and mouthed a silent "No."

Mere seconds later Jimmy reappeared on the stairs. "They opened the display case!" Tears were visible in his eyes. "They threw it down on the ground."

"Oh my God," Maria said breathlessly.

"May the saints preserve us," Garrett echoed.

"They damaged my Mego action figures!"

Dan felt like he was about to cry. "I'm sorry, Jimmy, I'll—"

Jimmy's voice erupted. "They took them out of the plastic wrappings! *They're ruined!*"

Dan rose to his feet, staring helplessly. "Jimmy. I'll reimburse you for—"

"You can't. They're priceless. They haven't been made since the 1970s. You'd have more luck landing an *Action Comics* #1 than a Mego Superman."

"Well, to be slightly objective about it...they are kind of aggressively ugly."

"What difference does that make? They're collectors' items."

"Right, right." He wrapped his arm around Jimmy's shoulders. "I'm sorry about this. I'll find some way to make it better. Promise."

"You can't."

"I will."

"I don't even want them anymore. Not after those invaders have handled them. I feel violated."

Garrett arched an eyebrow. "Jimmy, do you think you'll be needing a grief counselor?"

Maria jabbed him in the side.

A voice emerged from the staircase. "Ms. Morales?" It was Detective Kakazu. "Could I have a word?"

She rose. Dan started to do the same—then stopped himself. But he kept his ears alert so he could hear what they were saying.

"We found something," Kakazu explained.

"Where?"

"Dan's office. We would like to ask him about it."

"No."

"He might be able to explain it away and save us all a lot of trouble."

"Do you think I'm an idiot? You're not going to believe anything he says unless he tells you what you want to hear."

Kakazu's brows knitted closer together. "Ms. Morales, if I may remind you, I have known Dan for some time. We've worked on cases together. He has cross-examined me on the witness stand."

"So you hate his guts."

"I admire anyone as talented as I know him to be. Sometimes we have been on opposite sides of a case...but I have never known him to be dishonest. If he could explain the evidence, I would be inclined to believe him."

"Sadly, I am not inclined to believe you. And it wouldn't be your decision, ultimately, whether to use a piece of evidence at trial."

"Just a word. Please."

"Absolutely not. What's the evidence?"

Kakazu exhaled. "You realize I do not have to give you that information at this time."

"You will eventually."

"I don't now."

"Trade!" Dan shouted from the sofa. "He tells you what it is, I answer one question. Only one."

Maria almost shouted back, but she managed to contain myself. "You see why I'm reluctant. I have a loose cannon on my hands."

"I understand completely. But his proposal is acceptable. Will you agree to it?"

"Fine. What did you find?"

"A burner phone. Hidden in a small alcove. A loose board above a vent provided access."

"So what? A lot of people have extra phones."

"Hidden in the wall?"

"I'm sure there's a good reason."

"I'd like to ask what it is. And you promised." He took a few steps toward the sofa. "Dan? Would you care to comment?"

Dan spoke slowly. "I used that to make calls for my clients. Calls I didn't want traced back to me."

"Illegal calls?"

"Of course not. But let's face it, our constitutional right to privacy has virtually disappeared these days. The government—not to mention corporate America—collects data on us constantly. I keep that phone in case I need it."

"And have you used it recently?"

Maria jumped in. "We promised you one question. You had it. Now leave."

Kakazu tilted his head. "If that's the way you want it. But you know, he'll be asked about it at trial. And the prosecutor won't be limited to one question."

CHAPTER TWELVE

ELENA THOUGHT SHE WAS ON A BOAT, A BIG BOAT, BUT SHE couldn't be sure. She had been traveling for so long. She thought she'd been drugged and had no idea how much time she'd lost. She'd been beaten, hurt. Her clothes were torn. She wasn't sure...what they might have done to her. Her brain didn't seem to work the same way it once did. She was confused. Her memories were muddled.

She was lost. She knew nothing for certain.

The primary reason she thought she was on some kind of sea vessel was because she remembered how she used to get sick on boats, back in the day, back when her parents were still alive. They had always taken care of her. When she lost them to that car accident, right after her seventeenth birthday, she was completely lost, completely alone. No siblings, no family, no real friends. She couldn't stand being alone, so she began to wander.

She did at least have some money left to her, though she knew it would not last forever. Eventually she would have to get some kind of job, some legitimate way of making her way in the world. But she told herself that could wait. She needed to get her head on straight. Map out a future for herself. Although Spanish was her first language, she spoke excellent English. She could do anything. She wanted to go to college, to study art, to perhaps become an artist one day. She had always wanted to travel, though she never imagined she would do it alone. When she saw the email inviting her to join a special community in Guadalajara, it seemed as good a possibility as any. When she replied, they overwhelmed her with their sincerity and warmth. She needed a family. So she accepted the invitation.

As it turned out, the community was special, but not in a good way. Her first warning came when she saw it was surrounded by barbed wire fences. Entrance and exit permitted only by decree of the man in charge. They called it a commune. But after she had been there a few days, she realized it was closer to a cult.

Every cult needed a leader, someone others could depend upon, could be dependent upon. A charismatic soul who would make them feel better about themselves, if only for the briefest of instants.

She was certain David loved her. Sure, he was nice to everyone. That was how he kept the community together. That was how he kept everyone working the beanfields all day long. She knew he had been with some of the other girls. Who could blame him? They were so much prettier than Elena. But she still told herself he loved her best. She told herself she was his favorite. He told her, the first time they met. "You're going to be my favorite," flashing that wonderful lopsided grin of his.

Two weeks after she arrived, he raped her. Brutally. His eyes were wild and she thought he was on something, but she didn't know what. He didn't share it with her. He didn't share anything, except himself, in the most brutal way possible.

When it was over, after he finished, she cried. He told her to stop and she tried, but she couldn't. Tears spilled out of her like a faucet that could not be shut off. After a while, he became angry. He paced around the tiny closet he called a bedroom bellowing, waking everyone in the commune. He kicked the wall, then he kicked her. She was so scared she started trying to calm him, comfort him. The man who had raped her. She tried to ease his pain.

That's when he raped her again.

He wasn't there when she woke the next morning. She looked for him, but she found no trace, not in the house, not in the fields. She asked others, but no one would speak to her. Somehow, during the night, she had been excommunicated. She was no longer a member of the brotherhood of love.

That's when she decided it was time to go. But she didn't leave soon enough.

The men in the truck arrived shortly before noon. There were four of them and they were strong. She wasn't sure what their nationality might be, but they didn't look local, didn't look Mexican, didn't speak Spanish. They barely spoke to her, unless you counted the commands muttered in broken English. They forced her out of her tent and dragged her past the barbed wire fence.

"Get in truck."

"Why? Where are we going?"

"Get in truck," and this time, for emphasis, one shoved her so hard she almost fell to the ground.

She stumbled toward the black vehicle, so rundown she barely believed it could move. When she started to open the passenger-side door, the men laughed, loud and boisterous, as if something enormously humorous had taken place.

She hesitated. She wasn't sure what to do.

Three seconds was too long for them to wait. One of the men grabbed her hair at the scruff of the neck with his filthy hands and shoved her toward the back of the truck. Her head banged against the metal. Slowly, she climbed into the flatbed. It was covered with hay and dung. A hog tied by a rope squealed.

She travelled that way for three days. Not until the third would she admit to herself that David had sold her out—literally. He took what he wanted. Then she became a piece of merchandise to be bought and sold by men far more powerful than herself.

She was alone, and friendless, and lost. Who would rescue her? Who cared enough? Who even knew she still existed?

She wasn't sure she still existed.

Now she was on this huge hard metal ship. She didn't know where they were going. She didn't have anyone to ask. She sat in almost complete darkness. They brought her food, just enough to keep her alive. There was no toilet. She found a place and took care of it. She tried to stand as long as she could, but eventually she had to sit. In all that squalor.

That's what her life had become. Squalor. From the moment she woke each morning till she went to sleep at night. If she could have killed herself, she would have. That was perhaps the worst, most pathetic aspect of her existence. She was so helpless she didn't even have the ability to take her own life.

Only one thing had changed, here, on this voyage of the damned.

She was no longer alone. There were others, other girls.

One morning she heard someone crying. And for once, it wasn't her.

She couldn't see well enough to chart a path. She didn't know who was in there with her. But she could follow that voice. High-pitched. Young.

Crawling on hands and knees through the filth, she made her way to the endless sobbing.

"What's wrong?" she whispered.

The wailing stopped. She heard a sharp intake of breath.

"It's okay. I'm not going to hurt you. Why are you crying?"

Much time passed before she heard a response. "My tummy aches."

Probably from hunger. "Where does it hurt?"

"Down low. Near my waist." She had a Spanish accent, but her English was easy to understand. "I've never felt anything that hurt so much."

That didn't sound good. "How old are you?"

"Thirteen."

Too young. But any age was too young for a life like this. "Where are you from?"

"Tijuana. My parents took me on a trip. I was shopping in the marketplace. And—And—"

"Men grabbed you?"

A long pause. "Yes."

"Have you seen your parents since?"

"I'm sure they are missing me. I'm sure they are looking for me."

Elena hoped that was true. It would be so much more pleasant to think there was someone out there who loved this girl enough to search for her. Much more pleasant than believing she had been sold. "I'm sure you're right."

"Where are we going?"

"I don't know. What's your name?"

"Isabella. My parents call me Izzy."

She reached out with her left hand. "Show me where it hurts."

Izzy guided her hand to the lower right side of her abdomen. She pressed in, then released it.

Izzy screamed.

Jesus in heaven. Could this be appendicitis?

She was no doctor. But she knew appendicitis was serious. If Izzy's appendix was not removed soon, she would likely die. In excruciating pain.

And she didn't think their captors were likely to call for a surgeon.

Izzy continued sobbing, squirming, trying to escape the pain.

Something triggered inside Elena. Izzy had suffered too long. So had Izzy. They all had suffered too long. Endured too much.

But she was still alive, and while she lived, she would not surrender.

This little girl had no one else in the world. This little girl needed her. And even though the odds against her were a trillion to one, she would make the attempt.

She would find a way to help Izzy, to help them both. Or die trying.

CHAPTER THIRTEEN

DAN FELT GUILTY THE MOMENT HE ENTERED THE JAILHOUSE. IN the first place, he had told a lie. That was never a good idea, but even less of a good idea when the bar association was trying to yank your license.

But the main reason he felt guilty was because he was breaking a promise to Maria. She was working hard to save him and he was not helping. He knew she cared about him. It showed.

When she told him to stay away from Camila, she was giving sound legal advice. The prosecution alleged that the two of them engaged in a criminal conspiracy. Why give them extra ammunition? The prosecution would be alerted about this visit instantly. The conversation would likely be recorded. The last thing they needed was another smoking-gun recording introduced at trial.

But he had to see her. His feelings for Camila were strong and intense, and had only strengthened since they'd been separated. He hadn't felt anything like this for so long—he couldn't even remember when it happened last. High school? She was gorgeous, sure, but more importantly, she was smart, and strong, and so accomplished. She had transformed this town during her time as mayor, and now she was in line to be equally effective in the US Senate. She could be exactly what this country needed right now.

And he missed her.

When Camila saw who sat on the other side of the Plexiglas screen, her first words were straight to the point. "You shouldn't be here."

"You could've refused the visit."

"I thought I was meeting my lawyer. Not someone pretending to be my lawyer even though he couldn't be because we've both been charged with the same pack of lies."

"I doubt I have to tell you this, but this conversation is probably being recorded."

"Good. Let the scum behind this farce know how much contempt I have for them."

"It might be best not to antagonize anyone."

"You can be accommodating. I will dance on their graves."

That answered his first question. Had she given up? Not hardly. "How are you doing?"

"How do you think? I'm in jail for a crime I didn't commit. Again. I have work to do, a campaign to run, but instead I'm here. Plus, I look like hell."

"I think you look beautiful."

"Stop. No one behind bars looks beautiful. Probably wouldn't be a good thing if I did. It would only make me more of a target."

"Camila, you are so—so—you are—"

"Spit it out, Romeo."

"You are very important to me."

"How romantic. I'm important. Like an excellent pair of sneakers."

"You know what I mean." He fell back in the clamshell chair.

He had been desperate to see her again. But this wasn't going well. "I hate to see you like this."

"You and me both. Even if I'm exonerated, some people will always prefer to believe I'm a killer. This accusation will haunt me forever. Many pundits are already saying my political life is over."

"Others have overcome worse accusations."

"Are there worse accusations?"

"Your campaign staff is handling this magnificently. They're spinning it as a purely political attack. An attempt by extremists to take you out of the race."

She shrugged. "What else could they say? I started this race as a low-polling underdog and this is not helping. But I do have an alibi, you know."

"Yeah, me. I was with you all night."

"No, I mean a good alibi. Before I came to the party at your office that night, I was at my campaign office. At least ten other people were with me. If it turns out the murder occurred while I was still at the office, I have an ironclad alibi. Where were you before the party?"

"I went to the beach. Spent some quiet time. Alone. Went kitesurfing. Blew off some steam."

"Any witnesses?"

"Not that I'm aware."

"Damn. Should've known. These bastards have us by the short hairs." Her head dropped, forehead to the countertop.

"Camila?" He pressed his hand against the acrylic screen. "I miss you."

She raised her head. Her eyes softened a bit. "I miss you too, you stupid, sentimental man."

"This too shall pass. The circle will be unbroken."

"How many clichés can you utter in a single breath?"

"You might be surprised." He pressed even harder against the screen. "You're the most important thing in my life."

"I will be a happy woman when this is finished. When I'm out of here. Back on your boat."

"Really? What do you like best about the boat?"

She smiled. "You're there."

"I could say something about how you really rock my boat."

"Please do not."

"This isn't easy for me to say, but…but…"

Again the smile. "I know. You don't have to say it."

"But I will. I love you."

She pressed her hand against the other side of the screen. "And I you."

CHAPTER FOURTEEN

MARIA STARED AT THE HIDEOUS TABLEAU BEFORE HER, THINKING this was the most disturbing, most inhuman sight she had ever observed.

Somehow, as she struggled through law school, supported by her beloved father who wanted her to build a better life for herself, she never envisioned it leading to this. A filth-ridden back alley. A bloody fence. The scent of the ocean mingling with the stench of death.

"It was worse when the body was still here," Detective Kakazu noted.

No doubt. The corpse was gone, but the smell lingered. She could see holes in the fence where the stakes were used. In her mind, she could visualize the entire scene, the helplessness Belasco must have felt. Overpowered. Injured. Mutilated. Then murdered. Or did the killer leave him there for a long time before delivering the killing blow, allowing him to bleed slowly to death, his life's energy seeping away, each moment more excruciating than the last?

She shook her head violently, trying to force those images

out of her brain. "How can you stand it?" she asked Kakazu. "Do you get used to this sort of thing eventually?"

Kakazu gave her a flat response. "Sadly, yes."

She shook her head. "I never will."

"First crime scene?"

"Does that surprise you? I've been a criminal lawyer most of my career. But I never felt the need to view the horror in situ."

"Dan does. All the time."

"That's Dan. He wanted to come to this one, but I forbade it."

"And he let that stop him?"

"Only because he knew I was right." She crouched down and scrutinized the alley. She expected to find the rotting food, the stench of alcohol. They were behind Beachcombers, after all, a popular if somewhat sleazy bar near the marina.

Empty crates barely concealed human waste. Someone was using this back alley as a toilet. Probably homeless people. This strip of the waterfront had an above-average share. Camila had created many homeless shelters. But it seemed there were never enough. And some people refused to go, claiming they preferred life on the streets. She didn't know whether to believe that, or to attribute it to the mental illness that led to homelessness in the first place.

"CSI techs have already been over this, right?"

"Of course," Kakazu replied. "I would never have let you in otherwise."

"Then why the boots and gloves?" She pointed to the protective gear marring her stylish Dolce & Gabbana ensemble. "Isn't that overkill? If you've already got what you want?"

"You never know. A new lead might send us searching for something new. But that's not the primary reason we have to be careful."

"What is?"

"The fact that grasping defense attorneys are always looking for ways to criticize the way we gather, store, and process evidence."

"That's our job."

"Yes, I know. On the witness stand, your job is to make all police officers look like bumbling stooges. Never Dick Tracy. More like Laurel & Hardy."

"Actually, I don't do that. Neither does Dan."

"Dan has put me through the wringer in court on numerous occasions."

"But he never questioned your integrity. Or your competence."

"He's above average, as defense attorneys go." Kakazu glanced at his watch. "But he's still a defense attorney. Well, now he's a defendant. Which some of my colleagues feel should have happened a long time ago."

"Jake, you know damn well Dan did not commit this murder."

"I don't know that. And frankly, neither do you."

"He's not the type."

"There is no type. Unless you're talking about serial killers. And this was not the work of a serial killer."

"You're sure?"

"Look at those photos. This is not the product of insanity. This is the product of outrage. Anger. Vengeance."

"I don't know. Looks pretty crazy to me."

"Crazy in a human way. Not a twisted psychosexual maniac way."

"Your distinctions elude me."

"That's because this is your first crime scene."

She pivoted around. "You can pontificate all you want, but you've known Dan for years. You cannot seriously believe he would commit this brutal, vicious crime."

"I'm sorry, Maria, but none of us truly knows what lies in the heart of another. We can make guesses based upon external appearances, but we do not know. If there's anything I've learned in my many years on the force, it's that anyone is capable of anything, given the right circumstances. We all have a breaking point."

"This is not how Dan would handle a desperate situation."

He gave her a long look. "This may have been the only way to save himself. Or the woman he loves."

"You think he did this for Camila? Is that the fairy tale you're planning to tell at trial?"

"I'm not the prosecutor. I have no idea what their theory of the case will be. But I do know this." He took a step toward her. "I'm only telling you this because I genuinely...appreciate you, Maria."

What? Was Kakazu coming on to her?

"Your partner is in a massive amount of trouble, and so far, I have seen no indication whatsoever that he is being framed. I get why you're representing him. You had no choice, given the circumstances. But...don't get too attached. That will only make it difficult to detach. When it becomes necessary."

She turned away abruptly. This conversation was pissing her off. Kakazu thought he knew everything because he studied at Oxford and had a fancy British accent. But this time he totally missed the mark. She was sure of it.

Absolutely. She was sure. *Right?*

"DRT?" Which she knew was cop slang for, Dead Right There.

"We don't know yet. But the medical examiner should be able to tell us soon."

"I can tell you right now. He was killed somewhere else, then dragged here and pinned to the wall."

Kakazu arched an eyebrow. "And you know this...how? I assume it isn't because Dan confessed."

"Common sense. And observation."

"I thought that was your partner's schtick."

"Maybe I've learned a thing or two in the time we've worked together."

"Please explain."

"Take a step back. Look at the scene from the rear." She led him to the entrance point. "Imagine that the crucifixion spot on the fence is the focus. Twelve o'clock. You enter the alley with a body. How do you get to the fence?"

Kakazu squinted. "By...walking?"

"If Belasco was able to walk. But why would he come back here willingly? Surely he would know he was never coming out alive."

"He might be drugged."

"But then he wouldn't be walking. Not without help."

"Maybe he thought it was some kind of rendezvous. Maybe they met here all the time."

"I don't buy it. Squint a little and stare at the point where the body was found. Notice anything unusual?"

Kakazu hesitated several moments before answering. "A path."

"Exactly. The crates and trash and debris have been rearranged to create a clear passage to the only point on the fence strong enough to hold a body. And I don't think that could be done at the last moment, especially not when they risked being spotted. That had to be done in advance. By a murderer who planned to bring a corpse in later."

"The killer might have a travois or similar device to help port the body."

"And that would require a path."

"If a body was dragged in here, there should be traces."

"Except that it rained that night, remember? The police report said that when the officers responded to the anonymous call, they found the body in the rain."

"That is true. But it's not proof."

"Let me show you something else." She marched all the way to the fence. "See any signs of a struggle?"

"If he was affixed to the wall—"

"And he stood there calmly while someone pounded something through his chest? I don't think so. If he were still alive, he would start struggling as soon as he saw the stakes, if not before. And after he was staked, he would thrash and squirm and try to get free. See any signs of damage to the fence, other than the stake holes?"

"No. But there is blood."

"Some. Which means one of two things. Either the murder was so recent that rigor had not set in...or the more likely, though more disturbing possibility."

"Which is?"

"The killer collected the blood at the time of the murder. Saved it. Then splashed a little around the fence."

"To make it look like he was killed here when he wasn't. But why go to all that trouble?"

"To confuse you, super-cop. This is more proof that this whole horror show was planned by someone with a specific goal. A motive. Once we figure out what that motive was, we might be able to figure out who killed him."

CHAPTER FIFTEEN

MARIA PACED AROUND THE LONG SEMICIRCULAR SOFA IN THE middle of the living room—what they called the lobby of their office.

"Of course the grand jury returned an indictment. Did I really think anyone was going to do us a favor? No one has so far."

Garrett sat in the center, watching as she passed by in a blur. "The grand jury does what the prosecutor wants. It's a farce. A constitutionally required waste of time."

She crumbled the document in her fist. "But it still hurts to see it all written out on paper."

"Should you put that in the file?"

"I made copies."

"So you could rip them all up in anger?"

"How well you know me." She continued pacing. "This is infuriating. As if it weren't enough that the cops destroyed our beautiful workplace."

"Mr. K is sending cleaning and repair squads."

"And a carpenter, I hope. They tore this place to shreds. Just for spite."

"To be fair, they did find at least one significant piece of evidence tucked behind the wall. And they took other items they haven't identified yet."

"That burner phone doesn't prove anything."

"I agree. But the prosecution would be remiss not to examine it. So we can't say the destruction was completely unnecessary."

"You're much too logical, Garrett. It's simpler to hate everyone and everything they do."

He smiled a little. "You're stressed."

"Who wouldn't be? We even got a letter from the neighborhood association. Can you believe it? Complaining about the holes the cops dug in the yard. Like that was our idea."

"Regardless of whose idea it was, it's an eyesore."

She made a loud growling noise. "Would you stop being reasonable already? Why can't you get angry like everyone else?"

"I understand what the cops are doing, and why they do it." He checked his watch. "Ready to go?"

"Sure. Absolutely. Fine."

"You think you should take a Valium or something?"

"I don't use drugs. I meditate."

"Fine. I'll wait in the car while you meditate."

"No." She grabbed her Louis Vuitton purse. "Let's get out of here. Before Dan shows up and wants to come with us."

"The Belasco family would never let him through the door."

"That wouldn't stop him from trying."

The Western Hills Country Club was known throughout St. Petersburg as the swankiest, priciest, and most elite private club in the city. Maria had heard about it for years but knew she would never be a member. First and foremost, because she didn't want to be a member. She didn't like golf, she didn't like tennis, and she didn't like snobs. But she also knew she would never be invited to join. She was doing fine in the money department, thank you very much, but she still might not have enough for this crowd, or the right color skin, or the right connections. Her hard-working immigrant father struggled to give her a better future, but the one thing he couldn't manage was connections.

They wasted ten minutes before the grounds guard would let her onto the property, even though Evelyn Belasco had left her name. Was it the Jag he didn't like? Her Gucci jeans? Or, as she suspected, her Hispanic complexion. She did eventually get in, but the guard's attitude was grudging at best.

She had never been on the grounds before, never been behind the veil. She had to admit, it was impressive, landscaped to perfection. The main road led to a roundabout encircled by small buildings. The pro shop. The ice cream parlor. The arcade. The card room. The four-star restaurant. A ring of palmettos and topiaries created a beauty that was artificial enough to be perfect but not so perfect that it seemed artificial.

She was too proud to ask for directions, but she did eventually manage to find the nineteenth hole, not far from the pro shop. They had to park and walk past the pool to get there. A few kids were swimming. Several women were sunbathing. Seriously? In this day and age? There were only two things, she reminded herself, that we know for certain will kill you—smoking and sun. Why would anyone volunteer for either?

"Have you been here before?" she asked Garrett.

"Of course not. Way outside my league."

"Belasco was a prosecutor. You were a prosecutor. I thought you might understand these people better than I do."

"I can assure you that Belasco's government job did not get him his Western Hills membership. He had family money. He used to spend more on his campaigns than the district attorney earns. Which is why that fortune is mostly gone now."

"Was he having financial problems?"

"Not sure. But I do know that Belasco took out a million-dollar life insurance policy on himself. So his heirs' financial problems should soon disappear."

She passed through the front doors. After a few moments, she spotted the widow sitting at a corner table. She assumed the young man seated beside her was her son.

Maria had needed all her persuasive powers to convince Evelyn Belasco to meet with the lawyer representing the man accused of killing her husband. She suspected someone in the prosecutor's office thought it was good idea, or at the least, assured her it couldn't make any difference, because they had an ironclad case. She reminded herself not to push the privilege.

She extended her hand. "Mrs. Belasco? I'm Maria Morales."

Evelyn Belasco peered at her for a long moment. "Nice to meet you. This is my son, Christopher. We call him CJ."

Maria nodded in his direction. He appeared to be in his early twenties.

She also noticed the half-filled drink on the table. Pina colada, she thought. She was a wine girl herself. She suspected it wasn't the widow's first, judging by the alcohol in the air and the glassy cast to her eyes.

See? Ha! Dan wasn't the only person capable of making astute observations.

Garrett also introduced himself. "Thank you for meeting with us."

"Whatever," Evelyn said. "I'll play the game."

Maria was perplexed. "The...game?"

"Jump through the hoops. Be a good girl. But make no mistake. I know your partner killed my husband. And we will move heaven and earth to see that he rots in jail until the time comes to stick a needle in his arm. I hope he's currently enjoying his freedom. Because his days are numbered."

Well. This was off to a good start. "Can you tell me about your husband? I have to apologize. I've always worked criminal law, but I'm rarely in the courtroom and I never spoke to him. Never even said hello."

"Pity. He would've liked you."

"Because...he got along with his professional colleagues?"

"Because you're a hot little Mexican spitfire. He went in for that."

Maria bit back her natural instinct to chew the woman out for making racist, sexist remarks and maintained her composure. "Did he...have a wandering eye?"

"Who the hell are you, lady?" This was the son, CJ. "My father is barely in the grave and you want to trash his reputation?"

"I'm following up on your mother's comment."

"Chill, CJ," Evelyn said. "The more we cooperate, the sooner this will be over."

Maria stuck with the son. "You were close to your father, then?"

His hesitation told her a great deal.

Evelyn jumped in. "No one got close to George. Not really. He was self-sufficient. That's part of what made him a success. He had that single-minded focus most successful men have. The ability to block everything and everyone out and focus on the prize."

"Did that include his wife?"

Evelyn took a slow pull from her drink. "Are you sure you haven't worked in the courtroom? You seem like a crossexaminer to me."

"Just asking the obvious questions."

"Mm. George and I got along okay. We had an understanding. But I wouldn't fool myself into thinking I was his whole world. Any more than he was my whole world."

We had an understanding, she said. Not a marriage. "He had...other associations?"

"As did I."

"Is that what your son is so angry about?"

"No. He's angry because George was a crappy father. Does that surprise you? No one gets as far in the world as George did by being a homebody. He was distant, absent for the most part. And when he was around...he was incredibly hard on his son. Not a coddler."

"He was a cruel control freak," CJ said through clenched teeth. "He killed—"

"CJ!" Evelyn shot daggers with her eyes. "Be quiet."

Maria cleared her throat. "Look, I'm sorry, but I have to follow up. Did you say your father...killed someone?"

Evelyn sighed heavily. "We lost a daughter. CJ's sister. Annabel. Years ago. Car accident. A tragedy. No one's fault. But the boy blames his father."

"He could have prevented it," CJ said. "He could've saved her."

"No one could have saved her."

"Especially since he was never around."

Maria drew in her breath. "Could someone please tell me what happened?"

Evelyn took another slug from her drink. "Annabel was my youngest. CJ's little sister. She developed a bad drug problem. We sent her to rehab. Several times. Nothing helped. One night she came home...completely messed up. George didn't know what to do. He threw her out of the house."

"And she got in a car and drove," CJ said, eyes burning. "He killed her."

"Oh, he did not," Evelyn said. "It was...unfortunate."

Maria wasn't sure which direction to go next. "You indicated that George kept long hours?"

"I didn't quite say that," Evelyn replied. "I said he wasn't at home."

"Someone told me that, at least after his mayoral campaign began, he was usually out of the office by five."

"That's probably true. He was happy to delegate the small stuff to people whose time he considered…less valuable."

"But he didn't come home immediately, I gather. Where did he go?"

Evelyn raised a hand and signaled for a waiter. "You would have to ask him. And since that's impossible now, I guess we'll never know."

Garrett leaned into the conversation. "Ma'am, I knew your late husband slightly. I used to work in his office, and though he may have been imperfect, he was a good, efficient manager who got his work done on time with a minimum of messing around."

"Well…thank you."

"What's more, so far as I could tell, everyone in the office thought he was a terrific man—which makes what happened all the more inexplicable."

"Not really." Evelyn pointed to her glass, ordering a refill.

"Forgive me for touching on this awful subject, but do you know anyone who would have any reason to kill your husband?"

"Other than your partner?"

"Indeed. Perhaps a vengeful criminal? Your husband was responsible for putting many people behind bars."

"Indirectly. He ran the office. But he rarely entered the courtroom himself, not after he became district attorney. I can't imagine this was a grudge match."

Maria jumped back in. "I've been to the crime scene. And the horrible manner in which he was killed does suggest there might have been...personal enmity involved. Did he ever receive threats?"

"Not to my knowledge."

"You indicated that he was having...other relationships. Could his death be the result of an outside relationship?"

"A woman scorned? A jealous husband? Please. Tramps might steal his wallet, but they're not going to lure him into a back alley and plug him full of holes."

"What about at the workplace? Any rivalries there?"

Evelyn accepted the fresh glass and took a deep slug. "Now you're on the track of something. There was definitely someone in the office who wanted him out of the way."

"And that was...?"

"Jazlyn Prentice. Who I believe is a close friend of your client."

CHAPTER SIXTEEN

MARIA COULDN'T BELIEVE WHAT SHE WAS HEARING. JAZLYN? THE epitome of logic and self-control? "Wait a minute. I know Jazlyn. She's about the least likely person to commit a murder I can imagine."

Evelyn appeared completely unruffled. "I never said anything about the woman committing a murder. She's too smart for that."

"Then you're saying Dan did it? For Jazlyn? That's absurd."

She felt Garrett's hand lightly touch her shoulder. She knew what he was telling her. Calm down. They wanted Evelyn to keep talking, not to get angry and stomp away.

Evelyn stirred her drink with her finger. "You are aware that the two had a...relationship. Right?"

"If you want to use that word. They were professional colleagues."

"They went out together."

"One date."

Evelyn smiled broadly. "In the public eye. But no one knows for sure what happened outside the public eye. They were certainly seen together a great deal."

Maria could feel heat rising to the surface of her skin. These accusations were outrageous. But if this woman was willing to peddle them, how many others would be? "There was nothing romantic between Dan and Jazlyn. They worked together—on opposite sides of the courtroom. That's the only reason they were seen together."

"Are you sure about that?"

"Yes, I am." She was supposed to be getting information out of this woman. Instead, she was defending Dan against preposterous claims—and not doing it well.

"The whole situation stinks," CJ said. "Who ever heard of a defense attorney and a prosecutor being buddies? And why was he always beating her in court? Prosecutors don't bring charges unless they're certain they can win. I learned that from my father, if nothing else."

Maria blinked. "Are you suggesting Jazlyn was throwing cases?"

Evelyn titled her glass. "Women have done stupider things for men."

"Not Jazlyn. Not in a thousand years."

"Given the right circumstances, most women will do whatever it takes." Evelyn grabbed her handbag and lit a cigarette. Just when you thought she couldn't possibly be any viler, she was. "To defend her children. Anything. To survive. Anything. To protect the man she loves. Anything."

"Dan didn't need protecting." Maria stifled her irritation. "I don't think they'll allow you to smoke in here."

"Honey, they'll allow me to do anything I want in here." She blew smoke in Maria's direction. "I don't think Jazlyn planned the crime. Your partner was the manipulator. Why would he initiate a relationship with her? He could do better. He slept with her for information. That's why he kept winning all those cases. That's how he built his renowned winning streak."

Maria could barely contain herself. "That is absolutely…inaccurate."

"Truth hurts, doesn't it?"

"I haven't heard any truth yet."

"Mind you, I'm not saying there wasn't anything in this for Ms. Prentice. She wanted to be the district attorney. Still does, obviously, since she's running. And that meant my husband had to be eliminated."

"No one on earth wants to be DA that much. The job doesn't even pay well."

"It's not about money. Not with her. She wanted what the man had. But she couldn't beat him. He could outspend her six ways to Sunday. The only way she was going to get what she wanted was if George met an untimely end."

Maria was about to erupt, but Garrett leaned between them. "If I may ask, are these theories your actual beliefs?"

"Why else would I say it?"

"Perhaps it's my imagination, but I thought perhaps you were baiting us."

"Why would I do that?"

"Why would you light a cigarette in the middle of a conversation? No one will appreciate that. Even your son scooted away."

Evelyn grinned, then rubbed the cigarette out on a saucer. "I like you. You're direct. And you pay attention. That's more…formidable."

Garrett turned his attention to CJ. "Is this your theory of what happened, too? Some sort of lovers' pact rubout so Jazlyn Prentice could be DA?"

CJ looked uncomfortable having the focus of attention shift to him. "I don't know who was sleeping with whom. But I know Daniel Pike killed my father."

"And how do you know this?"

"It's obvious."

"It's not obvious to me."

"Have you heard that recording? They were plotting against him."

"Dan and Jazlyn aren't on that recording. It's Dan and Camila Pérez. Those two actually were in a relationship."

"I think Pike had a lot of relationships. He was a player."

"Judging from what your mother has said, so was your father. Is that why you were angry with him? Were you mad about the way he treated your mother?"

"My mother deserved better. Much better."

Evelyn waved her hand in the air. "Ehh. I'm doing all right."

Maria tried to pick up the thread. "You don't seem terribly sorry that your father is gone, CJ."

"I didn't want him murdered, if that's what you're implying."

"But this must be better for your mom. She stands to gain quite a bit of money from an insurance policy, right? She'll be free to use it any way she wants. And you'll be free of a father who was rarely around and criticized you constantly when he was."

CJ slammed back in his chair, his arms wrapped around himself.

Evelyn made a cackling sound. "Not bad, lady. Two points for you."

"I was with friends at a party the entire night my dad was killed," CJ said. "Tons of witnesses. And about a thousand selfies."

"Could you email me some of those?"

Evelyn shook her head. "Maybe I could. CJ is perhaps the one millennial on earth who doesn't know his way around a laptop. Completely computer illiterate."

"I'll use my phone, Mother."

Evelyn waved her hand at the waiter. Another drink so soon? "I never believed that stuff about Pike and the mayor."

Maria was puzzled. "It's well known the two were in a relationship."

"Well known isn't always true."

"You think the relationship was…some kind of…sham?"

"I'm not saying they didn't all conspire to kill my husband. But the rest of it? Pfft."

"Now I'm confused. Was it Dan working with Jazlyn, or Dan working with Camila?"

"Or all of the above."

She squinted, trying to make sense of it. "Are you saying Dan and Camila weren't really in a relationship? Because let me tell you—I've seen them together. They were."

"Putting on a show. Building an alibi."

"That's not even—"

"That Pérez woman? She's a dyke if I ever saw one."

Maria's lips parted wordlessly.

"He was a beard, that's all. All she cares about is herself. She wanted my husband gone too. They'd known each other a long time. He knew the real dirt, and that's what worried her. Secrets. Stuff she didn't want to come out."

"Like what?"

"Pérez is into chicks. I see it in my Twitter feed every day."

"That's what some people always say about strong women."

"There are memes all over Facebook. Photos. It's a fact."

"Because you read it on the internet?"

"Because it's true. Obviously."

"Meaning…confirmation bias. You believe stories that reinforce your preexisting beliefs without questioning their accuracy?"

"You want to know what's fake, sweetie? Your insistence that Daniel Pike was some kind of crusading hero. He's a womanizer, a fraud, and a con man. Who only cares about himself. And he killed my husband."

A well-built man Maria did not recognize handed Evelyn a

slip of paper. Her demeanor changed immediately. She sat up straighter. Her face relaxed.

"Tomorrow at ten a.m., Evelyn," the man said. He looked strong, like he spent a lot of time in the gym. He was at least ten years younger than Evelyn. "I'll be handling the massage myself. Try to arrive about fifteen minutes early, if possible."

"I'll be there."

"See you then." He made a small salute and departed.

Maria tried to maintain a straight face. "Friend of yours?"

"Look, George had plenty of friends. Why shouldn't I?"

"And why did he have so many friends?"

"I tried, okay? But whatever it was that man liked, he wasn't getting it from me. He married for the arm candy, not for the tiger in bed. He was a man of unusual interests. Which is not a crime." Evelyn paused. "And it doesn't matter. Your partner is going down."

"How can you be so sure?"

"I talk to people. I've still got connections. Your pal has pulled his last Houdini. This time, even he can't escape." She scribbled a signature on the check and pushed uneasily to her feet. "If the courts don't take care of Daniel Pike, I'll find someone who will."

CHAPTER SEVENTEEN

JIMMY STROLLED INTO THE COURT CLERK'S OFFICE BEARING A serving tray covered with a plastic lid. The plastic was thick enough to make it impossible to see what was inside. He whistled a happy tune, hoping Shawna would hear.

His wish was granted. The head of the office emerged from an office in the rear. "Stop already, Jimmy. The answer is no."

He laid the tray on the counter. "I haven't asked the question yet."

"Think of this as *Jeopardy*. The answer precedes the question. And the answer is no."

He grinned. "Then the correct response is, 'Can Shawna resist any dessert brought by Jimmy Armstrong?'"

Shawna was a short woman and a bit on the heavy side. He had known her for many years and she had provided him with useful courtroom intel on many occasions. She had a nephew Jimmy knew had seen some tough times as a teen. He was in college and seemed to be getting his life back on track, mostly due to Shawna's support. "I brought enough for the entire office. Do you have the right to deny these culinary delights to your colleagues?"

"I do. The people made me County Clerk. I have an obligation to fend off corruption in all forms."

"You wound me." Jimmy pressed his hand against his chest. "I would never suggest anything that might compromise your integrity."

"Uh-huh."

"I know that you're a pillar of the community."

"Good. Then take your tray and vamoose before—"

Jimmy removed the plastic cover. "*Voila!*"

Brownies. Still fresh enough to emanate chocolatey goodness.

Shawna twisted her lips into something like a frown. "This is supposed to tempt me?"

"Of course not. This is simply supposed to brighten your day."

"Did you get these at a bakery?"

"Perish the thought. Homemade."

"Don't tell me that you made them. I know better."

"This is my colleague's work. He's the kitchen whiz."

"Dan?" She did a double-take. "I suppose he does have time on his hands these days." She stepped closer. "Not drugged or anything?"

"Seriously?"

"Maybe you're trying to knock the whole office unconscious so you can crawl into the files and remove all the charges against your buddy."

"Because that would work."

"No telling what you might have up your sleeve." She hesitated. "Brownies are fattening."

"Not these. Low sugar, low fat. Gluten-free."

"How is that even possible?"

"I gather black bean is the critical ingredient. Lots of cocoa, of course, but barely any sugar, no butter. Healthy brownies."

"Two words you don't often hear spoken together." With an

air of resignation, she grabbed one of the treats and took a bite. "That isn't terrible. Though I might've preferred more sugar."

"Wouldn't we all?" He nestled in close to the counter. "Look, Shawna, what's the lowdown on this judge? Hembeck."

She took another bite. "Now we're getting to it."

"I'm not asking you to reveal confidential information. Just your general impressions. You must see the woman every day."

"True enough."

"What do you think? Do you like her?"

Shawna shrugged. "Meh."

"Meaning no?"

"She's not really friendly, if you know what I mean. Not unfriendly exactly. But...distant. Business oriented. She's never going to be one of the girls."

"I know she's in line for a federal seat. Conservative?"

"Every criminal case she's handled to date has resulted in a conviction."

That wasn't promising, but it also wasn't that surprising. Prosecutors rarely went to trial unless they thought they had the defendant dead to rights. "What about sentencing?" In Florida, in most cases, though the jury rendered the verdict, the judge delivered the sentence.

"To the max. Almost always. Even on drug crimes. Even on white-collar crimes."

That was unusual. Especially in this era, when prisons were woefully overcrowded. Many people advocated alternate forms of punishment for non-violent criminals. "She did grant Dan bail."

"Yeah. But why? Some people on the internet are saying she wanted him on the street so someone could rub him out. Saving her the bother of a controversial trial."

"I find that hard to believe."

She shrugged. "Merely repeating what I read."

He reached into his coat pocket. "I've got a motion in limine I want to file."

Shawna made a tsking noise and shook her head. "Mistake."

"Hembeck doesn't like motions in limine?"

"Hates them. Says it's like asking her to decide the case before the trial has started. She'll hold it in abeyance."

"This is not trying the case. It's deciding what evidence can be presented at trial."

"Hey, don't kill the messenger. Only repeating what I've heard."

Great. "Well, I'm still filing the motion. Anything else you know about her?"

Shawna thought for a moment. "She has an autographed football from a Buccaneers game in her chambers."

Sports. That was a language he didn't speak at all. Maria would have to bring Garrett with her when she wanted to talk with the judge. "Thanks, Shawna. How's your nephew?"

A smile rose on her face. "Very well, thank you. He aced Organic Chemistry."

"Terrific."

"Yeah. I don't even know what that is, but they tell me it's a tough class. He's really turned himself around."

"Because of you. Those tuition payments must've taken a big chunk out of your savings."

"Yeah." She fell quiet for a moment.

"Did they finish the courthouse sweep? Find any listening devices?" During a previous case, Dan had become convinced someone was eavesdropping on the private consultation rooms.

"No. They spent a bundle but they didn't find anything. Probably nothing to find. I can't imagine anyone would do something like that."

"Two words. Conrad Sweeney."

Shawna's eyes drifted downward. "I've heard of him..."

"I'm not surprised." Jimmy didn't have Dan's gifts, but there was something strange about the way Shawna's face tensed when he mentioned Sweeney's name. "You probably wouldn't see him in the courthouse, though. He works through minions. Finds someone he can buy off, then wrings them dry. Destroys lives in the process. I wouldn't be surprised if he was behind this whole mess with Belasco."

Shawna gave him a long look. "Jimmy, you're a nice guy. But you must know that everyone is completely convinced your pal murdered Belasco. That recording speaks for itself."

"Not to me." He started to leave, but Shawna stopped him. "Wait. Someone left something for you. I figured you'd be in soon."

"Because I miss you."

"Because you always want something." She pushed a sealed envelope across the counter. His name was written in ink across the front.

"Thanks." He took the envelope and started out the door. By the time he'd reached the elevators, he had the letter out.

It was written in rigid block lettering obviously intended to disguise handwriting.

I KNOW WHAT YOU NEED.

Okay, that was mysterious enough to grab his attention.

He flipped the paper over and found a time and meeting place.

What? There was no way he was doing that.

He sighed. Except maybe for Dan.

He shoved the paper into his pocket. Why was someone setting up a meeting in this mysterious Deep Throat way? Why not tell him whatever they wanted him to know?

He didn't have the answers. But he knew he would make the appointed rendezvous. Even if the voice inside thought it was the stupidest thing he could possibly do.

Even if it meant someone might be planning another murder.

CHAPTER EIGHTEEN

CAMILA SCRUTINIZED THE PACKED COURTROOM. AN IMPRESSIVE turnout. She would like to think this was a sign of positive community engagement with local affairs—but she knew better. Most citizens' engagement with their communities these days was minimal. These people were gossip hounds, interacting with their community on the TMZ level. They would never show up for a city council meeting. But they were all over a juicy murder case.

Her attorney, Gary Davenport, was a big-firm lawyer charging big-firm fees, but he had a rep for getting the job done right.

"Do you have Daniel Pike's win-loss record?" she asked.

"I don't have it and I don't want it," he replied. "That's a trial record. I make sure my clients don't go to trial. Why roll the dice at the craps table when you can win before the game begins?"

"That...does make sense."

"No disrespect to a fellow attorney. But Pike is a showboat. A truly great attorney makes sure their clients never go anywhere near a trial."

Davenport told her a bail application was useless, despite the fact that her alleged co-conspirator had succeeded with one. Among other problems, she didn't have the financial means to meet the likely bail and no bondsman would cover that much money.

Instead, he recommended that they just win the case.

"Which leaves me in jail forever pending trial."

"Watch. This is why you're paying me the big money."

Beverly Garfield was at her station. The prosecution ice queen seemed uncomfortable, perhaps even a little baffled—like, if we aren't going to discuss bail, why are we here?

The only person in the courtroom who appeared more baffled was the man in the white coat, Dr. Zanzibar, the city medical examiner. Wasn't the white coat rather cliché? It did make him stand out, she supposed, and lent him an air of authority.

Judge Fitzgerald entered and called the court into session. "I understand we have a motion to dismiss the charges against the defendant?" the judge said, obviously somewhat incredulous.

Davenport rose to his feet. "That's correct, your honor."

"And we vehemently oppose," Garfield said. "This motion is completely frivolous."

"If I may explain," Davenport said, "although we will make a brief evidentiary showing, this is a motion to dismiss. The prosecution has no case. This is a wrongful prosecution. And…" He paused long enough to create interest. "…I can prove that in less than an hour."

"Well now," the judge said, peering at the pleadings through his readers, "that's an offer I can't refuse. Please proceed."

Camila watched as Davenport put Zanzibar on the stand. This must be a change of pace for the old pro, she thought. Being called to the stand by the defense rather than the prosecution.

Davenport established the doctor's credentials and his years of experience, then moved directly to the case at hand. "You were asked to investigate the murder of George Belasco, correct?"

Zanzibar stroked his beard. "I was contacted shortly after the body was discovered. I immediately dispatched a team from my office. As soon as the CSI techs were done photo- and video-graphing the body, they carefully removed it and brought it to the morgue."

"What did you do then?"

"As soon as possible, I performed an autopsy to determine the cause of death and to establish whether there were any unusual circumstances."

"What did you determine?"

"As to the cause of death, technically it was loss of blood to the brain due to excessive bleeding from six gunshot wounds."

Davenport nodded. "And as to unusual circumstances?"

"The tox screen found nothing. He did not appear to have been drugged or poisoned. Hadn't eaten anything that bothered him. Drank too much coffee, but that wasn't a factor in his demise. But I did detect some unexpected results with respect to liver mortis."

"Can you explain to the court what that means?"

"It's a simple concept. Once the heart stops pumping, blood tends to settle at the lowest point of gravity. Since the victim had been pinioned to a fence, you would expect that lowest point to be the feet. But it wasn't."

"So that tells you…"

"That the body was moved after death. In other words, Belasco was killed somewhere else, while in a different position. Then moved to that alley and nailed to the fence."

Camila heard an audible murmur from the courtroom. She assumed they were all pondering the same question: Why would anyone do that? Why go to the enormous trouble of dragging a hard-to-manage corpse to a back alley, then go to the even greater trouble of driving stakes through it?

"Did this conclusion surprise you?" Davenport asked.

"Not really. I'd seen photographs taken at the crime scene, and they showed relatively little blood on the fence or on the ground at the victim's feet. If he had been killed on the premises, I would've expected to see far more."

"Did your examination produce anything that suggested where the victim was actually killed?"

"I'm afraid not. That's beyond medical science. That's something for the detectives to determine."

Davenport flipped a page in his outline. "Dr. Zanzibar, I'd like you to focus on the time of death. We know the body was found around midnight. But do you know when George Belasco was actually killed?"

"I do."

"And how was this determined?"

"The primary indicator is stomach contents, although there are others. Internal body temperature is a strong indicator. Rigor mortis typically sets in after about three hours, so the degree of bodily stiffness can also be an excellent gauge."

"Given all the evidence you viewed and all the examinations you conducted, what did you determine with respect to the time of death?"

"Approximately seven p.m. that evening, though I would allow a margin of error of about forty-five minutes on either side. Not all bodies deteriorate at precisely the same rate."

"Thank you. No more questions."

The judge glanced at Garfield, who simply shrugged. "No cross, your honor." In other words, Why should I?

"Anything further, Mr. Davenport?"

"Yes. With the prosecution's indulgence, I would offer into evidence the following fourteen affidavits."

Garfield's eyes widened. Fourteen?

"May I ask what these affidavits contain?" the judge asked.

"Of course, your honor." He passed the documents to the bailiff, who in turn walked them to the judge. "They are all from witnesses who can testify that they were with Camila Pérez, in her office, at the time George Belasco was murdered, according to the government's own expert."

The judge rifled through the documents, obviously impressed. "Fourteen?"

"Yes, your honor. My client was still at the office and many people work there. They all remember the boss being present at the time the victim was murdered."

The judge arched an eyebrow. "Impressive." He peered over his glasses. "Ms. Garfield?"

"Your honor, we object to the admission of these affidavits. I can't cross-examine an affidavit."

"What would she say if she could?" Davenport asked. "But in an effort to accommodate the prosecutor, I have six of these witnesses on the premises at this time, ready to take the stand. And I could call the rest if necessary. What's more, we have footage from a security camera active on the date in question in the parking lot outside my client's office. It shows when Camila Pérez left the office." He paused. "And it was long after the victim was murdered."

The judge tapped his glasses against the bench. "I'm beginning to see why you brought this motion at this time."

"Your honor," Garfield said, "the People most strenuously object to this."

"Grounds?"

"The whole—the whole—motion is premature. I haven't talked to these people and and—I wasn't given advance notice and—"

"But Mr. Davenport makes a sound point. These people know where they were and who was with them. And there are fourteen of them. Do you seriously believe fourteen people joined together to perjure themselves?"

"Well...no."

"I suppose we can call a few to the stand if you like. But it seems like an enormous waste of time."

Camila could almost see the wheels turning in Garfield's brain. "Your honor, Camila Pérez was a co-conspirator. Even if she wasn't at the scene of the crime and didn't pull the trigger, she could still have been involved."

"But you've charged her with first-degree murder. You've asked for the death penalty."

"True..."

"It's not first-degree murder if she wasn't present."

Garfield was obviously fumbling. "It could be...conspiracy to commit a felony. Maybe felony murder."

Judge Fitzgerald checked the pleadings. "You haven't filed those charges."

"We could dismiss and amend."

"You could. But as of this time, you have not done so. Correct?"

Garfield pursed her lips. "That is...correct."

"Well then," the judge replied. "This motion isn't completely frivolous, is it?"

Camila felt a tingling inside. She tried to suppress her excitement. She didn't want to be disappointed. Was there a chance this might actually work?

The judge turned toward the defense table. "Mr. Davenport?"

He nodded. "I think your honor has already anticipated what I have to say. We have the time of death, given to us by the prosecution's own expert. We have more than a dozen witnesses, plus a security camera, telling us that Camila Pérez could not have committed the murder at that time. That evidence has not been challenged and frankly, I believe it is unassailable. Let me add, the prosecution has not yet filed a conspiracy claim, and I don't think they will. Their prosecution is based upon an audio recording of two people talking, maybe saying things they shouldn't have said, but never saying anything that would rise to the level of criminal conspiracy. That claim requires real evidence of an actual plan to commit a felony. At this time there is no concrete evidence whatsoever that Camila Pérez had anything to do with this murder."

The judge seemed almost reluctant to agree, but forced to do so. "I can't argue with that. Even if the DA filed such a claim, the court would be forced to dismiss it unless they can adduce more evidence."

"And let me make one more observation," Davenport continued. "This is not the first time my client has been victimized by false accusations. The previous charges were false, politically motivated lies brought by opponents to derail her career. Can we see this latest batch of trumped-up charges any differently? Look how much negative publicity she has already incurred. Look how much time she's spent in jail while her opponents are on the campaign trial. Enormous damage has been done, and in service of what? More bogus charges that turn out to be unsupported by the slightest wisp of truth."

The judge listened attentively, not speaking, but not disagreeing.

Davenport proceeded. "The proper role of the courts is to protect the citizenry, not to harm innocents, not to be a tool for those who would manipulate the system, who think political decisions should be made behind closed doors. Camila Pérez is a fine woman with an outstanding record of public service and it's time we stopped letting her opponents use the judiciary to short-circuit an exemplary career."

Davenport appeared to have the entire room in the palm of his hand, hanging on his every word. The reporters in the gallery were scribbling notes at the speed of sound.

"Your honor, I respectfully request that the defendant's motion be granted and that these charges against my client be dismissed."

"Any further discussion?" the judge asked. No one spoke. "The motion will be granted. The court apologizes to the defendant for what she has suffered. And hopes she will continue her work without any further interference."

The judge slammed his gavel and the courtroom erupted. A near-deafening cacophony spread across the room. Reporters shouted questions at Camila. Some people applauded. A few even had tears in their eyes.

Davenport crouched beside her and spoke quietly. "That's what I'm talkin' 'bout."

Camila looked at him, barely able to speak. "You are a miracle worker."

He winked. "Remember that when you get my bill."

Reporters shouted questions at her. "Mayor Pérez, will you continue your senatorial campaign?"

She turned toward them, beaming. "First I'd like to get out of these hideous orange coveralls." Everyone laughed. "But as soon as I'm free, I will be back on the campaign trail. Count on it. And my opponents had better look out." Her eyes narrowed slightly. "Because I'm coming for them."

CHAPTER NINETEEN

Dan set down his phone and shouted loudly enough to be heard throughout the office.

"Camila got off! All charges dismissed!"

Barely a few moments later, Maria emerged from her private office and threaded a path through the housecleaners and carpenters working to restore the mansion to its pre-search-warrant glory. "You mean she's out on bail?"

"I mean she's out. Period. Charges dismissed. Full stop."

Maria whipped out her phone and started tapping. "How can that be?"

"A lot of co-workers were prepared to testify that she couldn't have possibly pulled the trigger at the time of death."

"Where does that leave you?"

He plopped down on the sofa. He could barely describe all the cascading emotions rushing through his body. First and foremost—relief. When he last saw Camila, at the jailhouse, it almost tore his heart in two. He knew she desperately wanted —*needed*—to be somewhere else. Now perhaps he would witness a return of the Camila he knew and adored.

The second wave of emotion related to himself. How was

this going to affect his case? Would this be perceived as another chink in the prosecution armor? Or, as seemed more likely, would this cause them to intensify their pursuit of him?

"Leaves me holding the bag, I fear. Except now I'm holding it alone. I'm all the cops have left to avoid looking like total fools."

Maria shoved her phone into her tight jeans pocket. "It would be sweet if we could ride her gravy train. But you have no alibi witnesses."

"Aww, you don't want to cling to Davenport's coattails. You'll come up with your own brilliant success strategy."

"You hope. Why are you still here? Aren't you going to run off to see Camila?"

"No. Her attorney thinks it's a bad idea. She doesn't need a lot of paparazzi pics showing the two of us together. She needs to return to the office and show people her focus is on politics. She's got a campaign to run and a lot of lost time to make up for."

"That might not be as difficult as you imagine. If my Twitter feed is any indication, Camila's a rock star."

He scooted closer so he could peer at her iPhone screen. "What do you mean?"

"People see her as a martyr to the progressive cause. She's been charged twice now, and both times the charges proved to be groundless. Memes are reminding the world that Dr. King was also thrown into jail by the forces that opposed progress. As was Gandhi. According to the internet, the powers-that-be perceive Camila as a major threat to their privileged lifestyle."

"A poster child for the underprivileged."

Maria kept scrolling. "Look at this. It says she beat the attacks that come to anyone who tries to bring down the hegemony. She did more than persist—she survived." She looked up from the screen. "Her handlers could turn this sow's ear into a silk purse."

"And to think, I knew her when she was just a sweet little co-defendant."

"Look at her approval ratings! Her numbers are going through the roof. She's barely out of jail and she's already the frontrunner." Maria put the phone away. "I think your girl is going somewhere, Dan."

He tried to maintain his poker face. "Of course, if I don't beat the charges, she'll be going without me."

"Even if we can't use her success in the courtroom, I think we can use her success on the internet. Try to alter public opinion. I told you about the social media consultant—"

"Judge Hembeck won't like it if she thinks I'm campaigning for acquittal."

"You won't have anything to do with it. You can't control what internet trolls do, right?"

"I can't even control what my lawyer does."

She gave him a sharp eye. "Coincidentally, I can't control what my client does."

He grinned a little. "No wonder this relationship works so well. We're basically two control freaks, each completely unable to control the other."

"That does sum it up rather nicely." She stared at him for a moment. "But seriously. We need to go full-out on this. Webpage, Facebook, Twitter, the whole nine yards. Prepare to be anointed in the InstaCommunity. Jimmy's already laid the groundwork."

"Wonderful. Where is Jimmy, anyway?"

"I don't know. Said he had some kind of meeting."

"With whom?"

"He was kind of mysterious. Not forthcoming on the details. Told Hank he might be out late. Should we be worried?"

"Nah. He's probably buying new action figures on the black market."

"By the way, I think we should not push the motion in

limine. Jimmy says our judge hates evidentiary hearings in advance of trial."

"Well, isn't that too bad. We need to kill that recording."

"Do we, though? Time to face reality, Cragheart."

Uh-oh. Anytime she hauled out his Gloomhaven name, he knew she was preparing to say something he didn't want to hear. "Meaning?"

"Everyone has already heard that tape. It's all over the internet."

"We can weed out jurors who have already heard the recording and formed an opinion about it."

"We can weed out the jurors who will admit they've already heard the recording. Which is not the same thing. What do we accomplish by trying to suppress it? We irritate the judge and probably gain nothing."

"This sounds like a risky strategy."

"Strategy is my forte. When the prosecution attempts to use the recording at trial, I'll object. The prosecutors still don't know who sent the recording to them. They can't put it into evidence without a sponsoring witness. Who exactly will that be?"

"They'll use the cop who first saw the email."

"And that lucky devil will not be able to explain where it came from or how it was recorded. Won't be able to testify as to authenticity."

He thought long and hard about it. He didn't like the idea. His approach had always been to constantly be on the attack. If someone hits you, you hit them back harder, immediately. But he wasn't running this case. And if he wanted Maria to be at her best, he should stay out of her way. Let her run her own show.

"I will yield to your strategic analysis, Maria. I can see you've given this a lot of thought. Which I very much appreciate."

"But you're not convinced."

"I'm never convinced of anything. Trial practice is mostly

preparation, but there's a lot of shooting from the hip too. You're the one who's going to be standing up there yakking. You need to do what you think is right." He took another breath, then added, "I trust you."

She inched slightly closer. "Really?"

He peered back at her. Something was going on behind those lovely brown eyes, but he couldn't quite read it. "Yes. In fact, there's no one on earth I would trust more. I know you can do this."

A strange expression crossed her face. "Stop. I'm going to get choked up."

"Nah. Just get out there and fight."

CHAPTER TWENTY

DESPITE THE FACT THAT HE WAS ENTERING A BUSY LOCATION THAT was basically an indoor amusement park, Jimmy couldn't resist the temptation to tread carefully, to practically tiptoe. He knew someone, somewhere, was watching him.

Why would his mysterious correspondent pick Play Date for a rendezvous? He'd never been before, but he knew the general concept. Sort of a Hey Dey, Trade Mark, Urban Adventures on steroids. Higher, faster, scarier. Thrills for people seeking something with a little more edge—though still not edgy enough to actually be life-threatening. Supposedly.

He stepped up to the young woman behind the front counter. "Mmm….can I come in?"

She beamed a Disney smile at him. "Of course. Do you want the All-Admission Pass, the three-day pass, the Super-Saver…" She paused for a moment. "Or the senior discount?"

His jaw lowered. He was forty-six. "I don't think I qualify." He tried not to be offended. The woman looked seventeen at best. Probably everyone over thirty looked senior to her.

Or maybe Maria was right. Maybe it was time to ditch the cardigans.

"Okay. Regular admission then? Or do you want to go à la carte?"

He had no idea what that meant. He scanned the list of activities on the marquis behind the counter. Laser tag. Paintball. Arcade. Go-carts. The list went on and on. How did they fit it all in one location? Bowling. Trampolines.

All that bouncing around sounded dreadful. His eyes traveled down the list. Road rally. Rock wall. Ropes course.

Ropes course? As in, strap me up in a harness and haul me into the air?

He remembered what the note said, after the address. NO MICS FORTY FEET UP.

Of course. It was always the thing you dreaded most.

"One ticket for the ropes course."

The young woman arched an eyebrow. "You're sure about that?"

He was starting to get angry. "Is there an age restriction?"

"No." She licked her lips. "But there's a weight restriction."

Okay, he had maybe twenty pounds he didn't need, but this was even more irritating than the remark about his age. "I'll be fine. You need to get out of your skinny Gen Z ripped-jeans world and show some respect."

She held up her hands. "Ok, Boomer. Chill."

He handed her a credit card. "Don't you mean, *chillax*?"

"Whatever." She ran the card and handed him a ticket. "Enjoy your aerial experience."

"I will. Afterwards, I think I'll try skydiving."

To Jimmy's relief, the attendant running the ropes attraction didn't have any problem with him. The kid wrapped the nylon netting between his legs and around and beneath his shoulders, gently tugging to make sure it was secure. He hooked the carabiner to thick sturdy wire overhead, then made sure Jimmy's helmet was secure.

"Ready to go?" he asked.

Jimmy wished he didn't need to speak. He was afraid his voice would flutter. "Of course." He started up the steps that would take him to the first station.

What kind of crazy person thought this was fun? Hauling yourself into the air? Why? It looked like this course went quite high, as high as the ceiling would permit. You were supposed to maintain balance as you crossed narrow blocks, loose zigzagging steps, plank bridges, even single-wire paths.

He supposed there was no real risk or the place wouldn't be allowing it. No matter how uncoordinated you were, or how poor your sense of balance, the harness would prevent you from tumbling to your death. In fact, given how tight the line was, it would prevent you from doing much of anything. He could probably deliberately step off the track or take a big jump, but even then, he wouldn't go far. The helmet seemed irrelevant. Probably more for appearances than anything else, or maybe something an insurance company required in case someone tripped coming down the stairs.

He took a deep breath, trying to calm himself. He needed to get out more, not just to the courthouse and back. Maybe his life had become too sedentary—writing briefs, talking on the phone, gaming. And perhaps he did eat a bit more than he should. But he loved food. Was it his fault he was surrounded by great cooks, Dan at work and Hank at home? He was really the victim here...

He plunged across a path that required him to hopscotch between alternating blocks, all while moving steadily upward. People were buzzing in the arcade beneath him, but there were only a few up on the ropes. He supposed that must be why this meeting place was chosen. No bugs, no one to overhear or record a conversation on a cellphone.

He found a resting place in a corner between paths and looked around. On the plank bridge he spotted a teenager with long hair and an Eminem T-shirt who was having a much harder time than he getting from one side to the other. Ha! Youth wasn't everything. Experience counted...even if his experience with athletic endeavors was scant at best. He saw a man in his thirties skittering across the swinging steps with a certainty that suggested he had done this many times before.

But who was his mysterious correspondent?

Before he had a chance to give it more thought, he heard a voice speaking quietly behind him. "Scared of heights?"

He jerked to attention. "Of course not. This is perfectly safe."

"Safe from prying ears." It was a woman's voice. He did not recognize it. But he couldn't turn enough to see her face. "You're Jimmy Armstrong, right? You work with Daniel Pike."

"I certainly do. You know something about the Belasco murder?"

"Maybe. I...knew George."

He remembered what Maria told him about her meeting with Belasco's widow. "You were his...girlfriend?"

"In a...vague sort of way."

"Lover?"

Her voice elevated a bit. "Dominatrix."

CHAPTER TWENTY-ONE

JIMMY TWISTED AROUND ENOUGH TO SEE HIS MYSTERIOUS informant. She was tall, and her face was partly obscured by the helmet. Her dark hair had a blue streak.

She pointed to a small alcove on the other end of a long double-wire path. "Think you can make it over there? It's the closest thing to a chat spot up here."

"Sure." Jimmy soon realized that this next stretch of the course was the most difficult. He supposed that was why the alcove was on the other side. After all that exertion, you need a breather. There were no steps to rest your feet on this path. One strong but skinny wire below, and another overhead to grip.

Could he make it across? Yes. Was it easy? No. He suspected you were supposed to glide across using your sense of balance, but he found himself almost hauling himself across, clutching the upper wire for dear life.

When he finally made it to the other side, he all but collapsed. The woman followed close behind. Her eyes were wide open, exhilarated. "That was fun!"

"Yes, 'fun' is just the word I was thinking of." He sat on a flat board jutting from the wall. "I can share this seat."

"That's okay. I'm fine." She paused. "Thanks for coming. I know it was a leap of faith."

"If it helps Dan, it's worth it. Do you know Dan?"

"No. But I knew George Belasco. And I don't think your guy had anything to do with his death. I wanted to talk to someone, but I definitely did not want to get on the DA's radar. I heard you frequented the court clerk's office, so I left a message for you."

"What do you know about this case?"

"Not much. But George was involved with a lot of sketchy characters."

"And you know this because you were his…dominatrix?"

"George was into the kink. And he wasn't getting it at home. So he came to me. Have you met his wife?"

"No."

"She's an uptight society witch. Nasty. Mean. Smokes." She shuddered. "Has a thing going on with her masseuse at the country club. Disgusting."

"So…Belasco was looking for some outside comfort?"

She leaned sideways, letting the tug on the carabiner hold her upright. "I'm not sure 'comfort' is the right word. But he was looking for something. He showed up about the time I started working in this profession."

This was a profession? "Where were you working?"

"At a downtown BDSM dungeon."

Dungeon? That sounded appealing. "Is this in St. Petersburg?"

"Oh yes. And completely legal, too."

"BDSM…?"

"Bondage, domination, sadism, masochism."

"Of course."

"I was a history major in college and, well, do I need to say it? I was having trouble finding work. Didn't like teaching. I answered a rather mysterious ad and found myself interviewing for a job as a dominatrix."

"What...kind of material did they cover in the interview?"

"Not much. Maybe I flatter myself, but I think as soon as they saw me, they wanted me. The interview was more about developing my secret identity."

"Dominatrices have secret identities? Like Superman?"

She laughed. "Yes, but for different reasons. No one would be intimidated by the regular me, the history nerd who likes to read and take long candlelit baths. So we developed my alter ego. Mistress Suspiria."

"Sounds like a character in a horror film."

"It was meant to intimidate. What I liked was that it allowed me to use a wide variety of accents. On different nights, I did British, French, Spanish. With George, Mistress Suspiria had a Russian accent, kind of like Boris and Natasha. And about that subtle. I wore bright red lipstick, high heels, and provocative outfits. Leather pencil skirts. Corsets. Vinyl. But my favorite was the catsuit."

"Comfortable?"

"Not at all. But damn, I look good in it." She purred. "Mistress Suspiria was strong, unapologetic, sometimes tough, sometimes gentle, sometimes dirty, sometimes sweet. Whatever the situation required."

"Whatever puts the man on edge."

"No. Exactly the opposite. Whatever makes the man feel safe. You have to understand that...all people are different. Tastes are not universal. Some men want to be mothered. Some men want to be told what to do, to be dominated. They want a place where they feel safe enough to remove the mask, to shed the armor, to become the little boy quivering inside, full of trauma and pain and heartache."

"And that's good?"

"Yeah. Because once they surrender to that, they can heal. And after they heal, they become better men."

He couldn't believe he was having this extremely adult conversation in the middle of a high-rise theme park. "I had no idea being a professional dominatrix was so…spiritual."

"I understand that you don't get it. But that's because you're gay, right?"

"I…don't see…"

She laughed again. "Don't be embarrassed. I knew ten seconds into this conversation. You don't react the same way most men do. Nothing wrong with that. In fact, I like it. Nice change of pace."

"Glad I could be of assistance," he mumbled.

"And you're Catholic, right?"

"Okay, this is getting downright spooky."

"So you understand the concept of confession."

"Yes, but—"

"Well, that's what dominatrices really are. Not sex toys. We don't even have sex. But men end up kneeling in front of me and confessing all their sins. Asking for forgiveness."

"Which you grant."

"Of course. That's what makes them feel whole again, so the healing can commence. They need someone who listens without judging. Without constantly criticizing or looking for openings to make negative comments. Men have feelings too, and insecurities. Sensitivities. Nothing wrong with that. Given the way our culture runs, full of toxic masculinity, my hat goes off to men who are courageous enough to deal with their problems in a way that doesn't hurt anyone. Going to an underground dungeon might seem weird to you, but who's harmed? No one."

"Where does the bondage come into it?"

"Some men need to be tied up before they can connect to their deep-seated emotions. Before they can let it all hang out."

"Did I hear you say…there's no sex involved?"

"Never."

"Including George Belasco?"

"Absolutely. Sure, I crack the whip, literally, and some men get off on it, but traditional sex is off the table. Some men like to masturbate at the end of the session—after they've asked for permission. But far more often, the session ends with men talking about their emotions openly, wanting to hug me or kiss my feet to show their gratitude."

"I've met George Belasco," Jimmy said. "I've seen him at work. I have difficulty picturing him kissing your cat-suited toes."

"He had to wear his armor in public, of course. People expect that from the district attorney. But behind the scenes...he opened himself up to me." She paused. "And that's the problem."

She repeatedly glanced over her shoulder. He noticed a couple staring at their alcove with envious eyes. "What do you mean?"

"Turned out, George had some major sins to confess. He was involved in seriously bad stuff."

"Like what?"

She glanced over her shoulder again, then proceeded. "Like...trafficking."

"You mean...human trafficking? Sex trafficking?"

"I'm not sure about the details. But I know he was involved with dangerous people. And I knew it weighed heavily on his conscience."

Jimmy knew there had been a recent surge in human trafficking in this area. The proximity to the coast, to foreign nations, made this a relatively easy drop-off spot. "Why would he do that? He had a first-rate legal career."

"Yes. But not nearly as much money as people thought. His family inheritance wasn't as substantial as some believed, plus he spent a ton of it getting himself elected. And that horrible harridan wife spent compulsively. He needed a surge of income or he was going to face serious public humiliation." She hesitated. "Have you heard of a man named Conrad Sweeney?"

Jimmy had to stifle a laugh. "Yes, that name has popped up once or twice."

"Like George, Sweeney's public persona is all goodness and light. But the reality is much darker."

"He might be the man to see if you need money. Sweeney's a billionaire."

"Except maybe not so much anymore." She leaned in closer. "George said Sweeney was experiencing some financial problems. Cash-flow issues. A major investment went sour in a big way."

Jimmy's mind raced. During the Ossie Coleman case, they learned Sweeney had invested in a new bio-quantum computing project that went belly up, and despite his best efforts, he hadn't been able to collect from his partner, who was now behind bars. Could that be the source of the problem? "Sweeney and Belasco both needed cash. And they turned to human trafficking?"

"Nothing legit was going to bring the kind of dough they needed. Not fast enough."

"How much did they need?"

"I'm not sure. I know what George told me while he was crying and kissing my feet."

"Did he mention any other partners?"

"Not to me. But his girlfriend might know more."

"Wait a minute. I thought you were his girlfriend."

"No, I was his confessor. But there was no sex. Most men do, however, want sex every now and again." She paused. "Most women too, for that matter."

"Belasco also had a mistress?"

"If you want to use that ugly word." She glanced over her shoulder. The other couple was heading toward their alcove. "I should get out of here." She jotted something on a scrap of paper and shoved it into Jimmy's hand.

"Wait. I have a thousand more questions."

"Sorry." She turned away. "Leaving."

"I don't even know your name."

"Better that way."

"How will I contact you?"

"You won't."

"I might need more information. Maybe when the trial—"

She whirled around, and this time her face showed more than a trace of anger. "Don't push it. I liked George. I want you to catch his murderer. But I will not get wrapped up in a trial. You know what would happen if I were publicly exposed? 'The DA's Dominatrix.' Do you know what the press would do with that? I'm not going to let that happen to his memory. Or to me."

She headed across another sky-high bridge, far faster than he could follow. She'd be out of the building before he could cross to the next station.

He had obtained some fascinating information. But was it useful? Would anyone believe it? Human trafficking? Hard to imagine.

Though not as hard as imagining George Belasco on his knees weeping, kissing a dominatrix's feet.

He wasn't sure what he should do next, other than getting off this scary aerial contraption. But he knew he had to keep searching. George Belasco had many secrets, and it was possible they led to his demise.

CHAPTER TWENTY-TWO

CONRAD SWEENEY STOOD ON THE DAIS, STARING AT THE CROWD that had gathered in the middle of the afternoon to watch him cut a stupid ribbon to open yet another women's shelter in Southside St. Petersburg.

He was pleased. No matter how much controversy swirled around this community, and how deeply involved he was, it never touched him. He was careful. He made sure there were buffers, layers of people and dummy corporations preventing anything from being traced back to him.

This was the ninth shelter he'd opened in the past five years, and yet he could still gather a crowd. The only difference between this and the previous openings was that Camila Pérez did not stand at his side. Though she was out of jail, she was busy managing her senatorial campaign.

"Ladies and gentlemen," Sweeney began. The microphones squawked. He signaled the sound man in the rear, who adjusted the gain. "We are gathered today to renew our commitment to everyone in this community, from the most fortunate to the least privileged, reminding ourselves that every human life is important and that we will leave no soul behind."

The crowd thunderously applauded.

What a load of poppycock. He literally believed not a single part of that contrived sentence, but it went down well with the masses—particularly those so little employed that they could turn out for this sort of twaddle in the middle of the day.

He had favored cracking a bottle of champagne over the cornerstone, but someone in municipal government thought that could be perceived as promoting alcohol abuse. Small minds, small ideas. He would have to content himself with the scissors.

"And so," he boomed, "let us open the doors to all those who might need this place. In an era when we finally give proper respect to women and the unique challenges they face, let us ensure that all, no matter how dire their circumstances, have a safe place they can go in a time of need."

Prudence handed him a large golden pair of scissors. He turned, moving slowly so the photographers could get as many shots as they needed, then cut the pink ribbon.

Enthusiastic applause followed.

"Okay," he muttered. "Get me out of here."

Prudence took him by the arm and gently guided him toward an exit she had prepared, totally guarded and completely immune from reporters lobbing questions.

As Prudence herded him toward the car, he started asking questions. He'd been out of touch for almost ninety minutes. In that amount of time, the entire world could have shifted on its axis.

"Bring me up to date," he said calmly.

Prudence needed no further instruction. "The press want a statement on the Belasco murder. Mayor Pérez's release. Pike's bail."

"They're not going to get one. I'm staying out of it." His upper lip curled. "Publicly."

"The bar association called. They're requesting your input on the vacant judgeships."

"I do have some thoughts on that. Tell them I'll get back to them. Are the disbarment proceedings against Pike moving forward?"

"Not really. They're waiting to see if he's convicted. If he is, that will make disbarment a no-brainer."

"And the Senate race?"

"The mayor is soaring in the polls. Up two points since yesterday."

His fists clenched. "How can that be? The woman has been charged with murder. Twice!"

"But completely exonerated. Both times. On the internet, everyone believes she was framed by secretive but powerful forces."

He tilted his head to one side. "Well, yes, there is that."

"She's an underdog. And America loves an underdog. Loves to watch them fight their way to the top."

"And then once they reach the top, America loves to watch them fall."

"True. But our mayor is still on the ascendency."

"Which baffles me. Perhaps we should finance a new opponent."

"A little late for that." She reached the limo, then opened the back door. "Not to mention expensive."

He slid his considerable girth into the back seat. "True. My cash flow issues have not been alleviated."

"Any luck with the Coleman suit?"

"No. The clan has closed ranks, completely isolated themselves from my partnership and all those involved in it. It will be a long time before that's resolved."

Prudence slid into the other side while Verity, Sweeney's driver, donned her chauffeur's cap and started the car.

"What about your…other enterprises?"

"I'm optimistic. But the future is always difficult to predict."

"If need be, you do have a gallery full of virtually priceless artworks you could liquidate."

He glared at her with cold eyes. "That will never happen."

"I'm just saying…"

"That will never happen." He exhaled heavily, then folded his hands in his lap. "Is Shawna producing any useful intelligence?"

"She is becoming…" Prudence paused, as if searching for the right word. "…somewhat difficult to work with. She seems… recalcitrant. I think she regrets getting involved with you."

"Has she offered to refund the money she took?"

"I believe that has been spent on her nephew's education."

"Then she can damn well deliver the goods."

"Agreed. But she's not happy about it. Someone paid for a surprise sweep of the courthouse."

"Sweep? Housecleaning?"

"Looking for electronic devices. Like the ones she has repeatedly placed at your direction. She managed to get hers out before they were detected, but just barely."

"I will need her at the ready if the Pike case goes to trial."

"And it will. Soon."

"With that skinny little Mexican girl representing Pike?"

"I assume."

"She has no idea what she's facing."

"She's talked to a lot of people. I believe everyone in Pike's firm has. They're not working on anything else." Prudence fell silent for a moment. "You think…this is the time to reveal your trump card?"

"Yes. We've slipped the noose around Pike's neck. Now we need to tighten the cinch. I don't want him to escape this time."

"You could try a more...direct approach to eliminating this nuisance."

"I doubt it. Ever since he was attacked and almost killed, he's been careful. He's got security people watching him."

"Rent-a-cops are easily eluded."

"He'll be on trial for his life soon. And that's so much better than simply killing him. Let him rot in prison, like his father did. Imagine the irony. The exquisite torture. I wouldn't be surprised if he took his own life. That would be majestic."

"Indeed."

"I gave Pike a chance to work with me. But he turned that down, like his father before him. Fine. I'm tired of his interference."

The limo stopped at his next appointment. Prudence started to exit, but he stopped her.

"It's time for this little drama to reach its conclusion, Prudence." He peered at her with darkened eyes. "This time, we finish Pike for good."

CHAPTER TWENTY-THREE

DAN HAD COME TO LIKE TEAM MEETINGS—OR AT THE LEAST TO not positively detest them. He'd learned the value of working with a team. He'd learned what a fine pack of partners he had and how much they could contribute. Plus he genuinely liked them and liked working with them.

But in this case, he wasn't really working with them. He was watching them work. He would never enjoy being sidelined.

The fact that his life was on the line probably also undercut some of the pleasure.

All four sat on elevated bar chairs circling the kitchen island, currently covered with papers and files. Maria sat at the far end. Since she would serve as counsel during the trial, she was taking the lead at this meeting.

"Okay," Maria said, "let's make sure we're all on the same page. We have to convince a bunch of random drivers licenses that Dan is innocent. The charges against Camila have already been dropped, so I would argue that, at this point, the audio recording proves nothing."

"That won't be the position the prosecution takes," Garrett

replied. "I can tell that from reading their trial brief. They're using the Becket theory."

Jimmy glanced up. "Becket?"

"Thomas à Becket. Saint Thomas, now. Murder at the indirect direction of Henry II. *Will no one rid me of this turbulent priest?* The prosecution will say the recording shows Camila expressing a desire to be rid of Belasco. Dan murdered him to please her. Even if she didn't actually participate or conspire."

"The better question," Dan said, "is when an unidentified someone illegally bugged my boat. Once they heard that conversation, they knew the perfect way to eliminate me."

"Great minds," Garrett said, tapping the side of his skull. "That's exactly what I was thinking. But how do we prove it to a jury?"

"I have a few thoughts on that subject," Maria said. "I've prepared a detailed trial strategy." She distributed three stuffed loose-leaf notebooks. "I would appreciate it if you all read this. And perhaps offered suggestions on how it might be improved."

Dan glanced at the first page. "Shouldn't the starting point be, 'Dan is innocent?'"

"No. Everyone expects us to say that. I want to shake the jury up, shake them out of their prosecution-favoring complacency. We need to provide an alternate theory of the case."

Jimmy looked concerned. "You're talking about pointing the finger in a different direction?"

"No, this is more about suggesting an alternative motive. Dan is being framed. And here's why."

Garrett cleared his throat. "Did you notice how Mrs. Belasco's demeanor changed when the man from the spa came to her table?"

"Hard to miss," Maria replied. "You think something is going on between them?"

"It's worth investigating."

"Wait a minute," Jimmy said. "Was he a masseuse?"

"He did say something about her massage appointment."

Jimmy snapped his fingers. "She's having an affair with that guy. Has been for a while now."

Maria arched an eyebrow. "And you know this...how?"

"I...uh...heard it from...an informant."

"When you went to that indoor playground? Did she have any proof?"

"I don't know."

"Did she have any other leads?"

"I'm working on it."

"You realize this trial starts tomorrow morning, right?"

"I'm working on it!"

Maria held up her hands. "All right. Stay cool. We could subpoena her, Jimmy."

"I don't know her name."

Maria stared at him. "You didn't even get a name?"

"We were forty feet in the air and dangling from a cable. What did you want me to do, tackle her?"

"Yes! Grab her purse, if necessary. Check her ID."

"She wasn't carrying a purse. Look, I'm on it. If I learn anything, I'll let you know."

"We need to be focusing on Sweeney," Dan said. "He's the one behind this. He's the one behind everything."

Garrett closed his laptop. "Dan...I know you've been under a lot of stress. I don't know how you're handling this as well as you are. I'd be scared out of my mind. But I wonder if your desperation to find an alternate theory has led you to...demonizing Sweeney. Making him the archfiend, the mustachioed supervillain—"

"He's all of that and more."

"And I also wonder if your...personal situation is impacting your judgment."

"What does that mean?" Dan slid off his stool. This wasn't

the first time Garrett had gotten in his face, and he was getting more than a little tired of it.

"You already know. That's why you're getting heated up. I'm talking about your father. You think Sweeney had something to do with his incarceration."

"It's a fact."

"Dan…if you could prove that for a fact, your father would never have been convicted."

"Are you saying my dad was guilty? I want to hear it from your lips."

Maria and Jimmy eyed one another with alarm, but neither spoke.

Garrett turned toward him. "Dan, I understand you believe your father was innocent. It's only natural that you would, given how young you were when he was incarcerated and how much you loved him. But you don't know for a fact that Sweeney was involved, and—"

"I know Bradley Ellison's testimony put my dad behind bars. And Ellison works for Sweeney."

"He does now."

"I think he did then."

"But you can't prove it."

"What the hell are you saying?" Dan was shouting. "That my father was guilty? Maybe you think I'm guilty too!"

Garrett stared at him, stone-faced, biting his lower lip.

"Okay, stop." Maria slid between them. "I think we all need to calm down."

"I do not need to calm down," Dan said, pounding his fist. "I need this son-of-a—"

"Stop. I'm cutting this off right now." She shoved Dan back onto his stool. "We're talking about the murder case. The one that goes to trial tomorrow morning at nine o'clock sharp. And we're not talking about anything else. Understood?"

Garrett glided back onto his stool. "Yes. Of course. I'm sorry."

Dan regretting causing trouble, making Maria's job tougher than it already was. He had a sore spot, and once again, it had caused him to behave badly.

"While you're reviewing my trial notebooks," Maria said, "please pay attention to the witness outlines. I've been working on these all week, but they are far from perfect."

Jimmy thumbed through the pages. "Looks pretty darn good to me."

"Not good enough. There must be something the prosecution is holding back."

Dan laid a hand on her shoulder. To his surprise, she placed her hand on his and squeezed. "Whatever happens, you'll handle it brilliantly."

"I hope you're right."

"Garrett's research is excellent," he added, without actually making eye contact with the man.

"Thank you," Garrett said quietly.

"Jimmy's briefs are always first-rate. And you're every bit as terrific, Maria. You'll be fine in there."

"I am lucky to have such a talented team. Everyone has performed their designated jobs masterfully."

"Except me," Dan said. "What's my job?"

"Keeping your mouth shut."

He should have known. "I will be like an Olmec head."

"Good. No talking. No reactions. No facial expressions. No head shaking. Nothing."

"You realize you're giving me the same advice I've been giving clients for years."

"Yes. But I worry that you think it doesn't apply to you. It does."

He waited a beat. "You know, like it or not, you're going to have to put me on the witness stand."

She sighed. "Yes, I know. If nothing else, you have to explain away that recorded conversation. I assume you can handle yourself on cross." She stared daggers at him. "If you keep your temper in check."

"Message received."

"We all know how sensitive you are. Especially on certain subjects."

"My father won't be relevant at trial."

"A smart prosecutor would find an excuse to bring it up. And we have to assume Garfield is a smart prosecutor. What really bothers me is, I have to deliver an opening statement, possibly tomorrow—and I don't have a good story."

"You have some good facts," Jimmy said.

"So does the prosecution. But stories beat facts. Every time. The jury can get lost in a quagmire of contradictory testimony. But they will remember a good story forever."

"What kind of story do you want?"

"A story that explains that Dan didn't commit this murder, that he couldn't have and would never have committed this murder. Plus a reason why someone else would. Inciting incident, conflict, resolution. Believable characters. It all needs to be there. That's how we beat this charge."

Jimmy shrugged. "Sorry. I only know superhero stories."

"Don't you see?" she continued. "This is a superhero story. Or should be. And Dan is the superhero."

Jimmy beamed. "Our Aquaman."

"If I can sell that to the jury, that he's a heroic figure fighting for justice while the villains try to take him down, we can win this." She closed her notebook. "Your life is on the line here, Dan. And I'm not going to let those bastards take you down."

THE CALCULUS OF DEATH

CHAPTER TWENTY-FOUR

ELENA FORCED HERSELF TO STAY AWAKE, LONG AFTER NIGHT HAD fallen, long after the last serving of that slop they called dinner, long after the guards locked them in the hull and retired for the evening.

This was the night they made their move. She and Izzy were getting off this filthy boat.

She had to bide her time, even though Izzy continued to scream. Perhaps it was appendicitis, perhaps it was something else. All she knew was that their captors refused to help.

She could see why. There were many girls on this slave ship, and if they lost one, they still had more than enough to turn a profit. Unsurprisingly, there was no doctor on board, no health care plan for girls abducted and carted off to…the worst life she could possibly imagine.

She could endure a great deal. She could make herself wait for the right moment, the perfect opportunity. But Izzy could no longer wait. Every day, more poison might be seeping into her system. While the ship was at sea, she waited, knowing that even if they managed to escape, there was nowhere they could go.

But now the situation had changed. The boat had docked. They had landed. She did not know where. But there must be land on the other end of the gangplank. Somewhere to run. Somewhere she could seek help.

Would they have to run? Jump? Swim? She wasn't sure. But if there was land, there must be a way to get to it. Someone would care about them. Someone would care about Izzy. Someone would bring her the medical aid she needed so desperately. Someone would save them from a life of sin and degradation before...

Before.

The men came for her last night, when others were asleep and there was nothing she could do about it. They left Izzy alone, thank God. Because she was so young? Because she was sick? But they did not ignore Elena. They leered. They mumbled cruel and lustful words. Some she did not even understand, though these days she spoke English more than she spoke Spanish. Still, she grasped the intent behind the men's words.

They put their dirty hands on her. She begged them to stop. She wanted to cry out, but the one they called the Captain put his hand over her mouth. He wore a large knife in a leather sheath at his waist. She knew what that meant. She tried to stifle her pain. She was not completely successful. But she did not scream. She took her mind to another place, far from here, before everything became so dirty, so ugly. After the Captain finished, others followed.

They made her feel empty, hollow, rotten from the inside-out. They made her want to die, anything to take herself away from this place of horror.

But she would not die. If she killed herself, they won. They triumphed over her and every other girl they had taken against her will.

She would not let that happen. She would be the one who triumphed.

In time. In time.

She had learned how to remove her mind from her body long ago, when she was with David. After he took her by force, it was impossible to continue pretending that he cared about her. He cared about nothing but himself. She was one of many interchangeable bodies, not so much a moment of pleasure as a moment of domination. A reminder of his vast superiority.

And yet, even David was better than the men on this boat.

If she could stop them from coming again, she would. If she could get Izzy the help she needed, she would.

She nudged Izzy from her slumber. She felt bad about it. She knew that the time when Izzy slept was the only time she did not feel pain.

"Let me sleep," Izzy murmured.

"No. It's dark. It's quiet. We must go."

She had explained this to the girl before, but she was so young, no naïve, and so miserable, it was hard to know how much she had truly absorbed. "Do you want to get off this boat?"

"Yes..."

"Then now is the time. Tomorrow will be too late. We have a chance. We must take it."

Izzy rubbed her eyes with tiny fists. "The door is locked."

"Not completely."

They had given her a comb. Because she begged for it. After they were done with her. One of the men complained that she was ugly, and she said she had no way to comb her hair. She said she wanted to make herself pretty for them, before the next time. And they believed her.

While they laughed and preened, she wedged the plastic comb into the space between the door and the wall. When they left and closed the door, it did not quite close all the way. They assumed the door would lock automatically behind them.

But it didn't. The lock did not engage.

This was her chance. In all likelihood, the only one she would ever get.

She helped Izzy to her feet. Fortunately, they had nothing to bring. "Should we tell the others?"

"No." She would like to help everyone. But fifteen girls could not move quietly. It was just barely possible that two could. Once they found freedom, authorities, doctors, then she would tell them about the other girls on the ship. Right now, they needed to escape.

She pulled on the door. Even if not locked, it was jammed. She pulled harder and felt it give the tiniest bit.

This would work.

She heard a clicking noise, then the door yielded.

It creaked. She froze.

She had never noticed the squeak before. But then, it had never been this quiet before. She pulled slowly, but that did not make the hinges any quieter. She opened it wide enough to allow the two girls to pass through, no more.

One cautious step at a time, they made their way down the passageway outside. She had only been here once. She did not know the way out, but she could see they were up high. She had imagined they were in the lowest cargo hold of the ship, but that was not true. The gangplank would be beneath them. They needed to move down. Silently. Without being heard.

She knew someone would still be awake, a sentry, perhaps several. But if they remained quiet enough, there was a tiny chance of success.

On this occasion, the fact that they had been given no shoes, that they were barefoot, worked to their advantage. Bare feet on a metal floor made little noise.

She found a stairway leading down. She pointed. The

descent was almost pitch black, with a small sliver of light creeping through the cracks.

She took Izzy's hand and led her downward.

She decided to take the stairs as low as they would lead. It was possible that would take her below the exit level. She had no way of knowing. But that seemed like the best place to start. If she was wrong, they would work their way back up again.

But what if this was where the men slept? The thought halted her steps.

What should she do then?

She could see Izzy peering at her, trusting her, scared to death but assuming that her protector had all the answers.

She could not let that girl down.

She made her feet move again. Slowly. Slowly...

Three levels down, she heard snoring. And detected movement.

This time she froze for good reason. She pointed behind her.

Back up, Izzy. Quietly. Back up...

Izzy's foot hit the wall. It made a noise. Not a huge noise, but a noise.

They halted, too scared to take another step.

Something moved. Something murmured.

She felt her heart race. Was this it? Had they come so far only to be captured again? There was no telling what these monsters would do to her if they felt threatened.

She took another step backward, taking Izzy by the hand.

Nothing stirred.

She kept moving backwards until they returned to the last flight of stairs. She moved a little faster. Maybe that was more dangerous, but her heart was pumping and she could barely keep her head together. She had never felt so scared in her entire life, not even when she was taken. They had done so much to her already. If they discovered she was trying to leave...

Izzy started to speak. She hushed the girl. Izzy needed reassurance. She hugged her tightly, but that was as much as she was going to get now. They couldn't afford to speak. Not one word.

Elena started up the stairs, one quiet step at a time. If the men slept on that lowest level, then likely the exit ramp was above them. At least that was what she hoped.

When the stairs arrived at the next level, they stepped out and tried to explore. Even if the gangplank was not down, there would be a door, or hatch, or some way to get outside.

Down the corridor she saw a patch of light streaming in from the outside.

That must be it! If they could just be lucky a little longer, if they could rush out while none of the sentries were watching...

Freedom.

She gripped Izzy's hand all the harder, tugging her forward. They reached the opening, the light, the taste of freedom. It was some kind of small door. She placed her hand on the knob—

"Going somewhere?"

Panic sliced through her entire body. Her eyes opened impossibly wide.

She turned to run, but two men stood behind them, blocking her path. She whirled around again.

She knew the man who stood before them, the man who had spoken. She had seen him before. He was the leader of the men who put their filthy hands upon her.

The Captain.

"You wish to leave?" He spoke English, but a thick accent made his words difficult to understand. "Did you not enjoy my attention? I gave you my best. Did you want more?"

She bit her tongue. If she spoke what she was thinking the result would not be good for her or Izzy.

Unfortunately, the Captain took her silence as poorly as he would have taken her words. He slapped her hard on the side of her face, so hard her head slammed into the bulwark.

Izzy screamed. But Elena did not. She kept it all locked inside.

"You will have more of it," the Captain snarled. "More of me, more of my men. Every day. Many times a day. All day long."

"Leave her alone!" Izzy screamed.

He ignored her, shoving her aside. "And then, when we are done with you, and only when we are done with you, we will dispose of you."

Her eyes narrowed, but she did not speak. She did not cry out. She remained silent.

"Such a pity. You could have been valuable to us. But you are not worth the risk you present. One stray girl could bring down the federales. We cannot risk it."

"Leave her alone!" Izzy screamed again, and this time the Captain hit her so hard she fell to her knees.

"Unfortunately for you, little one, you do not entice me as your foolish friend does." He glanced at the two men behind her. "Kill her."

"No!" Elena could hold it in no longer. She screamed and begged, but it made no difference. The Captain only hit her again, making her lips bleed. And the two men dragged Izzy away, kicking and wailing.

"I hope you are satisfied," the Captain snarled. He grabbed her by the hair and jerked her head upward. "We would have been good to you, in our way. You would have been cared for. Fed. Clothed. But no longer. Your ingratitude has caused your young friend's death. And you will suffer worse."

She clenched her teeth, trying to be brave. But inside, helplessness overwhelmed her. There was no hope now, nothing she could do, no chance of escape.

"You may comfort yourself with this knowledge, you young whore. Your friend will die fast. With no more pain than necessary. But it will not be the same for you."

He clenched her hair even tighter and forced her face close

to his, close enough to taste his rotting breath. "We will carry you far from this ship. And then we will feed you to the sharks. They will have a frenzy, chewing away at your flesh, gnawing at your bones. They will eat you alive. And you will have no one to blame but yourself."

CHAPTER TWENTY-FIVE

DAN STARED AT THE FACE IN THE MIRROR. A STRONG WAVE HIT the boat, tilting it ever so slightly to the left. Unexpectedly.

He cut himself shaving.

And winced. And swore. Bad enough to enter the courtroom an accused murderer. Worse to go in looking like Scarface. In the past, he'd entered the courtroom like a superhero, chest puffed out, cape flying, sweeping in to save the day. Zorro without the mask, Clark Kent without the glasses—

Stop.

He was angry at himself. He kept it on the downlow, beneath the surface, but he had screwed up and he knew it.

When did he stop being smart? Did he think he could hop and skip his way out of danger forever? It wasn't that long ago that three brutes met him at his boat and almost killed him. Now he was being framed for a death penalty crime. When was he going to get the message?

The worst was—he'd put Camila in danger. She'd managed to get those charges dropped, thank God. Maria said her poll numbers were soaring, but he knew there would always be a taint. He should've stopped that conversation dead. He should've had the boat swept for recording devices. He should've done a million things...

He stared at the increasingly haggard-looking face in the mirror. Your stupidity and carelessness have brought you down. You, and the woman you love.

And then there was that fight with Garrett. What was that about? Not the first time the two had clashed. Garrett's perpetual empathy for the prosecution never rubbed him the right way. But what Garrett said was not completely without merit and he knew it.

His life had been shaped by his father, more specifically, by what happened to his father. What killed his father.

Was Garrett right? Was that trauma still hanging over him like a shroud, impairing his judgment, influencing every decision he made?

One thing seemed certain. It was time for him to deal with this. When this case was over, assuming by some miracle he wasn't behind bars awaiting execution, he was going to make a serious effort to get to the bottom of the mystery surrounding his father. It was time for him to learn the truth and deal it. One way or the other.

He rinsed his face, dabbed a tissue on the wound, and grabbed his cell.

Camila picked up on the first ring. "How are you?"

"Cut myself shaving. Stings a bit."

"That's not what I meant. How do you feel?"

"I'm fine."

"Don't lie to me. You're about to go on trial for a crime you did not commit. No one would feel fine."

"I'll get by. I always do."

"Dan, you don't have to play the hero with me."

"I don't know what you mean."

He heard her sighing heavily on the other end of the line. "I think I know you better than you know yourself."

"Not saying much," he mumbled.

"I should have come over last night. I will come over tonight."

"That's probably not a good idea."

"I'm speaking in Tampa tonight. Fundraising dinner. I can get to St. Petersburg in an hour. Expect me."

"I still don't think—"

"Did I ask what you think? I'll be there around eleven. Until then, stay strong. A lot of people love you. Not only me." She paused. "But especially me."

He rang off and realized he was smiling. That had to be the truest definition of what it means to be a partner, a soulmate. Someone who knew what you needed and provided it—whether you liked it or not.

He splashed off and chose a suit. Neutral gray with a white shirt. The most ordinary suit he had. Okay, it was bespoke and hand-crafted, but it didn't scream dollars and cents. Nothing too flashy for this trial. Nothing that would attract attention in the wrong way. Okay, no one was taking away his Air Jordans. The jury would have to live with that. If you didn't look too closely, they could pass for black dress shoes.

The call with Camila had reminded him of one thing—he was probably the luckiest SOB on the face of the earth. Far luckier than he deserved to be.

He glanced back into the mirror. *So don't screw it up.*

MARIA STARED AT THE FACE IN THE MIRROR. SEVERAL LIGHT BULBS were out in her vanity, but she had never gotten around to replacing them. Come to think of it, she had never gotten around to buying light bulbs. Whatever. She'd been busy.

She stared at her inadequately illuminated visage. Too much lipstick? Not enough? It had been so long since she had actually spoken aloud with a jury present that she had almost forgotten how to do it. She wasn't worried about the judge. Professional women forgave one another's fashion faux pas. But the jury was an entirely different matter.

Statistically speaking, the jury pool would contain more women than men, more homemakers and self-employed than office workers, more old than young. What kind of face should she wear? How should she dress? Anything too flashy was out of the question. Stud earrings, nothing dangly. Light makeup, just enough. Hair pulled back, though she refused to put it up in a bun. Surely she could be moderately attractive without threatening anyone.

Dress suit, skirt, no scarf. High neck, normal bra, nothing that would attract attention from men or women. She had to be taken seriously, even by the most sexist pig who entered that jury box. She had to make them believe her when she told them Dan was innocent. They had to understand she was not another defense attorney trying to find a loophole to put her crooked client back on the street. Dan was the real deal. An innocent man.

She also knew that clothes and makeup would be the least important part of her work. Yes, studies had proven that attire matters, not only with the jury but with folks at home looking at photos. But even more important would be the expression on her face, the look in her eyes. Her sincerity had to translate.

She had considered punting this responsibility, roughly a thousand or more times. This was a death-penalty case, after all. There were at least a dozen lawyers in town with more experience. It wasn't that she didn't think she could do it. She got no pleasure from it. She was a strategist. She preferred to stay behind the lines, watching. Thinking. Let Dan put on a show. She preferred to generate the content that would ultimately make a difference.

She checked herself one more time in the mirror.

She knew how important this case was to Dan, but it was also important to her. Because Dan was important to her.

More than she cared to admit. She deflected the notion, laughed, teased, sometimes even pushed him away.

But she cared.

He looked so distraught last night. She watched him as they ate dinner, when he didn't know he was being watched. The creased brow. The dark circles around his eyes. The worry. The fear.

She had never seen him like that. Never seen him so vulnerable.

It brought back another image, unbidden. That horrible night he was attacked. She was the one who found him, sprawled out like a broken, dismembered doll. She stayed with him all the way to the hospital, all night long, never once leaving his side.

That night forced her to face her own feelings.

She grabbed her briefcase and pointed herself toward the door. One thing was certain. She did not have time for this now. She had a case to try. A life to save.

After that she could figure out what was going to happen next.

CHAPTER TWENTY-SIX

DAN WAS NOT SURPRISED BY THE CROWD IN THE COURTROOM. They had a solid turnout for the arraignment, for Pete's sake, and this was the actual trial. Maria told him the bailiffs stopped admitting spectators two hours ago. A few seats were reserved for media and relatives of the deceased, but the rest was first-come, first-seated.

He supposed this case had it all—sin, sex, politics, and murder. It was all over the internet, the evening news, and the papers. Some people were fascinated by crime. More than half the series on television involved crime-solving. True crime shows were enormously popular. He shouldn't be surprised that locals would take an interest in such a dramatic case. For that matter, he wasn't sure all the people sitting in the gallery were locals.

As he made his way to the defense table, following Maria's lead, he noticed Prudence Hancock sitting on the back row of the gallery. She must've arrived early to snare that seat. Or bribed a bailiff, who knew? She sat on the defendant's side. So she could heckle? Eavesdrop? Take snaps of their private documents? She'd been at his last trial, too—the one where he was the lawyer, not the defendant. Conrad Sweeney seemed to require daily reports on Dan's activities.

He was equally unsurprised to see Evelyn Belasco in the courtroom with her son, CJ. They were on the front row of the prosecution side. Maria had told him all about her visit to the country club. Sounded like Evelyn wasn't exactly mourning her husband. But she had to maintain appearances. It was possible the prosecutors asked her to be present. Few things could have as much impact on a jury as the grieving widow. She would never be introduced as such, but they would have little trouble figuring out who she was, especially since she was decked out in solid black.

He was more troubled by some of the unfamiliar faces in the gallery. Who was the tall woman with the blue streak in her dark hair? Or sitting beside her—but not speaking to her—the petite woman with the pixie haircut and the dimples. She looked far too sweet and innocent for this sort of show. What inspired her to spend the morning in this dour manner?

He nodded pleasantly at the two attorneys at the prosecution table, Beverly Garfield and Zachary Blunt—the Knife. Maria glared at him.

"Defendant," she muttered. "You're the defendant."

"I can still be friendly."

"Actually, no. I'll be collegial. You stay out of it."

"It's not like we don't know each other."

"As of this moment, they are not fellow members of the bar. They are your archenemies. They are the people trying their hardest to give you on a one-way ticket to a lethal injection. Being friendly is just perverse."

"It's my nature."

"To be perverse?"

"I meant—"

"Be quiet and sit down."

He assumed Garfield would take the lead as she had before,

though perhaps it was dangerous to make assumptions. Maybe it was a double act. Garfield distracted everyone while the Knife stabbed you in the back.

He had wanted to see Jazlyn before the trial began, but Maria advised against it. Jazlyn was already in an almost impossible situation, and Evelyn Belasco thought his relationship with her had motivated the murder. She would pounce if Jazlyn showed any indication of partiality. Much as he hated it, for Jazlyn's sake, he stayed away.

He didn't want any more of the people he cared about getting dragged down by his stupidity.

Judge Hembeck entered the courtroom and started the proceedings in her usual efficient, no-nonsense manner. Given the gravity of the charges, it was impressive how briskly she moved along. In fewer than twenty minutes, she steamrolled through the preliminaries and directed her clerk to call the initial jury pool.

Eighteen unknowns filed into the jury box. From this raw material, Maria would try to shape a panel favorably disposed to acquit. Good luck.

He supposed that the one, perhaps the only, advantage to being the defendant for a change was that he could focus on those faces in the box. He didn't have to memorize names. He didn't have to devise clever questions. He could simply pay attention—which was supposedly his strong suit. He could watch for tics, eye darts, micro-expressions, anything that might suggest someone was lying or keeping something to themselves. Which was good.

Because this time he couldn't afford any surprises. This time he was playing for his life.

DAN HAD SEEN JURY SELECTION TAKE DAYS IN OTHER CAPITAL cases. Judges tended to err on the side of safety, giving much leeway to the defense. If a case ended with a guilty verdict, as happened more often than not, there would be an appeal, and judges did not like being reversed. Therefore, they did their best to give the defense nothing to complain about. If the defense wanted to ask a particular question, it would probably be asked. If they wanted to exercise a peremptory challenge to a prospective juror, the judge was unlikely to stand in their way.

But this time the jury was a done deal by mid-afternoon, even though more than forty possible jurors were called to the box. Garfield was stern and firm but she was not a perpetual pain in the neck and did not make objections without a good reason. Maria handled herself magnificently, coming across as earnest and friendly while maintaining her professionalism. I'm a woman you can trust, she told them subliminally.

He hoped the jury got the message.

He and Maria agreed on almost everything, which also helped move matters along at a brisk pace. They both had done this enough to have a clear grasp of who they did and did not want on the jury. They didn't need jury consultants. They *were* the jury consultants.

"Very well," Judge Hembeck said. "We appear to have called a jury." She offered the venirepersons a long series of boilerplate instructions, mostly to make a record of the fact that the jurors were told how to behave, in case problems arose later. "And there's still time on the clock. We can have opening statements today and start calling witnesses first thing tomorrow. Ms. Garfield, would you like to present your opening at this time?"

It wasn't really a question, of course. Garfield rose to her feet, positioned herself before the jury, and launched in. After a few niceties and preliminaries, she went directly to the crime.

"Young people today talk about trigger warnings," Garfield said, a stern expression on her face. "I'm about to give you one.

This case centers around a horrific crime. Possibly the worst I have encountered in twelve years in the district attorney's office. The fact that it happened to one of our own, to a titan in the law enforcement community, the elected district attorney himself, makes it even worse. During this trial, you will see photographs of the crime. I apologize in advance. But there's no avoiding it."

Dan suppressed a bitter smile. There was, of course, a way of avoiding it. She could simply not do it. There was no law that required crime-scene photos. They had little to no evidentiary value. No one was contesting the fact that a murder occurred. But she wanted to shock the jurors. She hoped the violent crime scene would make them more inclined to convict someone, anyone, to erase the scene from their memories with a sense that they had done something about it.

Garfield spared no detail. "George Belasco was impaled against the fence like the martyred figure he was. Imagine the pain. Imagine the blood at his feet."

This went on and on. If anything, Dan thought she overdid it. After all, Dr. Zanzibar would testify that Belasco was shot elsewhere and was probably dead before impaled. Garfield was going for the shock and awe, but sometimes, even in a trial, subtlety produced surprising dividends.

Eventually, Garfield brought the case back to Dan. She was not supposed to argue in opening statement, only to preview the evidence for the jury, to give them a road map for what was to come. But of course, for an advocate, every time you open your mouth, it's argument.

"How do we know who committed this crime? During this trial, you will see that the evidence against the defendant is overwhelming. Shortly after George Belasco's body was found, the police received a recording of a conversation in which the defendant can be heard discussing and agreeing to George Belasco's murder. Substantial evidence will put him at the scene of the crime. Evidence will also show that the defendant and the victim clashed on repeated occasions. He has no alibi, no way to account for his actions. And that's merely the tip of the iceberg. When this trial reaches its conclusion, you will understand what happened. And what you must do to fulfill your duty as a juror."

She turned slowly, pivoting toward the defendant's table, forcing the jurors to look at him. "This heinous murder was committed by the man sitting complacently at the defendant's table. Daniel Pike, a defense lawyer who lives on a boat and likes to…kitesurf. He thinks he is above the law, that he will kitesurf away from these charges. It will be your job to ensure that he does not."

On that note, Garfield took her seat.

"Go get 'em, tiger," Dan murmured.

She rose and walked slowly toward the jury, speaking as she moved. "Well, that was certainly dramatic, wasn't it? Points to the prosecution for setting the proper Netflix true-crime tone. But this is not a television show, and you cannot make your decision based upon which lawyer is the most spinetingling. You must make your decision based upon the evidence—or, in this case, the lack of evidence. Because as Judge Hembeck will instruct, the prosecution has the burden of proof. We have no burden at all. We don't even have to put on evidence. The prosecutors must prove their case beyond a reasonable doubt. And if they don't, you must acquit. There is no other choice. They meet their burden, or you must acquit."

She reached the rail separating her from the jury and leaned gently against it. "In this case, they will not meet their burden. They cannot meet their burden. They do not have the evidence. And the reason they do not have the evidence is simple. Daniel Pike did not commit this crime. When this is all over, you will feel good about voting to acquit, because you will understand that Daniel Pike is an innocent man."

Maria took a short walk through some, though not all, of the prosecution's main points. She held back more than she said, and Dan knew why. There was little point in previewing your case to the prosecutors. The privilege of keeping secrets was one of the few advantages the defense had in a criminal trial. The prosecutors had all the power, all the support of law enforcement and usually the judiciary, but they were required to share their evidence in advance and to produce anything exculpatory even if they did not plan to use it. By contrast, the defense had no obligation to produce anything. They didn't have to share evidence. They didn't even have to produce a witness list. The prosecution would have no idea what their theory of the case might be until they heard it at trial. To maintain that advantage, Maria would avoid revealing anything during opening statement that the prosecutors didn't already know.

"Let me tell you a little about Daniel Pike. As you will learn when he takes the stand—because he will take the stand, although he doesn't have to—he has dedicated his entire life to the cause of justice. Yes, he has usually been on the side of the defense, but often in this world, it is the meek and the powerless who suffer most at the hands of what we call justice. Justice only becomes a reality if some brave soul is willing to stand up and fight for it. That's what Daniel Pike has been doing his entire adult life. He has personal reasons for doing so. It is important to him. He has built up this community's trust. And that is a trust he would never betray by committing a crime. Much less one so vile as this.

"Does everyone appreciate Dan's work? Of course not, and that's the real reason we're here today. Some people in power want to take advantage of those less fortunate. Sometimes law enforcement officers resent people who work for the defense, who protect citizens from false accusations. This is not the first time Dan has been targeted, and it will probably not be the last. Someone with less courage would have quit a long time ago.

But not Dan. And as the evidence will show, that is why he has been framed for this crime."

He saw several eyebrows rise in the gallery. She was making big promises. They would expect her to deliver. She was less overtly dramatic than Garfield had been. But in her own way, Dan thought she made more of an impact.

"Just to be clear," Maria said, making direct eye contact with each juror in turn, "let me say it one more time. My client is an innocent man. He has been framed. And by the time this trial is over, you will understand why."

CHAPTER TWENTY-SEVEN

THIS ISN'T MY FIRST MAJOR CHALLENGE, JIMMY REMINDED HIMSELF, as he watched Garrett clicking away at his laptop keyboard. He had, after all, grown up in this country, not only as a black man, but as a gay black man. Despite the obstacles he'd faced, he got himself through law school without parents to foot the bill. Managed to get a great job and a city-wide rep based upon his writing skills and his encyclopedic knowledge of everyone in town. He'd even married a doctor. Wasn't that supposed to be the 1950s be-all-end-all proof of social success?

He had never mastered the computer. He was functional, but nothing more. He preferred his phone—and yes, he realized that was a pocket-sized computer, but pocket-sized was all he wanted. Let Maria have the world of social media. He preferred people who were actually in the room with him. He'd text Hank in an emergency, but most of the time, he would rather be at home with his cardigans and his action figures, or acting as GM for a great session with players he could look in the eye. Cyberspace didn't do it for him.

But after days and days of trying, he had not gotten

anywhere trying to discover the meaning of the mysterious message the woman at the ropes course left him.

HONEY O'PLENTY.

What could that possibly mean? Was it a name? I mean, it couldn't be, right? Maybe a character in a video game or a porn movie. He'd put the name into Google and gotten nothing useful. Put it into his phone. Nothing. Even managed to find a local phone book—and that took some doing—but still nothing. Was this a person? Business? Location? He didn't know.

And while he was screwing around not getting anywhere with his only lead, Dan's trial had begun. He needed to find out why Belasco's dominatrix-confessor thought this might be helpful. But he had hit a dead end.

Which was what led him to do the one thing he never thought he would ever do.

He asked Garrett for help.

Not that he disliked Garrett. But Garrett was much more conservative, more reserved, more...okay, boring. Garrett was red-state conformity, and he was...something else altogether. He wasn't even sure where Garrett stood on the LGBTQ+ issue. He certainly never acted as if he bore Jimmy any animosity. But he was such a straitlaced individual, one had to wonder.

Necessity is the mother of invention, right? Garrett was the computer whiz on this team, and he desperately needed a computer whiz. So here they were...

Garrett's fingers moved at the speed of light. Jimmy didn't even try to keep up. "Spend much time on the dark web, Jimmy?"

"Of course not."

"You should."

"Sounds appalling."

"It's a disgusting place. But of course, that's why you have to go."

"I didn't think just anyone could visit the dark web."

"True," Garrett said, still clicking. "You have to know your way down the Silk Road."

"Excuse me?"

"That was the first online black market. There are more now. Fortunately, I know them all. Tor browser makes it easier."

"And you know this because…"

"Because our cases frequently bring us into contact with the scum of the earth. Which too often, these days, means the tech-savvy scum of the earth. The dark web has become a path to survival for drug pushers, terrorists, all manner of scum. Computers have made it harder to hide money or transfer money. Cell phones, and the ease of eavesdropping on them, have made it harder for scum to communicate. The solution is the dark web."

"Hard to believe our elected district attorney would be doing…dark web stuff."

"You're willing to believe that he'd get down on his knees in front of a woman in a leather catsuit and cry his eyes out—but not play around on the internet?"

"I see your point."

A few more moments passed while Garrett clicked. "Bingo."

"What've you got?"

"George Belasco's Bitcoin wallet. He used Empire Market, one of the newer online black markets. Bitcoin has blockchain security, so getting in isn't exactly easy. I already had his traditional bank account numbers from our discovery motions. He made an initial transfer of money from one of them to this dark account. That's how I tracked it back to him."

"Why would Belasco have a Bitcoin account?"

"That's become the most popular way of paying for illegal goods and services. Bitcoin was supposed to be this wonderful border-crossing universal currency. That hasn't happened yet, obviously. But it's great for scumbags who want to buy drugs. Or sex. Or people. Without leaving a trace. Bitcoin was key to recent ransomware attacks—you know, hackers lock up your files and refuse to release them unless you pay. In Bitcoin. They've held up entire cities. And dark-web purchases are now the fastest growing use of cryptocurrency."

Jimmy's eyes scanned a long document that looked like a scrolling ledger. He was impressed by how quickly Garrett appeared to assimilate the information. "See anything interesting?"

"Belasco used this account a lot."

"For what?"

"Hard to tell. Most of these payees are using pseudonyms."

"What are the possibilities?"

"Empire Market has pages of listings for fentanyl. Twelve grams for $1600 in Bitcoin."

"I can't afford to be an addict."

"You could get a patch for forty dollars. Plenty of other drugs, too. You like games, don't you? One of the new dark markets is called Monopoly."

"No thanks."

"Hey, what about this?" Garrett leaned closer to the screen. "Didn't you tell me the dominatrix had a blue streak in her hair? And she was tall?"

"Yeeeess…"

"Our deceased friend George Belasco was making payments on a weekly basis to an entity called Big Blue. And I feel relatively certain that was not IBM."

"You think it's her?"

"Do you know what she charged? This Big Blue got six hundred dollars a week. In Bitcoin."

"Holy smokes. Could she live off that income?"

"If she had enough guys who wanted to kiss her feet, yes." Garrett kept clicking and scrolling. "What about this entry? HOP. It pops up over and over again. Sometimes twice weekly."

"And that could stand for…Honey O'Plenty?"

"Why not? She didn't get paid quite as much as Big Blue. But more often."

"What service did Honey O'Plenty provide?"

"I'm sure I don't know. Though I could probably guess. You said he didn't have sex with Big Blue, right?"

"That's what she said."

"And judging from what I observed at the country club, he wasn't getting much action from his wife."

Jimmy pondered for a moment. It was starting to make a crazy sort of sense. "You think Honey O'Plenty is a prostitute?"

"A distinct possibility."

"What kind of prostitute uses the dark web?"

"The smart kind. You walk the streets, eventually you're going to get picked up by an undercover cop. But if you list your services on the dark web..."

"No one would ever know?"

"I hear the FBI is trying to police the dark web. But it's tough. Look at all this coding gibberish. How do you trace that back to a human being?"

"I don't know, but I need to talk to this woman." He paused. "I'm assuming it's a woman."

"Honey O'Plenty could be anyone. Or anything." Garrett pushed away from the keyboard. "There's no way to trace this back to the source. Few skid marks on the information highway. And the few that exist are tightly guarded. I doubt I would ever be able to hack into the source code. And an attempt could take weeks."

"Which Dan doesn't have." He scrutinized Garrett's face. He could tell something was happening in that tightly wound mind, but he wasn't sure what it might be. "Penny for your thoughts."

"I don't think we'll be able to hack our way to Honey O'Plenty. But she—if it is a she— might be interested in gaining a new whale."

"Is that a reference to my weight?"

"No. Street slang. Client. John. A whale is a super-rich john."

"I'm not that rich."

"You might need to be to get her attention. But I don't think it should be you. It will have to be me."

"And why, may I ask?"

Garrett smiled. "C'mon, Jimmy. You're gay."

"You think her gaydar will rat me out?"

"I think Honey O'Plenty will know you're gay immediately, and then she'll know she's being played. On the other hand, a conservative, seemingly normal unmarried guy like me might be able to get the information we need."

"Seemingly normal?"

Garrett grinned. "We all have our secrets."

"You really think this could have something to do with Belasco's murder?"

"There's no way to be sure. But it's clear that man was hiding something. Your dominatrix said he was connected to human trafficking. If he was running with those kinds of people, anything is possible."

"What a hypocrite he was."

"Amen to that." Garrett paused a moment, then turned back to the laptop and typed out a few sentences. "I'm going to reach out to her. I'll say I was referred by one of her clients. I'll offer twice her usual rate if she can meet me immediately. See if she takes the bait."

"And if she does?"

Garrett hit the RETURN key. "If she's interested in getting my money, she'll have to arrange a rendezvous."

"Then we can discover why George Belasco was paying her. Who his business partners were. And the more we know about that man..."

Garrett nodded. "The more likely we are to figure out who killed him."

CHAPTER TWENTY-EIGHT

DAN WATCHED CAREFULLY AS BEVERLY GARFIELD CALLED HER first witness. Dr. Zanzibar, the medical examiner, took the stand to establish that George Belasco had been murdered, not that there was any question about it. But death was an element of the charge of murder, obviously, so the prosecution had to make the point or risk being challenged for not meeting their burden of proof. It didn't take long. Belasco had been shot six times, moved, then nailed to a fence. Death set in before his body was found.

After Garfield finished, Maria rose to cross. Dan watched everyone with his usual close scrutiny. He knew Maria was nervous. He wasn't sure she had ever handled a cross-examination.

The witness, by contrast, seemed not nervous at all. If anything, Zanzibar appeared somewhat relieved. Perhaps he was flattering himself, but Dan suspected that Zanzibar was pleased he wasn't handling the cross this time. They'd been up against one another too many times in the past, and Zanzibar had never once left the stand with a smile on his face.

Maria plunged right into the heart of the matter. "Doctor, I've been to the crime scene, or rather, the scene where the body was found. It appeared the body had been brought there by the killer, possibly dragged or hauled in on some kind of device. Did it look that way to you?"

"I've never actually been to the crime scene," Zanzibar explained. "I'm a forensic detective, but I don't visit crime scenes. My work is performed in the laboratory. But what you described does seem consonant with what I determined about liver mortis, and what I observed in the photographs. Trash bins and debris appear to have been moved to create a path for the body. But I can't say with certainty that the person who transported the body is the person who committed the murder."

A good point. "And someone called in an anonymous tip that led the police to the back alley."

Garfield rose. "Objection. Outside the scope and knowledge of this witness."

She was right, but what did it matter? She'd be calling another witness later to establish what brought the cops to the alley.

"Sustained," Judge Hembeck replied. "Anything else?" The judge looked impatient, probably because none of Maria's points actually refuted anything Zanzibar said during direct testimony. She was laying groundwork for later arguments.

Maria continued. "You also reached conclusions as to the time of death, correct?"

"Yes. Earlier in the day. Around seven in the evening."

"And that's the only time the murder could have taken place?"

"With a margin of error of about forty-five minutes on either side."

"Dragging the body to the alley would've taken some time, right?"

"Since I don't know where the murder took place, I cannot say how long transportation would have taken."

"But the body was moved. After death. And this bizarre crucifixion scene was purposefully constructed."

"That is true."

"Thank you, sir. No more questions."

Maria slid back into her seat at the defense table.

Dan gave her a reassuring smile. "Nicely done, slugger."

"Oh stop. I didn't do a damn thing."

"You planted seeds."

"We'll see."

GARFIELD'S NEXT TWO WITNESSES WERE SIMILARLY NECESSARY though, Dan thought, extremely boring. First, she called the officer who took the anonymous call that led the police to the alley. Dan and Maria debated crossing, but opted against it. Someone obviously wanted the body to be found, which was hardly typical murderer behavior, but they couldn't be certain the call came from the murderer. Some innocent citizen might have stumbled across the corpse. Next, Garfield called the first officer on the scene, who sponsored the grisly photos and established a tight chain of custody for all evidence taken from the crime scene.

Garfield did not call the ballistics expert on her witness list, presumably because the police had never found the murder gun. Ditto for the paraffin test tech. No proof that Dan fired a weapon. Of course he had ample opportunity to wash his hands back at his boat. He had time to soak them in Purell for an hour if he wanted. Garfield opted not to open that can of worms.

"Your honor," Garfield said, "we decline to call the remaining forensic witnesses."

While the judge nodded in understanding, Maria rose to her feet. Her facial expression was angry. She clutched a piece of paper. "Your honor, bench conference, please."

Judge Hembeck nodded. Maria rose.

Dan looked at her perplexed. "What are you doing?" he whispered.

Maria walked to the bench, crossing over to the jury's side. Garfield followed close behind. The judge covered the microphone so the jurors couldn't hear what was being said.

Maria appeared agitated, forceful. She was obviously arguing, though it was impossible to tell what she was arguing about. The judge shook her head. Garfield remained silent.

The problem was, Dan couldn't imagine what they were arguing about. Maria didn't have any problems relating to ballistics, fingerprints, DNA, or any of the forensic evidence the prosecution covered today.

Maria ramped up the drama. She pounded the paper down on the bench, pointing. The judge continued to shake her head. Maria clenched her fists.

And then it hit him—this was pantomime. For all he knew, she was talking about the weather, or arguing that the air conditioning should be turned down. But that's not how it would look to the jury. They would see a defense lawyer fighting to get something into the trial, and being shut down.

They would spend the rest of the day wondering what the judge wouldn't allow them to see. And wondering if the prosecution case was as strong as Garfield indicated. Was it only strong because the defense wasn't allowed to tell all they knew? Were important secrets being kept from them?

When the show was over, Maria walked away from the bench with a frustrated, bitter expression on her face—and she pivoted around to make sure the jury saw it.

A moment later, she slid into her seat beside Dan.

"What were you discussing?" he asked quietly.

"I asked for a break. Said my tummy was upset. Garfield said I was stalling. The judge told me to get some Alka-Seltzer."

He nodded. "You are a tricky one."

"I learned from the best."

CHAPTER TWENTY-NINE

GARRETT ADJUSTED HIS TIE AS HE RODE THE ELEVATOR TO THE TOP floor of a ten-story apartment building not far from downtown. He knew the rent here was high. The location was favored primarily by business folk, those who preferred to live near their office. Married people with children might prefer a house in the suburbs, but those who were unattached had no reason to travel so far every day.

He used the reflective doors to check his appearance. Not that he was nervous or anything. But he had gone to a lot of trouble to arrange an immediate meeting with the mysterious Honey O'Plenty. And he had no idea what awaited him on the other side of the door. He had dressed in his worst suit and put on a tie that didn't really match. His goal was to create a character—a middle-aged, sex-starved loser with poor social skills.

He stepped off the elevator and scanned door numbers till he found 1006.

He knocked twice, resisting the temptation to tap out the "shave and a haircut" rhythm. He held his breath. No matter who or what opens the door, he told himself, do not show surprise. You were supposedly referred by someone who presumably told you what you were buying.

He braced himself.

The door opened.

The woman standing inside the apartment was drop-dead gorgeous.

She was petite, on the short side, but super-cute, with a dimpled smile and golden curly hair. She wore a dress—red, of course—with a plunging neckline that provided a clear view of impressive assets. He almost felt guilty looking, but hey, he was playing a part.

She gave him a sly grin. "Atty boy?"

That was the pseudonym he had used on the dark web to make the appointment. "That would be me."

"What do you think?" She shimmied her shoulders a bit. "Want to come inside?"

"Definitely."

She stepped aside and let him enter a first-rate apartment decorated in first-rate style. Clean. Nicely furnished. Lots of white. A plush rug that he suspected was chosen for comfort—when lying on it. A love seat that fit the same description.

"Sit anywhere you want."

He chose the love seat. He was less than astonished when she sat on the opposite side. Close.

So, prostitute? In a way, he was disappointed. With all the dark-web hugger-mugger, and Jimmy encountering a domina-trix, he had almost hoped for something more outré.

"Like a drink?" she asked, leaning forward in a way that couldn't help but attract attention.

"No, I'm fine."

"Well, what can I do for you, sugar?"

He cleared his throat. "What should I call you?" Presumably not Honey O'Plenty.

"How about Daphne?"

"Is that your real name?"

"I wish. I like it better. So what's up, Doc?"

"Well…what I had in mind was…somewhat unusual."

"Oh, baby, don't worry. I've heard it all. How can I make you happy?"

"I'm not sure where to start."

"Maybe we should review the pricing structure."

His eyebrow rose. He hadn't expected that answer. Although, all things considered, it made sense. "Okay…"

"My clients usually want the full experience."

"The…uh…full experience?"

"The girlfriend experience."

Okay, now he was confused. "I thought we were going to…"

"You can get that anywhere. You came here for something better, didn't you?" Her eyes twinkled. "Who referred you to me?"

"Um, actually…it was George Belasco."

The smile on her face faded.

"A long while ago. Obviously."

"George recommended me?"

"In a way." Okay, fine. "Look, the real reason I'm here—"

"Is this some kind of dog thing? Something involving animals?"

"A…dog thing?"

"You like to get down on your hands and knees. I pat you on the head and tell you you're a good boy. A very good boy. Then maybe we do it doggie-style."

He took a long deep breath. "Why would you think—"

"Your name. Atty boy."

"Uh, no. Atty is short for attorney. And…I'm a boy. Sorry. I've used the name online before. First thing that popped into my head."

"You're an attorney?"

"Yeah. Sorry."

"Don't be sorry." She scooted closer. "So you're loaded, right? Tons of money and no one to spend it on?"

He held up his hands. "Look, let me come clean. I didn't come here for...anything physical. Or any...experience. I came for information."

She stiffened. "About what? Me?"

"No. Not at all. About George Belasco. I represent Daniel Pike. As you probably know, he's been accused of murdering Belasco. But he didn't do it. And I'm trying to find out who did."

She scooted back as far as the love seat would permit. "You think I did it?"

"No. I mean, I don't know. I didn't know who you were till a minute ago. But I've learned that Belasco had a lot of secrets. And I'm trying to find out what they were. It might lead me to the truth about what happened to him."

"I did not kill George. I was never anything but nice to him. I was there when he wanted me, and I disappeared when he didn't. I gave him the full girlfriend experience."

He stopped short. "What exactly is this girlfriend experience?"

She frowned. "Why should I tell you? You're not a customer."

"I'm...curious."

She tilted her head. "And you're not a cop."

"Definitely not."

"Are you going to talk to the cops?"

"Not unless you know something relating to the murder." He paused. "I have no desire to get you into trouble. You seem like a...nice girl. In a way."

She looked at him, eyes narrowed. "I don't even think what I do is illegal. But I don't want to test that in court. It's not like I'm a hooker."

"You're...not?"

"No. It's not about sex. At least, not just about sex. It's the full platter. The complete girlfriend experience."

"Meaning?"

"There are many great guys out there, successful, rich, nice—but kinda lonely. Don't want to get married, but don't want to spend every night alone. Tech guys with limited social skills. Maybe a little autistic. Big business guys with limited spare time. They don't merely want sex. They want the perfect girlfriend. Someone they can spend the evening with and not be embarrassed about it. Someone pretty, sure, but also cultured, educated, able to carry on an intelligent conversation. Classy."

"And that's what you provide, Daphne?"

"Correct. I'm a college grad. Letters major. I'm well read. Culturally literate."

"And...selling that?"

"Why not? Pays better than teaching. My master's degree was just a piece of paper with a huge student loan attached. I could never pay that off teaching school. So I went a different route."

"And this..." He looked around the apartment. "Pays well?"

"I get $400 bucks an hour."

"For sex."

"For anything. I call it sugaring. Before, I was constantly getting hit on by older men. I don't know why. At first, I brushed them off. Then I started to think, well, what's in it for me? I told this guy, Look, I'm not interested in bloating your ego. But I do have loans. And living expenses."

"And he helped you pay them?"

"Yup. And I noticed that, although he did expect sex, what he really wanted—and what he really enjoyed—was a wonderful evening. Dinner at a nice place with a great-looking piece of eye candy. Intelligent conversation. Someone who understood what he was talking about. Someone who wasn't always babbling about clothes or pop songs or kids or repeating internet memes. Someone focused on him."

"And then sex."

"Like I said, the perfect girlfriend experience. I started posting on a website called GirlieGirls. They have an app, too. The idea was to hook sugar daddies up with sugar babies. But the dark web is even better. Safer."

"Do you have a lot of clients?"

"No. I'm quite selective. I basically have four guys in rotation, which leaves me a few nights off. That provides all the money I can spend and allows me to build a nice nest egg. I'm going to start a business of my own, once I have the startup capital. I don't want to be dependent on anyone. No investors, nothing. I've made my own way in the world. I'm build my future on my terms."

"These four guys...do you like them?"

"Do you like everyone you work with?"

He could see her point.

"But you still work there, right? If you're a lawyer, you've had clients you didn't care for. Probably couldn't stand. But you still worked for them. Look, it's a job. I do it for money, not fun. It's my business, and I'm the CEO. I've taken the male gaze and turned it around. I'm in control of it."

"I was not expecting this. It's...unusual."

"It's fairly common, actually. More girls like me around than you can imagine. We have websites and bulletin boards where we exchange information, ask about rates, share techniques. We trade tips on Tumblr. We have private Facebook pages where we discuss how to avoid law enforcement or guys with bad tempers. How to alleviate the aching from excessive spanking. How to pry money out of losers who won't pay up."

"You make this sound like an entire community of...proud working women."

"Why not? Is it better to slave away at some minimum-wage job? Flip burgers or sell shoes for a few bucks an hour? In my opinion, that's for people who lack imagination. Or who don't have the stomach for this kind of work. Every job requires you to do stuff you'd rather not do. How is this different? Get past the antiquated middle-class morality and you can see that it makes a lot of sense."

"How do you get paid?"

"Different ways. Can I show you something?"

"Sure." He followed her, getting a better view of this magnificent apartment. The almost wall-size window afforded a breathtaking view of downtown St. Pete and the ocean beyond. Every room was as well-furnished as the first. Gorgeous wallpaper. Gorgeous rugs. Not his area of expertise, but he knew quality when he saw it.

"George transferred money to my account every month. He had a dark web account with tons of cash. But some guys prefer to buy stuff. Chanel perfume. Gucci bags. I keep an Amazon Wish List fully stocked. Some of my guys log on every Saturday and buy whatever I list. That's how I got most of the niceties you see scattered about the apartment."

"Impressive."

"See the art on the wall? My sugar daddies paid for it. Trevor Carlson. Brand Coto. Working on a Hockney sketch."

"You're joking."

"I'm not." She took him into the enormous kitchen. Copper pans hanging from the ceiling. Two stoves. Two islands. Every appliance imaginable. And a refrigerator lit by a series of app buttons and a video display. "I even got a refrigerator from my boys!"

"Nice perks."

"But I never let the perks become the main event. They all have to contribute to the savings account."

They returned to the front living room. He took his place on the love seat, but she sat on the floor, spread out across the plush white rug. Perhaps now that she understood she wasn't going to be asked to perform, she felt she could relax a bit.

"Do you know how George came by that money in his dark web account?"

Some of the bubble in her personality faded. "I heard he inherited a lot of cash. But the way he threw money around...he needed a constant supply. And when he started that mayoral campaign, he needed even more."

"But you don't know how he got it."

She pursed her lips. "I think he was into something...dangerous. And he was...worried about it. The last night he was here... something was on his mind."

"Do you know what?"

"Sorry."

"Human trafficking?"

"God. I hope not."

"Murder?"

"I don't know." She paused. "Nothing's impossible."

"When was the last time you saw him?"

"The night before he was murdered. He was worried. Distraught." She opened a drawer in the coffee table, revealing a necktie and iPhone and a few other personal items. "He left some of his stuff here. Can you imagine? Who leaves their cellphone?"

"He must've been distraught. Did you ask what was bothering him?"

"All night. All through dinner, drinks. But he wouldn't tell me. One time he muttered, 'They must bring the boat here.' But when I asked what that meant, he wouldn't explain."

They must bring the boat here? Was he investing in the tuna industry? Or was someone shipping something far more profitable?

"Did he say anything else that might be important?"

"Oh, he went on and on about his wife. She was getting it on with some sleazebag at the country club. George paid her membership and her spa fees, which was basically paying off the male prostitute. Geez, I'd rather be doing what I do any day of the week."

"Anything else?"

"He worried about his son. CJ. Those two couldn't see eye to eye. Every time they talked it turned into a shouting match. And George was worried about this election. And he worried about that guy. The big bald guy."

"Conrad Sweeney?"

"That's the one. Talk about a whale. I could make room for him on my client list. But George said he wouldn't be interested. He said Sweeney only liked people he could control."

"Could you do that? I mean…him?"

She allowed herself a small smile. "I could let him feel like he was in control for a little while. A guy like that could fund my startup without blinking."

Practical to a fault. "Do you know what George was doing with Sweeney?"

"I knew he regretted ever getting involved with the guy. Wheels within wheels, he said, when he talked about Sweeney. So many plots going at once it would take a gamemaster to unravel them all. They had some kind of risky business venture. But I don't know the specifics."

Something bothered him. "Daphne, do you think George… trusted you?"

"I know he did. He may not have told me everything, but when he didn't, it was because he was protecting me. And he never lied to me. Never once. Never led me on. Never told me BS about plans to divorce his wife. We treated each other like adults." She paused. "The weird thing is…I miss him." She leaned forward on the rug, almost catlike. "You seem like a nice guy. What's your story?"

"Is this a…professional inquiry, Daphne?"

"With me, sugar, it's always a professional inquiry. You seem like a straight arrow. You must have some bucks. But you're not wearing a ring. And you're not gay."

"How do you know?"

"I know. And I haven't filled George's slot in my appointment book. If you'd like to give it a try…"

Garrett rose. "Extremely tempting, I assure you. But no."

She tossed her head to one side. "If you change your mind, you know how to contact me."

"I do. And no worries. I see no reason to share anything you've told me with the authorities." Which was quite a thing for a former prosecutor to say. But whether he approved of her lifestyle or not, she didn't appear to be doing anyone any harm.

He started toward the door, then stopped. "Daphne…how much longer do you think you'll be able to keep this up?"

"What do you mean?"

"I can see you have lots of confidence, lots of enthusiasm. But that can't last forever. You're beautiful, but sadly, looks fade. At some point, you'll need to make a course correction."

"One more year," she said firmly. "That's all I need. One more year at my current rate of income and I'll have what I need to start my business."

"You're sure about that?"

"I am. I thought I was going to be done two years ago, but then I got a new idea for an expansion, and I knew that would require more capital."

"Uh huh."

"In fact, I was going to quit this year, but you know how prices have risen. And what the coronavirus did to the economy. The stock market is so unpredictable."

"And always will be."

"One more year. Then I'm out."

He looked into her eyes. "I hope that's true." Bizarrely, he found himself inclined to lean down and give her a Dopey kiss on the top of her head. But he resisted.

"Sorry I wasn't more help," she said.

"You were terrific. Thanks again." He smiled, then walked out the door toward the elevator.

He waited until Daphne was gone and the elevator doors had closed before he took it out of his pocket.

George Belasco's cellphone. Which he had taken when Daphne wasn't looking.

She might not know more about Belasco's nasty business enterprises. But if he left any traces of that business anywhere, it might be in the tiny little computer he now held in the palm of his hand.

CHAPTER THIRTY

DAN KNEW THE WITNESSES YET TO COME WOULD BE FAR MORE trouble than the previous ones. For starters, they had to deal with the physical evidence linking him to the crime. And then, of course, they would have to deal with the audio recording. No way Garfield would let the day end without making sure the jury heard that in stereophonic sound.

Deanna Folsom was Florida's preeminent skin and scalp expert, which was presumably why the prosecution went to the trouble of hiring her. Given that all she was doing was testifying about a stray scrap of skin, the prosecution could've used any marginally intelligent forensic scientist. Hiring her was a clear sign of how much the prosecution wanted to nail him.

Dan watched as Folsom took the stand. Older woman, probably in her early sixties. Open collar. Medallion hanging from a chain around her neck. Black sweater, the frequent choice of those carrying a few more pounds than necessary.

Garfield wasted no time establishing her credentials. Folsom had originally worked at FamilyTree, an online genealogy site that encouraged people to submit DNA samples so the company could provide a report on the donor's racial and ethnic background. The accuracy of those reports had been challenged, but that was true of all online genealogy sites. Whether the reports were accurate or not, these sites became huge depositories of DNA data.

Folsom hit on the idea of using that material to solve cold cases. She testified that the samples could be used to reopen more than 100,000 unsolved cases, or cases in which the verdicts were questionable. They could also be used, she claimed, to identify dead bodies. Many people challenged the legality, not to mention the ethics, of using this data. After all, donors didn't know their samples could be used to convict their third cousins. But according to Folsom, there were currently over three hundred pending cases using these volunteered DNA samples.

In the present case, they didn't need a family tree. The skin sample was found in the back alley on Belasco's shirt. The exemplar taken from Dan matched. The previous police witness had established that the skin was found at the crime scene, put in a plastic evidence bag, and kept under lock and key in the downtown evidence locker, except when taken out for testing.

"Have you had a chance to examine the skin fragment found at the crime scene?" Garfield asked.

"I have."

"Did you reach any conclusions?"

"It matches the sample taken from the defendant. Daniel Pike."

"And when you say it matches—"

"It's virtually identical. There's no question. It's his."

"Pass the witness."

Dan doubted whether Maria should even cross-examine. She was not going to shake this witness. They had hired an independent expert to run tests, and he had reached the same conclusion. Nonetheless, Maria marched dutifully to the witness stand.

"You claim that my client's skin was found at the crime scene."

"It's a scientific fact. Appears to have come from his scalp. People shed skin without realizing it all day long. You lose thirty thousand skin cells every minute. We leave a trail of skin everywhere we go. Most pieces are too small to be detected. But not all."

"Finding his skin doesn't prove he was the murderer, though, does it?"

Folsom smiled thinly. "I'll let the jury make that determination."

"In fact, it doesn't prove that Dan was ever in that back alley, right?"

"His skin was."

"It could have been planted."

"That strikes me as unlikely."

"Why?" Maria gestured toward one of the crime-scene photos introduced by an earlier witness. "The murderer obviously went to a great deal of trouble to create a dramatic scene. And sent alleged evidence to the police by email. The murderer did everything imaginable to incriminate my client."

"That's one way of looking at it."

"So why not also plant a little skin? Simplest thing in the world."

"Objection," Garfield said. "My esteemed colleague is asking the witness to speculate. Based upon no evidence at all."

"I'm introducing possibilities," Maria said. "Possible causes for reasonable doubt."

"And besides," Garfield continued, "the witness is not on the stand to imagine bizarre and elaborate scenarios that might theoretically exonerate the defendant. She's on the stand to talk about what actually happened."

Judge Hembeck nodded. "I'm going to allow the question.

But I will caution counsel not to drift too far into the realm of speculation. Stick to the facts."

"Thank you, your honor." Maria turned back to the witness. "Dr. Folsom, does the fact that this skin was found on the body prove that my client was the murderer?"

"It certainly doesn't look good."

"Please answer the question."

"I will grant you, there are other possible explanations." She paused. "But as a scientist, I believe in Occam's razor. The simplest explanation is usually the best one."

THE NEXT PROSECUTION WITNESS WAS LIEUTENANT GREG Richards, the computer-desk monitor who first discovered the audio recording sent anonymously to the police. Young man, barely thirty. Uncomfortable, like most witnesses. Missed a button on his shirt. Left foot longer than the right.

Once again, Maria tried to suppress the recording. Judge Hembeck ruled against her, explaining that she was welcome to discuss any failings on cross, but she felt Richards was an adequate supporting witness to identify and authenticate the evidence even if he didn't know who made the recording or who sent it to the police.

Barely minutes after Richards took the stand, Garfield played the recording for the jury.

"There are ways we could deal with the District Attorney."

"What do you mean?"

"We could have him taken care of."

"Just off him?"

"If he's on Sweeney's payroll, he deserves to be offed."

"You don't have to do that."

"For you, I would do anything."

"Likewise."

Dan and Maria exchanged a dire expression. It sounded bad. He knew that he and Camila had been kidding around. But taken out of context, it was incriminating. It sounded like two people who despised Belasco contemplating the possibility of eliminating him.

Richards described in detail the rigorous testing the police put the recording through to determine its authenticity, to ensure that it had not been edited, altered, or tampered with. They used voice analysis—so-called audio fingerprints—to prove that the two people on the tape were in fact Dan and Camila. No surprises there. Mr. K had paid even more prominent experts to scrutinize the tapes and they had reached the same conclusions.

Dan felt for Maria as she rose to cross-examine. He had been in the same situation on too many previous occasions. She couldn't let such a key piece of evidence pass without at least attempting to poke holes in it—but there wasn't that much to say.

"Lieutenant Richards, you've listened to the entire recording, right?"

"I've listened to what we received. The excerpt you heard was all that came in the email."

"But it's clear that was not the entire conversation?"

"I assume there was more to it."

"Something had to come before, and something had to come later."

"I couldn't say."

"Would you agree that it's impossible to judge what these people are saying unless you can hear the complete conversation in context?"

He shifted slightly. "No, I think it's perfectly obvious what they're saying."

"Is it possible they were joking?"

Richards stared at her uncomprehendingly. "Who would joke about murdering someone?"

"Oh, come on. Have you done it?"

"No."

"Never said, 'Just shoot me?'"

"That's different."

"Ever said, "I could tell you, but I'd have to kill you?'"

"Completely different."

"Ever gotten mad and said, 'I'm gonna kill you?'"

"No. And even if I had, so what? The voices on that recording aren't angry. They're calm and collected. They're planning a murder like someone might plan what to fix for breakfast."

"Doesn't that prove they weren't serious?"

"All I know is what I hear. Two people talking about taking out the district attorney."

This wasn't getting anywhere. "You haven't been able to trace the recording to its source, have you?"

"We know the email ultimately came from an coffeehouse on Elm Street. Who sent it, we have no way of knowing."

"Quite the coincidence, especially coming right after an anonymous call told you where to find the body. It's almost like someone was deliberately trying to frame my client."

"Or a concerned citizen was trying to make sure a slick lawyer didn't get away with murder."

Good comeback. "How do you think your informant obtained the recording?"

"I don't know."

"Listening devices would've had to be planted in advance, right? Which suggests a deliberate—and probably illegal—effort to get the goods on my client."

"Someone needed to get the goods on him. I can't fault anybody for helping the police do their job."

"If that's what they were trying to do." Dan could sense

Maria's frustration. It was always a mistake to expect much out of police witnesses. They had a job to do, and that job wasn't helping the defense.

"You're aware that one of the people on that tape, Mayor Camila Pérez, has been released from custody. All charges against her have been dropped."

"I did hear that."

"Wouldn't that suggest someone doesn't believe a murder was being planned in this conversation?"

"No." And the second he said that, Dan realized that asking the question had been a mistake. But it was too late to call it back. "It means she didn't actually commit the murder. But here you see the seeds being planted. Pérez wanted DA Belasco dead. So her lover took it upon himself to do it. She had an alibi at the time of the murder. But he didn't. There's a reason for that."

"Objection," Maria said, trying to correct her mistake. "He's speculating."

Garfield rose. "He's answering her question. She opened the door to this response."

"I have to agree with the prosecutor on this one," Judge Hembeck said. "Objection overruled. Anything more, counsel?"

Maria's teeth were clenched. "No. Nothing more."

"Redirect?"

"Yes." Garfield remained standing. "Since the defense lawyer has called the meaning of the taped conversation into question, I would request that it be replayed for the jury. So they can reconsider it in light of this testimony."

"This is duplicative evidence," Maria insisted. "The jury will get the recording and a transcript when they deliberate."

"Nonetheless," Garfield said. "I think it would be useful for them to hear it again at this time. While the testimony is fresh on their minds."

"That does make sense," Judge Hembeck replied. "Play the tape again, counsellor."

Dan swore silently. That cross-ex had gotten them nothing, and worse, had given the prosecutor an excuse to replay her greatest hits, to give the jury one more chance to be appalled by a stupid and ill-considered conversation.

He made a point of unobtrusively observing the jurors' facial expressions while the tape was played. They thought it was as worrisome as he did. Maybe not conclusive proof. But a strong basis for suspicion.

Like it or not, Dan realized that the farce they called "burden of proof" had shifted. The jurors now leaned toward conviction. From this point onward, the burden of proof would be on the defense to prove his innocence.

Otherwise, his conviction was all but certain.

CHAPTER THIRTY-ONE

GARRETT WATCHED THE LONG-HAIRED MAN AT WORK, REMINDING himself that he disliked every single aspect of this meeting. And yet, here he was.

"Making any progress?" Garrett asked.

The young man did not look up. His greasy brown hair hung low on both sides of his head, masking his face. His worktable was illuminated by a single bright overhead light bulb in an otherwise dark apartment. "Getting there. Slow work. Hard. Commercial data retrieval software won't work. He had several levels of government encryption."

"Will you be able to get in?"

"I'm optimistic. No guarantees."

"It's very important."

"It always is with you prosecutors."

"I'm not a prosecutor anymore."

His head tilted slightly. "Leopards can't change their spots."

Garrett watched as the kid opened a desk drawer and withdrew something that bore a disturbing resemblance to Michael Jackson's single glove. "What's that?"

"Fake fingers. I've got a bunch of them."

Garrett grimaced. "Is that necessary?"

"Essential. And just for the record, I'd work a lot faster if you'd stop interrupting me."

Garrett drew in his breath, then slowly released it. He hated what he was doing, he hated where he was doing it, and he wasn't crazy about this hacker he'd hired to undertake what was technically a criminal invasion of privacy. But the person whose privacy he was invading was dead and Dan needed help. So he would have to live with this.

After he left Daphne's apartment with Belasco's phone, he tried to open it, but it was protected with a fingerprint sensor. You had five attempts and then it retreated to a six-digit password. There could be something on that phone that might help Dan, might explain what dirty secrets Belasco had been hiding. But how to get inside? Even the FBI had trouble digging into iPhones. On more than one occasion they had asked Apple for help—and been turned down.

Then he remembered this kid, Colin Baxter. Garrett had prosecuted him back in the day for an email phishing scam. He was another scammer trying to get someone else's numbers to buy his Cheez Whiz. But he understood computers like no one Garrett had ever encountered.

Was it possible he could hack a cellphone?

As it happened, the kid was out on probation and taking classes for a programming degree at USF. He almost felt bad about tempting Baxter away from the straight and narrow. He didn't want to destroy the kid's future...

But then again, Garrett was working on the side of the angels. He had to prevent these people from railroading Dan. They had to find out what was hidden. What motivated Belasco's murder.

And if he had to break a few rules to get there...he would. And he wouldn't feel too bad about it, especially since Baxter was illegally downloading *Star Trek: Picard* episodes when Garrett found him at a coffeeshop…

The irony of the situation was not lost on him. How many times had he and Dan clashed over Dan's tendency to flout rules? Dan was always bending, if not breaking rules, and Garrett was always the conservative defender of the Way Things Were Supposed to Work.

But not this time. He knew Dan didn't commit that murder. But the prosecutors kept producing more and more evidence. It started with the audio tape and escalated so quickly it was clear someone wanted Dan put away. He knew he wasn't the only person who saw it. Some of the people in the DA's office had to be suspicious. But what could they do? They had the evidence. They were obliged to prosecute.

"I think we've got something," Baxter said. For the first time in half an hour, he looked up, laying down his small watchmaker's tools. He had removed the back panel of the iPhone, interfering with what appeared to be an incredibly complex motherboard. "Give it a minute to process."

"Could you possibly explain what you're doing? In layman's terms?"

"From the beginning?"

"We seem to have some time on our hands."

Baxter pushed his wireframe glasses up the bridge of his nose. "It started a couple of years ago. Not my hack of this phone. But the theory behind it. Some guys at Michigan State and New York University discovered these phones could be fooled by fake fingerprints digitally composed of common features derived from real fingerprints. They used computer simulations to develop a set of what they called 'MasterPrints.' Artificial fingerprints."

"And those MasterPrints can be used to unlock phones?"

"With a sixty-five percent success rate."

Garrett whistled. "Are these MasterPrints hard to come by?"

"Nah. They're on the dark web."

Of course. Wasn't everything? "So anyone can use them?"

"The researchers who generated them used a commercially available software program. The tricky part is getting the fake fingerprints onto the cellphone."

"I assume that's where the magic glove comes into play."

"Precisely. Apple knows about all this. They've moved to Face ID—which is also hackable—but that doesn't help older phones that still use fingerprints. The theory behind finger-print ID is sound. Full human fingerprints are hard to fake. But the finger scanners on phones are small. They don't take complete prints, like cops do when they arrest you. The phones only read partial fingerprints on one finger. When you're setting up the protection, phones usually take eight or so images. A finger swipe only has to match one of them to unlock the phone."

"That must increase the odds of success."

"You know it. It's like the phone actually has forty passwords and a hacker only has to match one of them. Which is more doable than you might imagine." He winked. "Especially if you have a programmable magic glove and a good set of Master-Prints. Also, I found a set of Belasco's fingerprints."

"How?"

"George Belasco was fingerprinted before he took the bar exam."

"Everyone is. It's required. They run a background check before they allow anyone to practice law."

"I found the files. They were not in a downloadable format and they were in poor condition, but I got some idea what Belasco's right index fingerprint looked like. I combined that with the information in the MasterPrint file. I processed all of that information, then burned composite prints onto this image-receptive glove. Each finger will have a somewhat different print. Variations on a theme. By my calculation, we have a forty to fifty percent chance of getting into this phone in the first five tries."

"You must not be the only person who can do this."

"Far from it. Some companies are developing anti-spoofing procedures. They suggest designing a phone to look for not only a print but perspiration, or deeper layers of skin."

"Which means your glove wouldn't work."

"Right. But no one has done it yet. Qualcomm developed a sensor that uses ultrasound to detect fake fingers. But no one else—"

He was interrupted by a pinging sound. "Time's up. The images have resolved. Let's see what we've got."

Baxter pulled the glove out of the burn box, placed it on his right hand, and extended his index finger. He placed the finger on the sensor at the bottom of Belasco's phone screen.

Nothing happened.

"Strike one," Baxter mumbled.

Garrett pursed his lips. "But you have four more chances, right?"

"Precisely." Baxter tried his middle finger.

Nothing happened.

Baxter started to look a bit worried. He tried his pinky.

The black screen disappeared. White light burst from the screen. A moment later they saw the time and the date superimposed over a photo of Belasco at some kind of party.

"It's alive!" Baxter cried.

Even though he'd been with the kid every step of the way, Garrett was amazed it had worked. He snatched the phone and started tapping apps. "How long do I have?"

Baxter leaned over his shoulder. "It's only half-charged. If you're going to be on it for more than a couple of hours, you should probably plug in. Oh, and while you have it open— change the password. If it requires another finger tap, we know which one will work. Program an easy numeric code."

"Good idea." Garrett went through the procedure he knew all too well for changing the password. He changed his passwords on phone and computers every ninety days. Some of his teammates derided him for his abundance of caution, but now more than ever he felt justified.

He tapped the iPhone app and scrolled through the list of Contacts. Belasco had hundreds of them. Since Garrett didn't recognize all the names, or even most of them, it was impossible to know whether these were legitimate or criminal. He could do a thorough check on each and every one. But that would take time, the one thing Dan did not have in great abundance.

He tried a different approach. He scrolled down the Recent list. Who had Belasco been calling shortly before his death? Who was calling him?

At the top of the list he found a long string of phone calls from an unidentified caller. The length of the conversations told him it wasn't a robocall or solicitation. But the number didn't match any of Belasco's contacts.

Why would that be?

On a sudden whim, he hit return on the number, initiating a call.

He waited...

No one picked up. Instead, almost immediately, he received an automated response telling him this line was no longer in service.

A burner phone, probably. Something someone picked up at a 7-11, used a few times, then threw into the ocean.

One more thought. He tapped on the Messages app. Had anyone been texting Belasco?

Yes. Many people. Most were business-related, campaign-related. A few had pictures attached.

Well, a picture is worth a thousand words, right?

He tapped the first to enlarge it.

And gasped.

He tapped another message with photos, then another.

He couldn't tell exactly where these photos were taken. But it appeared to be inside a ship, perhaps in the cargo hold.

And the hold was filled with young women.

Most appeared to be Latinx, though it was difficult to be sure in the low lighting. Their clothes were dirty, ragged coveralls. They looked like they hadn't been able to wash or groom for an eternity.

And they were chained.

He didn't need captions to know what he was seeing. Human trafficking, like the woman on the ropes course had suggested. Sex trafficking, probably, a blight that had plagued this part of the country for far too long. Dan's first case with this team had involved trafficking, ultimately traced to a rogue ICE agent.

But that man had been locked up for some time now. The traffickers must've needed a new contact. Someone else on the inside.

And who could possibly be more useful than the District Attorney? Except perhaps the Mayor—the office Belasco was campaigning for when he was killed.

If they could link Belasco to human trafficking, the list of possible murderers would explode. It wouldn't make the evidence against Dan go away. But it would give new meaning to the phrase "reasonable doubt."

He cycled through the photos. They were much the same. Except one, the last, was taken on land, at a St. Petersburg port.

The point of embarkation?

He hoped so. Because he recognized it.

If this was where these pigs brought their illegal imports, he knew how to find them.

But the risk? This was more than a local conspiracy. It was international. It involved cartels. It involved men who shot first and blinked later. Human trafficking was a billion-dollar business. There was nothing some people wouldn't do for that kind of money.

If he got in the middle of this, he might get some useful information. But it was far more likely he would end up dead.

He couldn't expect these photos to be admitted into evidence. He couldn't explain how he got them and he had no one to authenticate them.

He needed a witness.

"Success?" Baxter asked. "Did you find what you wanted?"

"The first step," Garrett said quietly, sliding the phone into his pocket. "Which I hope will not be my last step."

CHAPTER THIRTY-TWO

DAN WAS IMPRESSED BY HOW MANY PEOPLE STILL FILLED THE gallery of the courtroom. He would like to think that was some kind of tribute to his animal magnetism, but he suspected it was more the natural attraction of anything gruesome, similar to people staring at car wrecks as they drove by.

Jazlyn Prentice stood in the rear of the courtroom, watching. She didn't approach the prosecutors' table, her normal venue. That was someone else's bailiwick this time around. Presumably she was just monitoring.

He started to move in her direction, but one look was enough to tell him that was not wanted. She couldn't be seen consorting with the accused. That could compromise the prosecution. Could compromise the entire office. And it would be deadly to her run for DA.

He would keep his distance. But he missed her. Very much.

He started down the aisle toward Maria and the defendant's table, but before he got far, Garrett burst in through the back doors.

"Good to see you," Dan said amiably. "You haven't been in the courtroom much."

"Trust me, I've been busy. Still hoping to land something useful before you have to put on the defense case."

"Look, the last time we talked, I got—"

Garrett raised his hand. "Stop. You don't need to apologize for anything. I should probably apologize."

"No, I was—"

"You're under incredible stress right now. Probably the most it's possible to bear. I get that."

"Still—"

"Forget about it. Okay? Keep your eyes on the prize."

"Thanks." He noticed the stapled papers Garrett clutched. "May I ask what that is?"

"Research. Maria's going to try to keep out the eyewitness testimony."

"Won't work. Not with this judge."

"Do you blame her for trying?"

"Of course not. I would do the same. What's the objection?"

"Using legally dubious facial-recognition software to find witnesses. Photoshopping mug shots for a lineup."

"Good points. That won't work."

"If nothing else," Garrett said, "the jury will see Maria arguing about it. That alone might make them think twice about —" His head jerked to one side. "Daphne?"

The young woman seated on the second row obviously recognized him. Her face flushed pink. "Oh. Um. Hello."

This was the petite dimpled blonde Dan had spotted in the courtroom the first day of the trial. And Garrett knew her?

Garrett appeared confused. "What...brings you to the courtroom today?"

Daphne fidgeted with her hands. "Oh, you know. I was curious. My calendar was clear."

"That's not really an explanation."

"Well, I do have an...interest in the situation. As you know."

Dan stared at them both, hoping someone would provide an explanation.

"Dan, this is the young woman I mentioned. I'm sure you read my report. George Belasco's..."

Daphne finished for him. "Girlfriend."

"*Experience*," Garrett added. "I'm...surprised that you've taken such an interest in the case, Daphne."

"You know what? Something went missing from my apartment. After you left."

"I have no idea what you mean," Garrett replied, completely stone-faced.

"Uh-huh. Quite the coincidence. You know, I was trying to help you."

"I can assure you I appreciate your assistance. But since you were unwilling to testify, I was forced to explore other avenues."

Dan did not want a fracas in the courtroom. Nor did he want an accusation that might tarnish future evidence. "If you were able to help Garrett in any way, ma'am, you have my thanks."

Daphne flashed a smile, but she did not look terribly happy.

Dan noticed the woman sitting beside Daphne—who he also recalled seeing on the first day of trial. Tall, lean, with a blue streak in her hair. More pieces of the puzzle clicked into place. Something he read...in one of Jimmy's reports.

He pointed a finger at the tall woman. "Are you the lady Jimmy met forty feet up in the air? On the ropes course?"

The tall woman sighed. "I had a hunch this was coming next."

Dan extended his hand. "Good to meet you, Ms..."

She shook his hand. "You can call me Sam."

"Because that's your name?"

"Because that's what you can call me."

"Jimmy said you were in an...unusual line of work." If you

considered dressing up in black leather and watching men cry unusual. "Are you still at it?"

"I can give you a business card if you're interested."

"I'm a bit busy at the moment. But I think the jury would be interested in hearing what you know about George Belasco."

"Why? His personal kinks have nothing to do with his death."

Maybe. But it would definitely pierce the prosecution portrait of the man as a living breathing saint. Plus, she had mentioned human trafficking. "Best to let the jury decide whether something is relevant."

"I won't be used to trash a man after he's gone."

"We could subpoena you."

"I'd advise against it." She looked him straight in the eye. "You force me onto that witness stand, you won't like what comes out of my mouth."

He didn't need advanced observational powers to know she was dead serious. "I'd rather you volunteered out of a sense of civic duty."

"That won't happen. Leave me alone."

He glanced at Garrett and shrugged. They already knew what little she had to offer, and her testimony probably wouldn't be helpful. But why was she in the courtroom? Sitting beside Daphne. Who come to think of it, Garrett had only found based upon a lead the dominatrix gave Jimmy.

Maybe it was nothing. But it seemed damned peculiar. Like everything else about this case.

By the time he reached the defendant's table, Maria was ready to rock and roll.

"Optimistic?" he asked.

"Not remotely. But prepared. Which at the moment is the best I can manage."

Garfield called her next witness, another police officer, this time a Sergeant Dunlevy. He was like the Oscar show celeb who introduces the introducer. His only function was to explain how the police found the following witness. The one who would pin Dan to the scene of the crime.

Dunlevy took the stand. Thirtyish. Pale. Uniform was snug, especially in the rear. Shiny shoes.

"What was your assigned duty on the day in question?" Garfield asked.

"I was manning the front desk. Primarily reviewing email. The downtown office gets a ton of it."

"Did you notice anything out of the ordinary?"

"I saw several anonymous emails."

"Is that unusual?"

"No. At least fourth of what we get is anonymous. Email is the modern equivalent of the tip hotline. On this occasion, though, one was of particular interest."

"What about this message caught your attention?"

"It contained an image taken by a security camera posted on a nearby building. Off to the left, it was possible to detect someone not far from the alley where the body was found."

"Why was this of interest?"

"At first, it wasn't. Later, when we realized this was near the scene of a murder, it became more intriguing. We thought this might be a picture of the murderer. Once we eliminated that possibility, we knew we had a possible witness."

The jurors stirred. "Did you recognize the face?"

"Not at all. The photo wasn't great. Distant, fuzzy, above eye level, looking downward. I doubt we could have traced it on our own. Even if we had made the photo public, I doubt it would have led to anything."

"What did you do?"

"I uploaded the image to a software program we licensed from a company called Clearview AI. It's a highly sophisticated facial-recognition program. We have other recognition programs, but they mostly draw from photos in police records. This program draws from everywhere online, which puts vastly more photos in its database. According to Clearview, it reviews more than three billion photos."

"That's impressive."

"The program gave me additional photos of the person in question, with links to the sites where the photos appeared. That allowed us to track her down."

"So it worked?"

"Beautifully. We identified the woman as Harriet Clooney."

"Thank you. Pass the witness."

Maria rose. "No questions. You honor, at this time we urge the motion we have already filed to suppress the next witness, Harriet Clooney, based upon obvious constitutional issues. Specifically, the violation of the right to privacy."

Judge Hembeck waved the lawyers to the bench. Dan followed. Why not? He was a lawyer, too, after all.

"I've read your brief, counsel," Judge Hembeck said, "and I have to tell you, I don't see the problem."

"Neither do we, your honor." This time it was Zachary Blunt speaking—the Knife. Apparently the niceties of constitutional law were his specialty. "If we thought there was any taint to this evidence, we wouldn't be using it."

Dan forced himself to suppress his reaction.

Maria stayed calm and put on her "reasonable advocate face." "Your honor, how much does the court know about this Clearview program?"

"I know it's popular with the police. Something like six hundred law enforcement agencies are using it. Everyone from our local cops to the FBI and Homeland Security."

"Because it works," the Knife muttered.

"But that doesn't mean it's constitutional," Maria insisted. "Some commentators have said there's a rush to get as much use out of it as possible before the courts shut it down. Since *The New York Times* first broke the story, Clearview has been under fire. Some companies, like Facebook and Google, have sent them cease-and-desist letters. Lawsuits have been filed. The AG of New Jersey has banned its use."

"We are not in New Jersey."

"But it's dangerous."

"So far," Judge Hembeck said, "no court has ruled it unconstitutional or illegal."

"Making this a case of first impression," Maria replied. "You could be the court that strikes a decisive blow for privacy rights."

Hembeck frowned. "The only thing I'm interested in is conducting a fair criminal trial."

"And I'm sure you will. But that doesn't mean you should turn a blind eye to illegal data gathering. Those billions of photos from social media were collected illegally."

"Arguably," the Knife inserted.

"Definitely in violation of the platforms' stated public policies. Their terms of service."

"If Facebook wishes to sue, I believe they have the means to do so," Hembeck said. "I don't see why we need to get involved."

"Because if you think about this," Maria continued, "the whole concept is terrifying. Once the use of this program is widespread, it will be impossible to walk down the street anonymously. Get this. The program comes equipped with programming language designed to pair it with augmented-reality glasses. Cops could walk down the street and ID everyone they see. They could instantly know who you are, where you live, who you know."

"Only a problem if you're doing something illegal," the Knife commented.

"I disagree. Cops could identify anyone attending a protest rally. Cops could trail an ex, or any woman who catches their eye on a bus. The stalker potential is frightening."

"But we're not talking about it being used by a stalker today," the judge said. "It was used by law enforcement to help them do their jobs. And it worked."

"That's how it was used today, your honor. What about tomorrow? I urge the court to rule that this program violates the privacy rights the US Supreme Court has said are part of the US Constitution. This is not the tool of a free state. This is the tool of a totalitarian government. If this becomes widespread, privacy will cease to exist. Some large cities, like San Francisco, have banned it."

"That was the act of politicians. Not cops. Cops need all the help they can get."

"They don't need this. No one does. This is beyond Big Brother. Even George Orwell never imagined anything so invasive."

The Knife waved his hand in the air. "I'm sorry, your honor, but this is pure hyperbole. Police departments have used facial-recognition software for decades. The only thing that's different here is the size of the database. If people are foolish enough to post pictures of themselves online, they have no one to blame but themselves."

"It's not always people posting pics of themselves," Maria rebutted. "This witness wasn't ID'd because of photos she posted. The best match was a pic her niece posted at a birthday party. She knew nothing about it. But it was still used to track her down."

"And no one has been harmed in the slightest," the Knife said. "I'm sorry, your honor, but this argument is the desperate ploy of a desperate lawyer representing a guilty client."

"That's a complete crock," Maria said. Her voice took on a palpable edge. "We don't even know how accurate this program is. The larger the database, the greater the chances of a mistake. Some people do resemble others. And they're all on the internet. If this court took a stand, it would force people to think twice about using this indiscriminately."

"It would start a chain of appeals that could go all the way to the top and cost the government a fortune," the Knife said. "Even though it has nothing to do with this case or her client's guilt or innocence. Do you think six hundred law enforcement agencies would be using this program if it were so awful?"

"Absolutely," Maria said. "Clearview is pushing it hard because there's so much money to be made. Government contracts can be enormously lucrative. The only way to stop this, your honor, is by banning its use in the courtroom. You can be the first."

The judge drew herself up. "I hear what you're saying, counsel. But I have to make a determination based upon what's best in this case. The software has not hurt anyone. To the contrary, it has enabled the police to locate a valuable witness. And I have to note that she is not complaining about this. Frankly, I'm not sure you have standing to raise this issue."

"It impacts my client, your honor." She glanced at Dan. "In a big way."

"Nonetheless, I'm overruling your motion in limine. The prosecution may call the witness. Ms. Morales, you of course are free to appeal."

And Dan knew she would. And maybe she would be successful, years down the line. But it would be too late to do him any good.

Harriet Clooney would take the stand. And she would place him at the scene of the crime.

CHAPTER THIRTY-THREE

DAN WATCHED AS THE KNIFE RETURNED TO THE PROSECUTION table. He and Garfield exchanged a pleased look of triumph. Everything appeared to be going their way. Their confidence was more than a little annoying.

And frightening.

"The prosecution calls Harriet Clooney, your honor."

Clooney was middle-aged, around fifty. Stiff collar. Kitty-cat lapel pin. Strand of pearls. She said she worked as a waitress at the Beachcomber, though Dan didn't recall seeing her there. Perhaps she was new. At any rate, that explained why she was in the area.

Clooney straightened herself and explained that, on the night in question, she was on her way home just after sunset but couldn't remember where she had parked her car. She reached for her phone because she knew Google Maps automatically recorded her parking place. "While I was standing there, a man raced out of the back alley."

"Did you get a good look at him?" Garfield asked.

"Fairly decent. He was moving fast."

"Could you describe him?"

"About six feet tall. Slender. Fit. Wore a stocking cap."

"Did you speak to him?"

"Oh my, no. He was gone before I could blink twice."

"What did you do next?"

"Nothing. I drove home and forgot about it. Until I got the call from Officer Dunlevy. I told him what I had seen."

"Did you identify the person you saw?"

"Yes. After I gave the police a description, they showed me five photos and asked me to pick the person I saw."

Garfield held up a pre-marked set of pictures. "Is this the photo array you reviewed?"

"Yes."

"Were you able to identify the man you saw?"

"Oh yes. It wasn't hard."

"Who did you identify?"

"Him." She pointed toward the defense table. Dan tried not to react. "The defendant. Daniel Pike."

"Thank you. No more questions from me."

Maria rose quickly, not missing a beat. "Quite a coincidence, isn't it?"

Clooney was understandably confused. "I'm...not sure what you mean."

"Your testimony. Everything you said. You were behind the club at just the right moment to see the suspect the police were already investigating. And better yet, you were photographed."

"I didn't know there was going to be a murder."

"Is it possible that you are mistaken?"

"About seeing someone leave the alley?"

"No. But I wonder if you had time to see the person in question well enough to be sure it was my client."

"I'm sure."

"Were you sure before the police showed you his photograph? Or only after?"

"Objection," Garfield said.

"It's a fair question," Maria replied. "The witness said she only saw the man for a fleeting moment. Can she really be expected to make a positive identification based upon that?"

"Well, she did," Garfield said.

"Based upon a brief glimpse, in a dark alley, after sunset—and the face was partly obscured by a cap."

"And yet," Garfield said, impatience creeping into her voice, "she made the ID."

"The objection is sustained," the judge said. "The question will be stricken from the record. Please proceed."

Maria continued. "I noticed that you didn't mention the hair color of the person you saw leaving the alleyway."

"I didn't see it. As you've already mentioned, he was wearing a stocking cap."

"Warm weather to be wearing a wooly cap." Maria glanced at the photo array. "But that explains why my client is wearing a stocking cap in this photo."

Dan turned away from the jury and winced, reminding Maria that never in a million years would he ever wear that ugly cap.

"The problem," Maria said, "is that my client has never been photographed in this cap or anything like this cap. This image has been digitally altered. Photoshopped. Your honor, I renew my motion to exclude this evidence based upon tampering by the prosecution."

"Which we oppose," Garfield said. "And we object to counsel making speeches in front of the jury. May we approach?"

Judge Hembeck waved them forward. Dan followed. The judge was also beginning to look impatient. This was the second bench conference in far too short a time for her taste. The defense was impacting her efficiency rating.

The judge covered her microphone. "What's your problem, counsel?"

"I've filed a brief on this, your honor, and I mentioned it at the pretrial conference. You said we'd take it up if the evidence arose at trial."

"I remember. What's the basis for your objection?"

"Isn't it obvious? The cops doctored my client's photo. They added a cap to make him look more like the description the witness gave them."

The Knife shook his head, making a tsking sound. "They don't seem to like any of our evidence, do they, your honor?"

"Because it's all tainted," Maria said.

"No, because it all points in the same direction. Your client is a murderer."

"Not true."

The Knife addressed the judge. "An eyewitness account is obviously of great persuasive value to the jury, your honor. There are no grounds for excluding this testimony."

"You doctored Dan's photo," Maria said, "to make him look more like what the witness was expecting to see."

"Standard practice."

"If you'd put a cap on all five of the photos, I might agree. But you didn't. Only on Dan's."

"We weren't trying to confuse the woman. We were helping her determine if the part of the face she saw resembled the defendant."

"You were stacking the deck."

Judge Hembeck held up her hands. "Okay, everyone calm down. Mr. Blunt, please explain what happened."

"It's standard police procedure," the Knife explained.

"Sadly enough," Maria muttered.

"Sergeant Dunlevy used photo-editing software to add a stocking cap to the photo of Daniel Pike he obtained from the internet. They couldn't find a shot of him in a stocking cap—"

"And never will," Dan murmured.

"So they created one. Police officers creating photo lineups often airbrush away a discrepancy or add fillers to make the non-suspect photos more plausible. Even the New York City police department, the largest force in the nation, does it. Regularly."

"You're altering photos to encourage witnesses to make positive identifications," Maria said. "It's unfair. What's worse is that you had Dunlevy on the witness stand, but you didn't ask him to discuss this. If you'd had him acknowledge and explain how the photo was altered, that would be different. But you tried to slide it through and hoped I wouldn't notice."

"It's not my job to make your case for you, counsel."

"No. Your job is to railroad inno—"

Dan jumped in. "Maybe when I take the stand, I can explain that I do not own and would not wear such an atrocious cap."

"Yes," the Knife said. "I'm sure the jury will be persuaded once they acknowledge the defendant's fine fashion sense. Look, your honor. The witness said she saw a guy in a cap. If we showed her no guys in caps, she would probably not be able to make an identification, even if we showed her the killer."

"I can see where you might be tempted to alter the dummy photographs to make them plausible," Maria said. "But altering the suspect's photo should be absolutely forbidden."

"Oddly enough, the department's policies are not drafted by defense lawyers."

"You already had Dan in custody. You could have created a true lineup. Instead, you used photos because they can be doctored. You knew that increased the chances of a positive identification. And once you tell the witness that the person they've been encouraged to ID is a suspect already in custody, they'll become absolutely certain they were right." She drew in her breath. "Even if they weren't."

"I hear what you're saying," the judge replied. "And let me say, for what little it's worth, that the court considers this a far more valid argument for the exclusion of evidence than the many others you've presented."

"Thanks...."

"But I'm still not granting the motion. You will be free to cross-examine the witness at length about her identification, but—"

"She's not the one who doctored the photo."

The judge's lips tightened. Dan tried to send Maria a mental message. *Don't interrupt the judge!*

"And if you wish," Judge Hembeck continued, "you may call Sergeant Dunlevy back to the stand and ask him chapter and verse about what he did to the photos. But I will not exclude the testimony."

"Your honor, I consider this a gross miscarriage of justice."

Judge Hembeck's eyes narrowed. "Counsel, since you're being honest with me, I will be equally honest with you. Whether you care to admit it or not, your client was identified at the scene of the crime, just as forensic evidence has put him at the scene of the crime, and just as an audio recording revealed him planning the crime. This evidence is completely consistent with everything that has been presented in this case. Your problem has nothing to do with the court's rulings."

Judge Hembeck leaned closer, lowering her voice. "Your problem is that all the evidence in this case demonstrates that your client is a murderer."

CHAPTER THIRTY-FOUR

DAN TRIED TO REMAIN CALM, BUT IT WAS BECOMING increasingly difficult. He was experienced in the art of not letting his emotions show, so he had no problem maintaining a stoic expression. But that didn't stifle the turmoil roiling inside. His stomach was tossing and turning, and for good reason.

This case was turning decisively against him. And he knew it.

Unfortunately, it was about to get much worse. Garfield told Maria she was only planning to call one more witness.

She saved her best for last.

"Your honor," Garfield said, "for our final witness, we call Ed Warner to the witness stand."

Warner was currently a resident of the St. Pete jailhouse, the same facility Dan had visited for far too long. He would like to think any sensible juror would disregard the kind of evidence he was about to offer. But sadly, he knew from experience that was not the case. Prosecutors used snitch testimony because it worked so well.

And Garfield had chosen to put this man on for her climax.

Warner made his way to the witness stand. They'd cleaned

him up and put him in a suit for trial. Nothing fancy, but enough to remove some of the jailhouse stink. He was a lean, wiry man with deep-etched lines in his face. Birthmark on the left cheek. White socks. A habit of rubbing right thumb and fingers together.

Garfield whipped through the preliminaries, establishing what the jury needed to know to understand the relevance of his testimony. "Mr. Warner, how long have you been incarcerated?"

"I've been locked up for about a year now. But to tell you the truth, this isn't my first time." If nothing else, the man seemed honest. Which of course was the best way to snitch. Appear forthright—then drop the hammer.

"You've had prior convictions?"

"Yeah."

"Felonies?"

"Four or five, something like that. Two counts of larceny. One for fraud." Warner shrugged, looking appropriately ashamed. "I wrote some bad checks."

Strategically speaking, that would be the one to emphasize. What person his age hadn't written a check that bounced?

"Have you been promised anything in return for your testimony today?"

"No," Warner said solemnly. "Absolutely not."

That response didn't surprise Dan. It might not be completely false. For someone as experienced as Warner, no express promise was necessary. He knew that if his testimony helped them convict the defendant, he'd see his sentence sharply curtailed. He'd probably be out in a few days once the jury decided to convict.

"Have you ever testified in a court of law?"

"Yes. Several times."

"How did that happen?"

Again the shrug. "I guess I just got one of them faces. People talk to me. Probably helps that I work in the library. People sit around together, people who are normally locked up by themselves. Only natural that they start gabbing. Sometimes they come to me for advice."

"For advice? Do you have an area of expertise?"

"I used to be a police officer. They all know that in the joint. Some think I might be able to help them with their legal problems."

"Do you?"

"I help when I can. But I'm no lawyer." With the last word, he glanced at Dan, presumably reminding the jury who in this courtroom was a tricky pettifogger.

"Does that have anything to do with your appearance in court today?"

"Yeah, I guess it does." He looked a little proud, a little downcast. "I still got law enforcement in my blood. I believe in justice. Right and wrong. I don't like to see anyone getting away with anything." He paused. "Especially murder."

To Dan, that sounded as contrived as anything he could imagine. But the jury seemed to be paying attention.

"Mr. Warner," Garfield said, "have you ever had occasion to speak with the defendant, Daniel Pike?"

"Yeah, once."

"When did that happen?"

"Not long after he was arrested. He wasn't in long. He managed to slip out pretty quick."

A gratuitous jab, probably intended to suggest that he had already gamed the system for special privileges.

"Where did you see him?"

"In the library. He was kinda playing the big man, like, look at me, I been to college, I got a law degree. Told people he could get them out of jail if they paid his gigantic fee."

"Did you approach him about representing you?"

"Nah. I been convicted. I don't think there's much he could

do for me. He was under the impression that I was some kind of investigator, and he wanted someone looked into. I had to tell him he was mistaken. I was a police officer once, but never a detective, and all that was a long time ago."

"Did that end the conversation?"

"No. You know how it is when two guys get to talking. Especially when they can't leave and there's nothing much to do. No one else was in the library so we were able to have a private conversation. Didn't take too long before he started in about George Belasco. We started grousing about how much we hated the guy. I mean, I didn't like Belasco much, but Pike absolutely hated him."

Maria rose. Dan knew she didn't really have an objection, because there was no valid objection. She wanted to interrupt the flow, to break up what was becoming an absorbing narrative. This story might be a complete pack of lies, but Warner was a good storyteller. He knew how to make it seem real.

And as Maria herself had said—stories trump facts.

"Objection," she said.

"On what grounds?" the judge asked.

"Credibility. He's a jailhouse snitch."

The judge shook her head. "You may explore that on cross-examination, if you wish. Overruled."

"Then on grounds of hearsay. I realize the hearsay rule doesn't normally apply to statements by the defendant. But in this case, there's no witness, no corroboration, and no reason for the defendant to admit things that could be used against him. There are no factors suggesting credibility. It's just gossip."

"Overruled. Ms. Garfield, please proceed."

That was fine. He knew Maria expected no better. At least she was able to remind the jury that this was a ratfink claiming someone said stuff completely contrary to their own interests.

"Did Mr. Pike explain why he hated George Belasco so much?"

"He said they had opposed one another in the courtroom many times, and Belasco played some dirty tricks."

Indeed. If Belasco had so many dirty tricks, why did Dan always beat him?

"Did he give examples?"

"No. But he said Belasco was connected to some powerful people. And they all wanted him out of the way. He also said Belasco was out to get his...." He squirmed. "A female friend of his."

That caused a stir in the jury box.

"Who was that female friend? The mayor?"

"No. Jazlyn Prentice. He called her Jazzy Jazlyn. With a wink, you know?"

Dan sat up straight. How did Jazlyn get in the middle of this? This sounded like the same nonsense Evelyn Belasco was peddling. What kind of prosecutor went after the woman who was ostensibly her boss? Was this some kind of internecine coup? Get rid of the boss so Garfield can be the new DA?

"Did he indicate that Jazlyn Prentice, the interim district attorney since this murder occurred, also hated George Belasco?"

"Not exactly. But she wanted to be the next district attorney."

"And Mr. Pike wanted to help his...female friend."

"And he did." Warner whistled. "In a big way."

"Did he say what actions he took?"

"Oh yeah. He gave me all the details, top to bottom. Said he lured Belasco to this club he liked. Beachcombers, I think it was called. Then he got Belasco outside and shot him. He talked about that for a long time. His eyes got wide and kinda spooky. Weird. Said he shot the man six times. Once for each time Belasco screwed him over."

Maria shot up. "Objection. Your honor, this is preposterous. No one would ever say that. Especially not to this...person."

"Save it for cross-examination," the judge said. She looked at Maria sternly. "And do not interrupt again unless you have a legitimate objection."

Gritting her teeth, Maria returned to her chair.

"Please continue," Garfield said.

Warner nodded. He took a moment to get back into character. "It was scary, honestly. To see someone get that way, to see the look in his eyes when he talked about killing. I think he must be one of those...what do you call it? Sociopaths. People who don't care about anyone else. Think they can get away with anything. Think they're entitled to do whatever they want cause they're smarter than everyone else."

"That must've been disturbing."

"More than that. Chilling. Earlier, I saw this guy walking down the hallway, shooting the bull with guys, laughing and kidding around. And then, all of a sudden, he's completely changed, talking about killing a guy in cold blood. Getting off on it."

Garfield gave the jurors a knowing look.

"Pike knew the body would be found," Warner continued. "He wanted it to attract attention. So he made it dramatic. He was sending a message. Don't mess with Daniel Pike. That was for the other people he said worked with Belasco, the rich and powerful ones. He was telling them, screw with me and you'll end up the same way."

"You mentioned that he made it...dramatic."

"Right. After he plugged the guy, he dragged the body to a back alley and pinned it up against a fence."

"And how did he manage that?"

"Oh, he came prepared. He had it all thought out in advance. He used this kitesurfing stuff."

Dan felt a clutching at the base of his spine. *Kitesurfing stuff?*

Now he understood why Garfield had mentioned his fondness for kitesurfing in her opening.

"Can you explain to the jury what you mean by that?"

"I can try. I ain't never been kitesurfing. Not in my income bracket. But there's this thing you hold onto. Like a handlebar. It's attached to the kite. You hold on and lean back and let it pull you forward."

"Something like this?" Garfield raised the device that had been used to pinion Belasco's body to the fence. It looked like the head of a trident, the two outer prongs being longest. And sharpest.

"Yeah. That's how he described it. Those ends aren't normally so pointy. He sharpened them so they would go through the body and stick in the fence. But it's strong. It will hold a body up for a long time."

"Actually," Dan muttered under his breath. "I prefer a fiber-glass handlebar…"

"I know," Maria whispered. "Hush."

Garfield continued, this time speaking to the judge. "Your honor, I have here an invoice from the Urban Adventure Gear Company. It shows that Daniel Pike purchased a new kitesurfing handlebar a few days before the murder occurred."

The judge nodded. "And I assume you're claiming this was used on the victim."

"Actually, no, you honor. This is for a fiberglass handle."

"Because that's what I use," Dan muttered. Maria jabbed him in the side.

"Our theory," Garfield continued, "is that the defendant bought a replacement. He had made his previous gear unfit for use by dismantling it and sharpening the outer points."

Dan glanced at the faces in the jury…and did not like what he saw. For many of them, the story was making sense—especially since Warner told it so well. Warner had developed his gift for storytelling into a perpetual Get Out of Jail Free card.

"Did Mr. Pike provide any more details about how he committed this gruesome crucifixion?"

"Oh, he didn't do it himself. C'mon, look at him. He's a rich lawyer. He probably hasn't done any real work in his entire life. He shot Belasco, but he didn't drag the body around or prop it up. He planned it. Provided the equipment. Then he hired someone else to do it."

"Hired someone? Who?"

"Carl or Card or something like that. Look, he's been putting crooks back on the street for years. He knows all kinds of scum, and some of them probably owe him a favor. I'll bet it wasn't too hard to find someone to do the dirty deed. Especially given the kind of money he has."

Dan had to be impressed, in a hideous sort of way. This was the kind of unnecessary detail that made Warner's story even more believable.

"Was there anything else Mr. Pike said about the murder?'

"Yes. The part I can never forget." Warner turned slightly so the jurors could see his eyes. "He talked about the buzz he got from drilling Belasco. He said after the first shot, Belasco begged him to stop. Pleaded with him. Even started to cry. But Pike didn't stop. In fact, he drew it out. The next shot went to Belasco's leg. That was sure to hurt—but wouldn't kill him. He wanted Belasco to suffer. For a long time."

The jury stared at him, stunned. The entire courtroom was deathly quiet.

Warner shook his head. "The look in that guy's eyes when he told me about it. I'll never forget that. I'll never forget his words. Pike said, 'That loser kept begging, crying like a baby. But he didn't die. I wouldn't let him die. I made him suffer.' And then he smiled. Can you believe it? Pike smiled."

Warner leaned toward the jurors. "That's why I had to testify today. This man is evil. He needs to be put down like the dog that he is."

VENUS ASCENDANT

CHAPTER THIRTY-FIVE

ELENA KNEW SHE NEEDED TO ESCAPE. SOMEHOW. SOON.

Ever since she'd been caught trying to escape with Izzy, they'd kept her under close guard, waiting. For what? They wouldn't tell her. The Captain had made a remark earlier about sharks...

She was watched at all times, night and day. She had been tied and gagged, the cloth choking her and removed only once a day so she could drink and eat the swill they called food. She had been chained to an iron ring on the wall. Her legs were sore. She felt dizzy. She was filthy, even worse than before. She was tormented by bad dreams.

They killed Izzy. Just as they promised. And they made her watch. She had to stand there, crying, screaming, begging, as they cut the throat of the young girl she loved...

Afterward, all she could think about was how much she wanted to die.

Why hadn't they killed her, too? It would be the simplest thing to do. She had proven she posed a risk, one that far exceeded any profit they might be able to earn from her.

Sharks...

They had all used her, abused her, so much that it barely registered any more. So much that she almost forgot that once she had a decent life, a clean life, parents who loved her, a home, a safe place to be. Now she was nothing. Now she was their lover who could never be kissed.

Now all she could do was wait to be killed. She had failed Izzy. She had *failed*...

And then she realized the truth. She had not failed yet. The only failure would be if she quit trying. She could not save Izzy, but she could honor her wishes. Izzy wanted her to live.

So she would do everything within her power to live. And if she died—she would die trying.

———

THE SHIP HAD LEFT WHEREVER THEY WERE DOCKED BEFORE AND they were once more at sea. Heading for an unknown destination. Endless hours of nothing. Waiting. Dreading...

When they finally came for her, she was more relieved than terrified. Though she felt both.

It was the Captain, the one who appeared to be in charge of everything. The other men seemed to respect him, although she suspected they would throw him overboard in an instant if there were any profit in it for them.

She noticed that he spoke loudly, so the other girls could hear.

"We have almost reached our final destination," he said. "And we have arranged a special surprise for you."

Two men forced her to her feet. They released her from the iron ring, though they tied her hands behind her back. The gag remained in place.

"The rest of you will go ashore tomorrow. To your new homes. You will be fed. Cared for. So long as you do as you are asked, you will have no reason to fear for your safety." He stepped closer to Elena. "But you could not follow the rules. You tried to cheat me, to rob me. *Me!* That I can never forgive."

He locked eyes with her. "You will be taken to a place I know, a cove not far from here where sharks swarm in abundance. Tiger sharks, the ones with the sharpest teeth and the nastiest tempers. The ones that eat people."

She bit down on her lower lip. Do not show fear, she told herself. Do not give him the satisfaction.

"We will put you into the water," he continued. "We will cut you, not enough to die, but enough to guarantee that you bleed. You will have to splash about to remain afloat. You will attract their attention."

She noticed that the men behind him were not grinning with the same enthusiasm that he showed. But they did not argue with him, either. They wouldn't. Couldn't. They would do as they were told. Even something so horrible as this.

"Overfishing has caused a scarcity in the sharks' normal feeding. They are hungry. They will be so glad to see you. They will chew at you. They will eat your flesh while you are still alive."

She did not make any foolish show of defiance. But she would not scream or beg. He could kill her, maim her. Feed her to these beasts. She had begged for Izzy, and it had not helped. She would not give him the satisfaction of seeing her beg ever again.

The Captain turned to face his captive audience. "The rest of you will be safe. Warm. Never hungry. Never lonely." He paused. "But I hope you will remember this. I hope you will recall the price of disobedience." His eyes darkened. "Do not cross me, girls. Because the sharks will always be out there. And they will always be hungry."

THEY PUT HER ON SOME KIND OF MOTORBOAT WITH TWO MEN SHE did not know. These young grinning idiots appeared to be new. Did the others refuse to carry out this vile execution? Did the Captain need someone fresh, two men desperate to prove themselves?

She tried to stifle her fear. This could be an opportunity, she told herself. Be strong. They will underestimate you.

The taller of the two was also the least confident. His smirk revealed a lack of certainty more than it did arrogance. "This will be your last meal," he said, shoving her into one of the seats, her hands still bound behind her. "And you will be the meal."

The other was little more than a boy. He still had pimples. She wondered if he was even twenty. He spoke few words but watched her constantly.

"Perhaps we will have a little fun with her, yes?" the taller one said. "Why not? A waste to let such prime meat be nothing but feed for animals." He stroked her under the chin. "I will appreciate you, little woman. Over and over again. Then I will feed you to the monsters."

Don't let him break you, she told herself. Don't let him win. There's nothing they could do to you that is worse than what you have already experienced. What you have already survived.

His arrogance will be the open door I need.

The tall one started the engine and zoomed away from the ship, travelling far faster than was necessary or safe. In a few minutes, she could see land.

They were near something. Florida, perhaps, though she could not be sure.

Could she swim to shore? Distances could be deceptive at sea.

No. She could do it. She could do it if it took her days. She would find the strength.

She had been pulling at her bonds since they boarded the boat. Carefully, without making a show, but gradually getting the job done. Her wrists were tied with some kind of cloth. Probably a strip off someone's shirt.

"There it is," the tall one said, pointing ahead like Ahab at the mast, like The Boyhood of Raleigh. "We will park. We will have some fun. Then we will feed the fishes."

If she was going to try, it would have to be now. Her hands shook and they were drenched with sweat. She ignored her racing heart and tried to focus her strength. She pulled as hard as she could at her bonds, twisting the cloth in opposite directions. They were not that strong. The men undoubtedly thought it didn't require much to subdue her, a weak female. She created just enough give to allow her to slip one hand out.

After that, it was easy. The next wrist followed. The gag after that.

Before the men noticed, she sprang.

Since the tall boy was busy driving, she tackled the other. She hit him hard, grabbing him around the waist and shoving him toward the edge of the boat. She knew she was not as strong as he was, so she had to surprise him, to win the fight before he could fight back. He cried out, flailing his arms, but he was much too slow to stop her momentum. He hit the side of the boat and doubled over. She hit her head but ignored it. She had no time to feel pain.

The boy wore a large knife clipped in a sheath at his side. He grabbed for it and brought the knife out. It scraped her on the side. She felt blood seeping. She ignored that too. She grabbed the hand holding the knife and banged it against the edge of the boat, the metal railing. The knife fell with a clatter.

The man driving the boat heard the noise over the roar of the engine. "What?"

She had no time. She shoved the boy again and he tumbled over the side of the boat, screaming as he went. The boat careened forward.

Who was fish food now?

The driver slowed the engine and released the steering wheel. The boat jerked hard to one side. They both dove for the knife but only succeeded in sending it skittering to the rear of the boat.

He threw himself on top of her, pinning her down, then punched her hard in the face. Tears rushed to her eyes. She tasted blood at her lips. She was hurt in more places than she knew. There was no time to catalogue them. She had to get away from this man. She was terrified, staring straight into the face of the demon, her arms shaking. Somehow, she had to break free.

"You have spirit!" he cried. He twisted her right arm above her head, as if trying to pull it off. She mustered as much strength as possible, but she could not get loose. All those days tied up, her muscles must have atrophied. He was powerful. "I need to steer this boat. After I tie you up again."

He reached for a strip of mooring rope, then stopped. Instead, he grabbed the front of her shirt and ripped it down the center. "Let us see what we are fighting for, no?" Spittle emerged on his lips. He tore her loose-fitting pants, cinched at the waist.

Her clothes fell to the side. "Later, I will have my fun," he said, literally drooling. "You will like it. It will be the last pleasure you experience before you are eaten alive."

He reached for the torn shirt—and that loosened his grip just enough. She jerked her right hand away from his. She knew she had mere seconds. She had to do something fast. What could she manage with one hand?

She jabbed her thumb into his right eye. Hard.

The man screamed. Both hands flew to his face. With her other hand free, she gripped his head, brushing his hands away. She pressed thumbs into both eyes. Blood trickled from the corners but she did not release him. He screamed and cried but she did not relent. She clenched her teeth as hard as she could and kept on pressing—

The crash took her by complete surprise. All at once, the boat shattered, splintering apart all around her.

Suddenly she was immersed in water. Thank God her hands were free. She could try to swim. She could try to survive…

The crashing tides buffeted her one direction, then the other. She tried to gain control. But she couldn't. The current was too strong. It tossed her back and forth like a kite in a hurricane.

Her head hit something hard. She shrieked, or tried, and saltwater rushed into her mouth. She spit and coughed, trying not to drown. For a moment, she thought her head had been split open.

No. Still intact. But it hurt badly. The pain was so intense she could barely think straight. She didn't know where to go. She didn't know which end was up. She had fought so hard, so long, and after all that, she would sink to the bottom of the sea and drown…

Calm, he told herself. Stay calm. Keep your wits about you. You don't need to know everything. You only need to know that you want to survive.

I very much want to survive, she realized. That's why I've been fighting, so hard, so long. I couldn't save Izzy. But I will save myself.

She detected light streaking through the water. That would show her which way was up, wouldn't it? She followed the path, letting her body float upward.

Her head broke through the surface just as she was sure her lungs would burst. She gulped in air, trying to restore herself.

She had come so close to dying. And yet, she endured.

Izzy would be pleased.

When she had calmed down enough to see clearly, she spotted land.

She also saw what remained of the boat. Some of it was burning, and she imagined that her captors were burning, hot and angry, a flame that would never burn cold. That boat would not take anyone anywhere again.

She saw no debris large enough to help keep her head above the water. For that matter, she imagined, the Captain might come looking for her, once he realized she had escaped. Maybe it was best she stayed beneath the surface of the water as much as possible.

She knew how to swim. She would get there eventually. She would be a wave aching for the shore...

She would have to be careful. Her clothes were gone and she knew she was injured. Her head...wasn't working the way it should. Thoughts came in bursts, in strange patterns. She seemed to remember things in flashes...

And none of that mattered. She had only one task now. She had to swim and swim until she reached the shore. She had fought so hard. She would survive. She would go on. She earned this.

She would do it for Izzy.

She told that beautiful girl there was something more, something beyond the present horror. Now she had to prove she was telling the truth.

CHAPTER THIRTY-SIX

GARRETT WALKED CAREFULLY, MEASURING EACH STEP, TRYING TO make as little sound as possible. He did not want to be heard as he crept toward the port office building.

He had never done anything this dangerous in his entire life. Never done anything so...stupid. Perhaps "risky" was the better word. What difference did it make? This was a desperate ploy to save Dan's life. But if it didn't work—and possibly even if it did —he could end up dead.

He had come unarmed. He was more likely to hurt himself with a gun than anyone else. But still...

The photos he found on Belasco's cellphone painted a grim picture. Kidnapped women forced into a life of slavery and degradation. Smuggled into the country against their will.

He'd done his research. Experts estimated that there were currently more than twenty-four million people trapped in modern-day slavery and exploited for forced labor. Roughly the size of the population of California. About seventy-one percent of those were female, sometimes girls as young as nine years old. About nineteen percent of the total were exploited for sex. Traffickers were always looking for children. Lonely kids separated from family and friends, or in poor relationships, easily manipulated and tricked. Human trafficking earned about one-hundred-and-fifty billion a year, but the majority of that, ninety-nine billion, came from sexual exploitation. The average profit generated by each woman in sexual servitude was about one-hundred-thousand dollars. According to the Department of Defense, it was the world's fastest growing business. Human trafficking had been reported in all fifty states, plus D.C. and all US territories.

Despite the worldwide prevalence of trafficking, the number of prosecutions was disturbingly low.

The morning news had been filled with stories about a young woman who seemingly rose from the water on a St. Petersburg beach, not too far from this dock. He felt certain this was the debarkation port visible in one of Belasco's photos. The press was calling the naked woman a mermaid, but given that she was injured and covered with blood, Garrett suspected her origins were less romantic.

He couldn't be sure, but he thought he spotted that same woman in one of the photographs on Belasco's phone.

This was probably where the traffickers brought their cargo late at night, under the cover of darkness, after they paid off the port authorities. He'd been here on a case, years before. This port had always had a bad reputation, and unfortunately, that pushed them even further in the direction of crime. They needed it to survive.

He slipped inside the unlocked building, then took a tentative step down the corridor. He saw a tiny light in the office at the far end, barely visible through the window in the door.

Someone was still here, long past midnight.

That was the person he needed to meet.

It had taken him hours to find a name. All his research, online and offline, produced a list of the people who worked here on a regular basis. There were many, and judging from external appearances, many were well-paid. Ridiculously well paid for people who worked at a loading dock.

There had to be an explanation.

Craig Emmer had worked here for more than a decade. He had a nice house on the north side, much better than you might expect for someone in his line of work. A wife and two kids. One went to a private school. Apparently she had some developmental disabilities. They had a boat. He liked to water ski.

How had Garrett learned all this? What advanced detective skills had he used to uncover the truth?

Facebook.

Like so many others, Emmer posted regularly. Garrett used a data-scraping bot to find people connected to this port. There were several, and all seemed to be doing fine financially. But one—Emmer—posted today that he was leaving town.

Why would anyone give up such a cushy job? There must be a reason, and it was possible that reason would lead to the information Garrett desperately needed.

He was all in on this one. All the chips in the pot. His life was in that pot, too, as well as his reputation and everything he held dear.

He took another step closer to the door. No movement inside. No sound. But he could see someone was there. The silhouette was visible through the mottled glass.

He placed his hand on the doorknob and turned it.

"I've been expecting you."

Garrett froze.

"Come on in. Let's talk."

Garrett didn't move.

"Do I have to insist?" The man in the swivel chair drew a Glock out of a drawer, then placed it on his desk. "Fine, I insist."

Perhaps he hadn't thought this out as thoroughly as he might've...

"I'm not planning to kill you," the man said. He whirled

around. It was Emmer. He was fortyish, bearded, and had a haggard expression. Cardboard packing boxes were stacked against the far wall. "Are you planning to kill me?"

"No. I just want some information."

"You're…not with the Captain?"

The Captain? "No."

"How did you find me?"

"Facebook."

"I haven't posted anything about my…business activities on Facebook."

"You mean, you haven't posted much. But your profile does show where you work. I used artificial intelligence to create a chain of connections. One thing leads to another."

"Clever. I should sue."

"You can't. Tech companies are protected by the Communications Decency Act of 1996. Despite the name, it protects social media outfits like Facebook from incurring legal consequences arising from what people post. They can publish hate speech, fake news, financial scams. Undermine elections. But they can't be sued."

"Seriously?"

"Yup. Some people are trying to change that, suggesting that even if they aren't subject to criminal prosecution, they should be liable to civil suits. There's been a little progress. Airbnb has been held liable for users who violated home-rental bans. But social media companies are being used for all kinds of criminal activities. Pimps use Instagram to lure kids into prostitution. Terrorists use it to recruit acolytes. The law needs to be changed."

Emmer squinted. "You some kind of lawyer?"

"That's exactly what I am. And I need information. To help my friend."

"What's his problem?"

"He's on trial for murder. Of the district attorney. But he didn't do it."

Emmer held up a finger. "I think I read about that."

"Then you understand how serious this is. Do you mind if I ask...what happened to you?"

"You mean, why am I leaving this business that has been so lucrative?"

"Exactly. Did you do something? Are they tossing you out?" Even as he said it, it didn't sound right. Human trafficking cartels didn't fire people—except maybe with a blowtorch.

"It wasn't that. They loved me. I did my job and did it well. Their shipments were never detected. Not once."

"Then what happened?"

Emmer held out his hands and stared at them. He appeared to be searching for words. "I...couldn't do it any longer."

"You're talking about the sex trafficking."

"Are you wearing a wire?"

"No. I'm not. Promise. What...changed your mind?"

He drew in his breath. "That girl. Elena. You must've read about her. The one who rose from the water like a phoenix from the ashes. Which is a good comparison, truth be known."

So he'd been right. That girl on the beach escaped from this trafficking ring. He could only imagine how much fortitude that demanded. "No one knows her story."

"I do. I know how hard she fought. She deserves her freedom. They wanted me to search for her, after they learned she'd escaped. I wouldn't do it. They threatened me. I threatened them. Stalemate. I agreed to leave the operation. And prayed to God they wouldn't take it out on my family."

Emmer pressed his hands against his face. "Did you see that girl? See what she looked like? She's a survivor. Tougher than the toughies. No way I was going to take away what she struggled so fearlessly to get." He paused. "She looks a little like my daughter. Made me think about how I'd feel if someone took her."

"That must be a..." Garrett noticed the bottle on the desk. "... a sobering thought."

"All those years, I turned a blind eye. Pretended like I didn't know what was going on. Like I didn't know how many lives they were destroying, how many people were being abducted and turned into slaves. I blocked it out of my mind." He exhaled heavily. "But once I saw the cellphone footage of that girl emerging from the water—I couldn't pretend any more. No way I would be part of any operation to take her out. She fought hard for her freedom."

The wheels inside Garrett's head turned fast. "You're afraid your former friends will take revenge. I have a solution."

Emmer's head shot up. "Yeah?"

"Come with me. Testify."

"You gotta be kidding."

"I'm not. I still have some friends at the prosecutor's office. I can get you immunity. Witness protection. You and your family will be relocated somewhere safe."

"Oh, the kids will love that. Instead of a big house with a backyard swimming pool, they'll have a room at a motel. Instead of a dad making tons of money, they'll have a dad working at Cinnabon."

"It doesn't have to be like that."

"Forget it. Wouldn't work. No matter where the feds relocated us, the cartel would find me. Just a matter of time. My best hope is that after they eliminate me, they won't feel the need to harm my family."

Garrett drew in his breath. There had to be some way he could make this happen. "Listen. My friend is about to be convicted of a crime he didn't commit. You could stop that. And you could buy yourself some freedom. Or at least some time. You could get out of the country."

"They'll find me."

"I work for a man with a lot of money."

"I have a lot of money. It isn't the answer."

His voice rose. "Then what is the answer?"

Emmer pivoted slowly, his head drooping. "There isn't one."

Garrett saw movement outside the window. Someone was coming. He needed to disappear. "Do it for your daughter. Show her what it means to stand up and be a man. Become someone she can admire."

"Wouldn't that be nice? But it's too late. And you've only got seconds to escape. Scram."

Garrett raced out the door. He scurried across the parking lot, avoiding the overhead lights. He didn't like abandoning anyone. But there was nothing he could do here. Emmer had created this situation. Now he would have to face up to his own actions.

He had reached his parked car before he heard the distant report of a gun.

He slid behind the driver's seat and drove as fast as he could.

CHAPTER THIRTY-SEVEN

DAN MADE BROWNIES, BUT AS GOOD AS THEY WERE, HE KNEW THEY wouldn't be enough. Years before, he'd found a brownie recipe attributed to Katherine Hepburn. He had his doubts that the famed actress invented it, but that didn't matter because it produced the best brownies he had ever tasted. Coupled with his special BakersEdge pan, which guaranteed every piece had a crispy edge, they were superb.

And that might help brighten the mood around the office. A bit. Despite the fact that the story Garfield was peddling in court was completely false, she had put on a dynamite case. When he looked into the jurors' eyes, he saw that they also felt she had met her burden of proof.

If he sat on that jury, he thought even he would be ready to convict.

Warner's testimony had been devastating. He saw why the man had been able to bail himself out time and time again with his concocted stories. He was good at it. He had a knack for adding just the right amount of detail to make it seem true. If the jurors thought Dan didn't seem the brutal type—well, he had a partner. If Warner had built a career writing crime fiction, he would probably be living on a yacht now, instead of lying his way out of jail.

The full reality of the situation weighed on Dan like a crushing boulder. He could go to prison. For a crime he didn't commit.

Just like his father.

The only thing that could prevent it was a killer defense, a gamechanger, something that turned the case on its heels and spun everything in a different direction.

But they didn't have that. Truth was, they didn't have much of anything at all.

Jimmy and Maria appeared dutifully enthusiastic when he brought the brownies into the mostly restored living room. The whole mansion had been cleaned or repaired, but it still didn't feel the same. They had all been too busy to shop, too busy to do any serious decorating. That would have to wait.

Maria stood in the center of the semi-circular sofa area. She was trying to hold it together, trying to keep the demons of despair at bay. But they all knew they were losing. Unless something dramatic happened fast, Dan was going down for the count.

"Okay," Maria said, staring at her notebook, "we need to determine what witnesses we want to call and in what order."

Jimmy was already on his second brownie, but the sugar rush did not appear to elevate his spirits. "What are the choices? What witnesses do we have?"

"We have to call Dan," she said. "I promised the jurors I would. Do we lead with him or finish? If we put him on first, the jury can hear what really happened, then hear others confirm it. Or we can save him for the grand finale. Go out with a bang."

"Who do we have that can confirm anything I say?" Dan asked. "At the time of the murder, I was completely on my own."

"We're still trying to find witnesses. I'm hoping to turn up someone who saw you at the beach. Someone who noticed you kitesurfing."

Jimmy's eyes turned downward. "I think we should stay as far away from kitesurfing as possible."

Dan nodded grimly. Now that the jailhouse snitch had turned his hobby into a murder weapon, it was probably best not to remind anyone.

"Jimmy, have you got anything?" Maria asked.

"Sorry, no. Wish I did. I talked to Shawna in the court clerk's office yesterday. She acted weird. At first, I thought she felt awkward because she knew things were turning against Dan in the courtroom. But there was more to it. I got a real sense of...regret."

"Regret doesn't equal alibi."

"Even if I had an alibi witness," Dan said, "the prosecution would say the man I hired was dragging the body around at my direction while I was somewhere else. It's brilliant, in its own evil way. They anticipated our moves and gave themselves a workaround. It's hopeless."

"Stop," Maria said. "Don't do that."

"Do...what?"

"Give up."

"I'm not. Exactly. But I am being realistic. Garfield is a smart cookie. The prosecution isn't privy to the defense strategy. So she anticipated everything we might say. Thought through the possibilities. And created a rejoinder for each and every one of them. She's headed us off at the pass."

"That sounds a lot like giving up." Maria's eyes were practically swimming.

"It isn't. But there are a few things I'd like to discuss with you."

"No. Dan. Stop." The first tear slipped from her eyes.

"I'm sorry, but it has to be said. I don't know how much time our defense will take. But it won't be long. And we can't assume the jury will deliberate forever. When it's over, if it..." He took a deep breath then started again. "If it doesn't go the way we hope, the judge will order the bailiffs to take me into custody immediately. There won't be time to do anything or to say what I want to say."

Maria collapsed onto the sofa. "Please stop."

"I've created a holding corporation and left instructions that in the event that I'm convicted, everything I own will be put into it. I've made you three, my partners, the administrators. I've opened a trust fund for Esperanza's education. And I've created an account to pay for my legal appeals...if the worst happens."

Maria covered her face. "If—If that happens, I will never stop trying to get you out. Never."

He smiled a little. "I know that. But still."

Jimmy leaned forward, touching his shoulder. "It isn't over yet, Dan."

"I know. But still. I left the deed to my boat on the refrigerator and—"

Maria raced out of the room toward the kitchen.

He glanced up. "Maria?"

She returned. "You son of a bitch!"

His eyes widened. He didn't think he'd ever heard Maria swear before. "Excuse me?"

"You really did bring the deed to your boat."

"If I'm unable to enjoy it, the administrators should sell—"

"You are giving up!"

"I'm just—"

"You love that boat. You would never even consider selling it unless...unless..." She ran out of the room.

Dan fell back against the sofa. "Well. I screwed that up."

Jimmy nodded. "You did." He reached for another brownie. "But this is hard on everyone. There's no good way to handle it. But there—"

He was interrupted when the front door burst open.

Dan's first thought was—cops? Again?

But it was Garrett, moving as fast as he could. He seemed excited about something.

"Sorry I'm late," Garrett said breathlessly. "I've been trying to track down—" He glanced around the room. "Where's Maria?"

"She's taking a break. What have you got?"

"I may know what happened. I mean, what really happened to Belasco. I can't prove it yet....but I have a lead."

As quickly as he could, Garrett relayed the high points, all the breadcrumbs he had followed since he stole Belasco's phone.

Jimmy looked at him incredulously. "What the ropes course woman said was true? Belasco was involved with a sex trafficking cartel?"

"Looks that way. Think about it. Who seems more likely to be responsible for the graphic execution-murder of George Belasco? A fellow lawyer, or a bunch of sadistic, evil bastards who buy and sell women for profit?"

Jimmy tilted his head. "I see what you mean. Can you get your source to testify?"

Garrett shook his head. "No. He's dead."

Jimmy swore under his breath. "Then we got nothing."

"Not quite. Did you read the news reports yesterday about the mermaid?"

"No," Dan said. "I've been kinda busy."

"Most of the local media is covering the bizarre story of a young woman who rose from the sea, naked and injured and babbling. She seemed completely dislocated, traumatized. Maybe in shock."

"And your point...?"

"I think her name is Elena. And I think she escaped from the traffickers. The ones Belasco was in cahoots with."

Dan rose from the sofa. "Where's the girl now?"

"Kindred Hospital."

"Let's go."

"She's being guarded by security—"

"Jazlyn can get us in." Dan grabbed his keys. For the first time in far too long, he felt a faint stirring inside. Hope. "I'll drive."

CHAPTER THIRTY-EIGHT

SWEENEY DRUMMED HIS FINGERS ON THE DESKTOP. HE HOPED HE was effectively communicating his impatience. He had no interest in subtlety.

His immense office was mostly dark. The skyline outside the huge backdrop window provided little illumination this time of night. Only one light was on inside the office, and that was the spotlight illuminating the Miró behind his desk.

Prudence stood at attention, just to Sweeney's left, hands behind her back, always at the ready. Bradley Ellison sat in the chair opposite. He shifted from one side to the other.

A single word was sufficient to get Sweeney what he wanted. "Report."

Prudence cleared her throat. "Garfield is doing an excellent job. Say what you will about her ice-queen persona, but it's working. The jury trusts her. She's efficient and effective. She built a strong case, used everything she had for maximum impact. I believe the jury is inclined to convict."

Sweeney's lips pursed. "The jury is always inclined to convict before the defense begins its case. I have to assume Pike's minions plan to change their minds."

She acknowledged the point. "They've asked the judge for a brief recess. They've found a new witness."

"And who would that be?"

"We tracked them to Kindred Hospital, but I don't know—"

Ellison jumped in. "Elena Alvarez." He paused. "At least she says that's her name."

"You doubt her?"

"The girl's mind is so addled she doubts herself. She's a keenly unreliable witness."

"But still they plan to call her. Desperation?"

"Perhaps. She does have a sad story. She's the young woman the press is calling a mermaid. It's all over the internet."

"How did she come to be in the ocean?"

"No one knows. She was injured. And exhausted. Docs say she was delusional, at least when they first found her."

Sweeney arched an eyebrow. "And you know this because…"

"Because I'm an investigator. A case doesn't have to be cold for me to do my job."

"Sounds like you've earned your pay. This time. How useful is her testimony likely to be to the defense?"

Ellison extended his hands. They shook a bit, and not due to the man's age. "I can't say. The girl wasn't even in St. Petersburg when the murder occurred."

"And yet, some connection must exist." Sweeney turned to Prudence. "Thoughts?"

"They haven't said anything I could overhear."

"Listening devices in place?"

"Yes. But Garrett Wainwright has taken the lead on this investigation, and he hasn't been speaking in any of the usual places."

"We need to know how they think this girl can help them."

"Agreed."

"And we need to be prepared to strike back. They're grasping at straws. This case is different from the ones that have caused Mr. Pike and I to clash in the past."

A small crease appeared between Prudence's eyebrows. "How so?"

"In the past, Pike always handled the trial. This time, his hands are tied. He has to let someone else run the show. Which must be driving that arrogant control freak insane."

"He does appear to be…bristling."

"Good. Let him squirm. But we have to assume that this mermaid is of some utility to them. We must be prepared to do something about it."

Ellison looked puzzled. "How do we plan a counterstrike when we don't know what the first strike will be?"

"The best counterstrike anticipates and precedes the first strike." Sweeney steepled his fingers, the soft pads of his fingertips bouncing against themselves. "We discussed this before, Prudence. Do it."

"You mean—"

"The souvenir we borrowed from the police evidence locker during Camila Pérez's murder trial. It's time that reappeared."

"It's on the exhibit list. Buried among hundreds of other items supposedly discovered during the search of Pike's office."

"And the officer will swear that's where he found it?"

"He has responded positively to my suggestions in the past. Especially when they were accompanied by more money than he's seen in his entire life."

"Good." Sweeney pivoted around and gazed at his Miró. "We have an opportunity to remove this perpetual thorn from our side. I will not let it slip through my fingers." His eyes seemed to sharpen their focus. "Not for some damned mermaid. Or anything else."

CHAPTER THIRTY-NINE

DAN HATED BEING STUCK IN THE COURTROOM WHILE GARRETT and Jimmy worked with the young woman in the hospital, but he had no choice. Judge Hembeck had given them some time, but she wasn't willing to put the trial on indefinite hold, especially not with the Knife huffing and puffing that this was all a defense ploy. The judge requested an offer of proof—in other words, a statement of what the young woman might say of relevance to the case. They hoped to have that soon, but in the meantime, the trial would proceed.

So Dan would take the stand. He hoped he could do himself some good. But at the least, it would buy them some time.

While he waited for court to resume, he noticed Evelyn Belasco in the front row behind the prosecution table. She was still coming to court each day with her son CJ. The prosecutors weren't in the courtroom at the moment, and Maria had foolishly left him alone.

Time for a carpe diem.

He walked toward Evelyn and spoke before she had a chance to yell. "Ma'am, I don't mean to disturb you. I wanted to tell you how sorry I am for your loss."

CJ spoke for her. "If you're so damn sorry, why'd you kill him?"

Dan remained calm. "I didn't."

The young man made a snorting sound. "Then who did?"

"We're trying to find out. Which is more than the police are doing."

Evelyn tilted her head. "Even I have to agree with you there. Seems like they stopped investigating as soon as they heard that audio recording."

"Doing the obvious is easier than investigating. Or admitting to the press that you don't know what happened."

"It was more than that," Evelyn said. "Some of the boys wanted the killer to be you."

"You may be right."

"I can't believe you're talking to him, Mother." CJ looked angry. "This man killed your husband. My dad."

"Yeah, maybe. But then again, your dad was a philandering egotist who lost our fortune and probably would've bankrupted us if he'd lived much longer."

"Mother!"

"It's not like I'm telling you anything you don't know, CJ. He was probably crueler to you than anyone."

Dan cocked his head. "That true, son?"

CJ wrapped his arms around himself. "It was tough love."

"I see." Could he possibly stir them up even more? "You look relaxed, Mrs. Belasco. Have you had time for a massage?"

Her eyes became slivers. "What does that mean?"

"I know you make regular visits to the country club spa. I prefer a nice Shiatsu massage, myself. How about you?"

"I don't know what you're getting at."

"I'm not—" Out the corner of his eye, he saw the Knife marching toward them. Uh-oh.

"What the hell is going on here, Pike?"

He raised his hands in a "back off" gesture. "Just having a friendly conversation."

"With my clients?"

"Your client is Pinellas County, Zach. Do you need remedial law schooling?"

"Don't get smart with me."

"I would never dream of being smart with you."

"I've heard about how you manipulate people to get what you want. These two are potential prosecution witnesses."

"You've rested your case."

"We might call them as rebuttal witnesses!"

"You need to chill." He turned toward Evelyn. "Again, I'm sincerely sorry for your loss." He returned to his own table... where he saw Maria looking about as happy as the Knife did.

"What was that about?"

"Being sociable."

"Do I need to give you the lecture again?"

"No. You're the lawyer. I'm the client. But you never know what I might turn up."

"All you did was piss everyone off. Make them even more determined to end you."

"Well, they can only execute me once." He settled into his chair. "I don't see how it can get much worse than it already is."

HE COULD FEEL THE ELECTRICITY IN THE COURTROOM WHEN Maria announced that he, the defendant, would take the stand. Defendants always have a fifth amendment right to remain silent and cannot be forced to take the witness stand. But Dan knew that when the defendant did not tell his story, the jury felt a little cheated. Like reading a novel but not getting the last chapter. It left them without closure, feeling that they were making a decision without having all the facts. Which didn't necessarily guarantee they would convict. But it was hard to shake the feeling that a silent defendant might be hiding something.

Taking the witness stand was a new and bizarre experience for him. He had coached a hundred witnesses on how to behave in court, but never once gave any thought to how he would do it himself. He tried to sit still, remain calm. Didn't grin, but didn't act miserable, either. Where should he look?

He decided to stare at Maria. She was soft on the eyes, after all. And if he looked at the jury, he might not like what he saw gazing back.

Maria began. "Mr. Pike, please tell the jury what you were doing on the evening that George Belasco was murdered."

And here the disappointment began. He knew the jury wanted some elaborate tale explaining that he was nowhere near the scene of the murder. Unfortunately, he didn't have that. "We had just completed a big case," he explained, remaining calm and natural. "It was a big win. We were planning a celebration later that night at the office. I decided to blow off some steam. I love the water." He smiled slightly. "That's why my partners call me Aquaman."

"Where were you?"

"The beach. Not far from where I dock my sailboat. I call it *The Defender*. I live on it."

"What in particular did you do at the beach?"

Maria wanted to go there, huh? Well, she was the master strategist. "For half an hour or so, I swam. Then I noticed that the wind was strong, so I tried a little kitesurfing."

The jury's reaction to the word "kitesurfing" was unmistakable. "How did that go?"

"Great. I normally prefer mornings, but this worked okay."

"Was anyone else there?"

"Not that I noticed. I mean, there probably were others passing by, but no one I saw."

"And you had no way of knowing that you would need an alibi later."

"Exactly." Smart woman. Maria was suggesting that normal people who haven't committed crimes don't go around collecting alibis, that it would be more suspicious if he actually had one.

"There was some talk earlier about the equipment you use when kitesurfing. Could you discuss that for a moment?"

"Sure. It's a simple rig, really. You need a kite, obviously. That's what catches the wind and propels you forward. A seat harness. A safety leash. The handlebar. That's the trident-shaped piece you hold. A surfboard to stand on. Water shoes. There's more stuff you can add if you like, but I prefer to keep it simple."

"What I'd like to talk about is the handlebar. A witness indicated that a handlebar was used to pinion George Belasco's body to the fence. Do you know anything about that?"

"I can't say whether that's true, though I personally doubt a real handlebar would be strong enough to do the job. I can say with certainty that the device used on Belasco wasn't mine. In the first place, I know where mine is. Plus, I use a fiberglass handlebar. I haven't used metal in years."

"But you have bought handlebars before."

"Yes, and for all I know that invoice the prosecutor waved around is accurate. But I got rid of that old-school metal gear a long time ago. Nothing of mine was used by the murderer. I can guarantee it."

"Was the use of kitesurfing equipment in this murder just a coincidence?"

"I don't think it was a coincidence. Plenty of people know I kitesurf. I think this was a deliberate attempt to frame me, like the audio recording and the anonymous emails."

"Objection," Garfield said. "Speculation."

The judge nodded. "Sustained. We need facts, counsel. Not guesses."

Yeah, yeah. The jury heard it. He planted the seeds.

Maria continued. "Let's talk about facts, then. Mr. Pike, do you have any factual basis for your belief that you were framed?"

"Think about it. That crucifixion on the fence was completely unnecessary. The victim was already dead. Why do it? Answer: to plant some kitesurfing equipment to frame me."

"Objection," Garfield said, louder than before. "This is still speculation."

The judge pursed her lips. "It's actually somewhere in the netherworld between speculation and argument. But neither is appropriate on direct. Sustained."

Maria nodded. He could see flashes of pink in her cheeks. She was more nervous than he'd ever seen her, inside the courtroom or out. "Let's talk about that witness. Warner. The man who claimed that you confessed to the murder. Have you ever seen him before?"

"Never."

"You're certain?"

"Positive. I have a good eye for details. Faces. If I'd seen him, I'd remember."

"But you have been in jail."

"After I was arrested on this charge, they locked me up. Took a while before I was released on bail."

"But you didn't talk to that man. Mr. Warner."

"I talked to few of the other incarcerated men. I had few opportunities, actually, and even when I did have a chance, I kept my mouth shut."

"Was there a reason for that?"

"Of course. I'm an attorney, remember? I'm all too familiar with jailhouse snitches and prosecutors' unfortunate tendency to rely on them, particularly when they have no solid—"

"Objection," Garfield said, springing to her feet. "The witness answered the yes-or-no question."

"Sustained."

Maria tried again. "Have you seen prosecutors employ snitch testimony before?"

"All too—"

"Objection. Relevance. What may have happened in the past has no bearing here."

Judge Hembeck thought longer this time before replying. "Sustained."

"Your honor," Maria said, "I will suggest that given Mr. Pike's years of service as a defense attorney, he's an expert on this subject. Therefore, he should be allowed to offer expert testimony."

"That's preposterous," Garfield said. "War stories are not expert testimony."

"I disagree," Maria said calmly. "Who around here would know more about snitch testimony and when prosecutors resort to it than my client?"

"And I object to the term 'snitch,'" Garfield replied. "Mr. Warner offered credible testimony based upon personal experience."

"He snitched to get himself out of jail."

"Okay, stop," the judge said, waving her gavel. "No more speaking objections. If you must offer your opinions, approach the bench first."

"I'm sorry, your honor," Maria said. But Dan doubted it.

The judge continued. "I will allow the witness to speak on a limited basis about his personal professional experience, as I would any witness. I don't think he needs to be certified as an expert to permit that. But I will not allow him to speak on specific cases that he has no knowledge about. And I have little tolerance for unsubstantiated attacks on the prosecutor's office or the law enforcement system. Do I make myself clear, Ms. Morales?"

"You do, your honor. Thank you." She turned back toward Dan. "Have you encountered snitch testimony before?"

"Yes. It was common in the Belasco administration, though I must say that some prosecutors refused to use it because of its inherent unreliability. It's become a last resort for some prosecutors—and some inmates. Warner admitted that he's done this before."

"He testified that the prosecution did not promise him anything."

"They don't have to. Warner knows how the system works. If his testimony gets the prosecution a conviction, he'll be rewarded."

Garfield again. "Objection, your honor. You instructed counsel to avoid attacks on the prosecutor's office."

"So I did." Hembeck gave Maria a sharp look. "Did you hear that part?"

"Yes, your honor. But with all due respect, that is how the system works, and I can't believe the court likes snitch testimony any more than we do. If I paid someone to testify, I'd be disbarred. But snitch testimony is just another form of paid testimony. And prosecutors do it with frightening frequency."

"And that is the end of this conversation," Judge Hembeck said, pointing her gavel. "If you want to write an op-ed piece for the paper, please do. But my courtroom is not your soapbox. This conversation is over. Move on."

Fine. She'd made her point. Made it quite well, in fact. He hoped the jury got it.

"Mr. Pike, did you in fact have a conversation with Mr. Warner?"

"No. Never saw him. Never spoke to him. Wouldn't have spoken to him if I had seen him. I'm not stupid enough to speak to someone like that. He's dangerous. Completely amoral. Thinks any lie is justified if it benefits himself."

Garfield shot up again, looking seriously angry. "Object to the witness offering psychological profiles. He's not that kind of expert." Her voice dropped. "Or any other."

"Sustained. Counsel, you've been told to move on."

"And I will, your honor."

"The whole idea is crazy," Dan said, not waiting for another question he knew would draw an objection. "Do I seem like I would get all bug-eyed gloating about killing another attorney? That witness has watched too many episodes of *Law and Order*."

The judge slammed down her gavel. "Mr. Pike! You know how courtroom procedure works. You will remain silent until you hear a question. And then you will answer the question. And that is all you will do."

"Yes, your honor." He tucked in his chin contritely. "My apologies."

"Mr. Pike," Maria said, "could you please describe the circumstances surrounding that audio recording the jury heard? Repeatedly."

"Of course. It was all a joke. Maybe not a funny one, in retrospect, but of course, we didn't know Belasco was about to be murdered. Belasco was interfering with a trial I was handling. Camila was with me on my boat. As you heard, she initiated a joke about taking Belasco out, which was funny at the time because that's about the last thing in the world she would ever do. I played along. That's all it was. Two people being inappropriately silly."

"Did you know you were being recorded?"

"Obviously not."

"Do you know who recorded the conversation?"

"Someone who, once again, was trying to frame me, obviously."

"Objection," Garfield said. "We've been over this."

"But this is different," Maria insisted. "That listening device wasn't planted by accident. It was already in place before the conversation occurred. That does strongly suggest that someone was out to get my client."

Judge Hembeck pondered a moment before answering. "I'll allow it. This time."

Maria continued. "Mr. Pike, do you know who sent those anonymous emails to the police?"

"No. But again…" He glanced at the judge and smiled. "It was not someone who wanted me to have a long and happy life."

Maria brought the examination to its conclusion. "Mr. Pike, did you murder George Belasco?"

"Absolutely not."

"Did you conspire to kill George Belasco?"

"No. I would never do such a thing."

"Were you in that back alley on the night of the murder?"

"No."

"Did Harriett Clooney see you near the alley?"

"No. She was mistaken. The stocking cap probably prevented her from making a reliable identification."

"Did you hire someone to kill George Belasco or to help you kill him?"

"Never."

"Thank you." She glanced at Garfield. "Your witness."

CHAPTER FORTY

GARFIELD WASTED NO TIME. SHE STRODE BEFORE DAN AND planted herself directly in his line of sight. "Mr. Pike, you have considerable experience with the criminal justice system, don't you?"

Really? That was her hardball? "I've been a defense lawyer for more than a decade."

"But your experience with the legal system…and the penal system…began long before that, didn't it?"

"I'm not sure what you mean." Out the corner of his eye, he could see Maria poised to object. But like him, she wasn't sure yet where this was going.

"Mr. Pike, your father was also arrested for murder, wasn't he? And convicted?"

"Objection," Maria said. "This is grossly improper."

"To the contrary," Garfield said calmly, "this is essential and necessary."

"No, it's potentially defamatory and completely irrelevant."

"I would ask the court's indulgence," Garfield said. "This is leading to a line of questioning that bears directly on the case at bar."

"How?" Maria said. "His father's case happened years ago. She's trying to embarrass him."

Or perhaps to suggest that murder runs in the Pike DNA, Dan mused. And to shake him up. Get him unsettled, not thinking straight. The more stressed he was, the greater the chance he would say something he shouldn't.

"If you'll recall," Garfield said, "Ms. Morales dug into the witness's past to accomplish her ends, despite being instructed not to do so by the court. I don't see how she can complain when I do the same."

The judge nodded. "Sauce for the goose. Overruled."

Proving once again how dangerous it was to hack off the judge.

Garfield addressed Dan. "Still waiting for an answer. Your father was convicted of murder, right? In fact, he died in prison."

Dan spoke through clenched teeth. "True."

"And ever since then, you've represented criminal defendants."

"I've dedicated my life to making sure no more innocent people are convicted. I know how that destroys families. Destroys lives. I don't want anyone else to go through what my family did."

"Is it the innocent you're helping? You have a reputation for being able to get anyone off. You've represented a fair number of drug dealers, right?"

"Accused dealers."

"How about Emilio López? Was he innocent?"

Damn. "Of the drug charges."

"And after you got him released, he was involved in a gang-land slaying. Six people died. Including at least one innocent bystander."

Several jurors pulled back their heads, obviously appalled.

"Waiting for an answer, Mr. Pike. True?"

His jaw remained tight. "True."

"It would seem you're not so much dedicated to the innocent as you are dedicated to the money. Perhaps, to use familiar words, you're a complete sociopath who thinks it's acceptable to do anything so long as it benefits him."

"Objection," Maria said.

"Sustained." But of course, the damage was already done.

Garfield withdrew a small silver object from a plastic evidence bag. "Mr. Pike, can you tell the jury what this is?"

"It appears to be a…flask." Something fired in the nether reaches of his brain. But he couldn't put it together fast enough…

"Would you like to tell the jury why this is significant? Or shall I?"

"I'll let you."

"Do you recall the case in which you represented Mayor Camila Pérez, who was also charged with murder?"

"Of course."

"And she subsequently became your…girlfriend, right?"

"Yes…"

"She's the one you're talking with on the audio recording."

"Yes."

"And you got her off the hook, right?"

"The jury found her not guilty. Because she was not guilty. And the true—"

"Please answer the question, as the judge instructed you. Isn't it true that a crucial piece of evidence went missing during that case?"

This is *that* flask? The truth slammed his chest so hard he felt like he was having a stroke. This cross-ex was a runaway train, but he was much too slow to stop it. "Yes."

"What evidence went missing?"

He stared at the evidence in his hand. "A silver flask. Found at the scene of the crime. A bakery."

"A vital piece of evidence that disappeared under mysterious circumstances, dealing a severe blow to the prosecution and contributing to the acquittal of your client. Who is now your lover. Mr. Pike, the flask you now hold was found during the search of your office."

"I don't believe that."

"I have an officer ready to testify in detail about finding this flask in a secret hiding place inside the wall of your private office."

"That can't—"

"Isn't it true that the flask you're holding is the one that went missing?"

The buzz in the courtroom almost drowned out his response. "I don't...have any idea. But I didn't—"

"I will submit, Mr. Pike, that you deliberately stole this evidence so you could win your case and protect your lover."

"That's not true. I had no way to—"

"You can deny it all you like, but the flask was found in your office. *You* are the sociopath—and compulsive liar—who believes he is above the law. Even the law against murder."

"Objection," Maria said.

Both continued speaking simultaneously, and between that confusion and the growing noise from the gallery, it became impossible to follow what was happening.

Garfield took advantage of the confusion. She kicked her voice up several notches. "Mr. Pike, I will submit that you are a clever, completely amoral man who thinks he can do anything. Even lying and tampering with evidence. You did it in your lover's case and now you're doing it in your own. Because you committed this murder!"

"That's not true. I never—" He tried to be heard, but no one was listening. The judge pounded her gavel for order, but it was almost useless. After several more moments of pointless pounding, Hembeck called for a ten-minute recess so everyone could calm down.

He knew Maria would do her best to smooth things over after the break, to rehabilitate him. But he also knew it would be impossible. Garfield made him look like a cheat and a liar. A murderer.

And that's what the jury would remember.

CHAPTER FORTY-ONE

IN THE CONSULTATION ROOM, DAN TRIED TO STIFLE THE GROWING panic that threatened to incapacitate him. "How did they slip that flask onto the exhibit list without us noticing?"

Maria looked crushed. "Blame me. How would I know that a missing piece of evidence from long ago would become relevant here?"

"We should have seen it coming."

"There are literally hundreds of items on the prosecution exhibit list."

"Deliberate misdirection. We're sunk."

Maria gripped his arms. "Don't panic. Garrett says the mermaid will be a great witness."

"Will she make the jury forget that I was a terrible witness?"

"We can hope."

He noticed she didn't attempt to persuade him that he wasn't a terrible witness. "Any idea where Garfield got that flask?"

"They say it came from your office. They have a sponsoring witness."

"Bull. I bet Sweeney has been sitting on it ever since the prior case."

"Honestly, it doesn't matter. Right now, we have to focus on using this new witness to turn things around."

"She doesn't know who killed Belasco. How could she? She was out at sea when it happened."

"She can still help." Maria attempted something like a smile. "I do have one pleasant surprise."

He arched an eyebrow. At this point, he couldn't even imagine.

"A surprise visitor." Maria left the room. And a moment later —Camila entered.

Without a word, he threw his arms around her and buried his face in her shoulder.

It was a long time before either spoke.

"I have...really missed you," he murmured.

"Likewise. How are you holding up?"

He stifled his first response. "The hardest part for me is over. I've already testified. And bombed."

"The trial isn't finished." She squeezed him tighter. "I think maybe I should hang around. I don't have anything pressing this afternoon."

"No. The future senator does not need to be seen with the likes of me." He kissed her again on the side of the neck. "Thanks. But we can't both go down because of this."

"I'm not going down. Have you seen my approval ratings? I'm perceived as the victim of a conspiracy. We need to convince everyone that you're a victim, too."

"I tried. When I was on the stand. Didn't work."

"But still—"

"You had an ironclad alibi. I don't."

She frowned. "We should've told them we were boinking on your boat at the time of the murder."

He gave her a surprised, but amused look. "That would've been a hard alibi to float. Since you were surrounded by a dozen people at the time."

"Well, I move fast." All at once, she pressed her lips against his. "I'm worried about you," she said after.

"I'm a little concerned myself." He paused. "But Garrett is bringing us a surprise witness. A mermaid, apparently."

"That sounds promising."

"We can hope." He hugged her again, and realized he was having a hard time letting go. He didn't want to let go. "Thanks for coming. Now get out of here."

"But—"

"Assuming I'm allowed out tonight, let's rendezvous back at the boat."

"And..." She swallowed. "If you're not?"

He looked deeply into her eyes. "Water my plants."

DAN COULD BARELY CONTAIN HIMSELF AS HE RETURNED TO THE courtroom. He knew all eyes were on him. They were still evaluating, contemplating, deciding who to believe.

Maria addressed the court. "The defense calls Elena Alvarez to the witness stand."

When Elena was first brought to the hospital, the doctors said she suffered from exhaustion, dehydration, and several serious injuries. She seemed to be in shock or some irrational mental state, probably brought about by all she had experienced, both before and after the boat crash that left her stranded in the Gulf near the Floridian shore. Her mental state seemed stronger now, but putting her on the stand was still completely unpredictable.

At the hospital, Elena told him she wanted to testify. He would've understood if her experiences left her terrified, unwilling to speak, but it was just the opposite. She relished the opportunity to strike back. She had looked him in the eyes and said, "I want to do this. Not for myself. For Izzy."

Elena settled into the witness stand. Visible bruising on the right side of her face. Underweight. Patchy hair. Simple black dress Maria chose.

Maria stood beside the defendant's table and offered her a smile. "Elena, would you please tell the jury how you came to be in this courtroom this morning?"

Step by step, Maria walked the young woman through her story. How she lost her parents in a tragic automobile accident. How she was lured into a cult by the man she called David. How he had taken advantage of her, and eventually sold her to a sex-trafficking cartel.

"I was so blind. I thought I loved David. I thought he loved me. Then he sold me like a piece of meat. He sold me to men he knew would hurt me." The aching in her face was evident, but she held herself together. "I knew I had to escape. But they watched me constantly."

Garfield rose. "Your honor, I mean no disrespect to this witness, who has obviously had a horrifying experience. But this is a murder trial and I'm not seeing even a tenuous connection."

"Give us a few minutes," Maria said. "You'll see the connection soon. And it's not tenuous. We're about to learn what this case is really about, what it has been about all along."

Judge Hembeck appeared intrigued. "I will allow you to proceed. But I expect this to link up soon."

"Understood." Maria turned back to Elena. "What happened after you were taken by the traffickers?"

In excruciating detail, Elena described the men, the boat, and the hideous conditions that she and the others experienced during their transit from Mexico to Florida. Stripped and hosed down. Given loose scrubs to wear. Sexually abused on a regular basis. Forced to live together in the hold of the ship. Fed once a day. Living in their own squalor. She described her attempts to escape and how she ended up swimming to shore on a Florida beach. She described a nightmare existence, and yet, not once did she seem to be feeling sorry for herself. She simply told what happened and let the story speak for itself.

"Were there any visitors to the ship during the voyage?" Maria asked.

"I only know of one," Elena answered. "I was usually down below. It's possible there were others I did not know about."

"How did you happen to see this particular visitor?"

"I was brought above decks to...service the Captain." Her eyes dropped, her shame evident. "I seemed to be a particular favorite. He said he liked me because I did not make a lot of noise."

Maria fell silent, perhaps to give the jury a moment to contemplate that. "You were brought out of the...cargo hold where the girls were normally kept?"

"Yes. I was brought to the bridge, the operations room. He barked a few orders. Leered at me, in his disgusting way with his disgusting breath. And I saw another man who had come to the ship in a separate vessel. Some sort of yacht or speedboat, I believe."

"Did you hear this man's name?"

"No. But I saw him. Quite clearly."

Maria picked up a folder on the defendant's table. "I have a pre-marked photograph, your honor. Actually, it's one of the prosecution's photos. Though just to be clear, it has not been Photoshopped or altered in any way."

Dan covered his mouth. *Bazinga.*

"Elena, have you seen the man in this photograph before?"

"That's him," she said. "That's the man I saw on the boat."

"Let the record reflect that the witness has identified Prosecution Exhibit 49A, which is a photo of the murder victim in this case, George Belasco. We originally gave the witness a stack of more than twenty photos taken from the district attorney's mugshot file. None of them were altered. The witness immedi-

ately identified this photo and has never wavered in her identification."

"It's true," Elena said. "I will never forget that face. I will
never forget any of their faces."

Maria nodded. "Did you hear any of their conversation?"

"I did. My English is good, but I only heard bits and pieces.
They seemed to be making arrangements to dock the boat in
Florida. The man you call Belasco made it possible for the ship
to enter American waters without being detected. He insisted
that the ship come there."

Because he was getting kickbacks from port officers on the
take, most likely. "Were there any disagreements?"

"Yes. Belasco and the Captain argued about something. The
Captain felt he had not honored his promise in some way. He
said if he didn't get what he wanted he would turn his ship
around and take the girls somewhere else. Belasco did not like
that idea. He insisted that payments had been made and his
partner was expecting the cargo to arrive." She looked at the
jury. "That's what he called us. Cargo. He said he had a lot of
money riding on this delivery and he couldn't afford for it to
fail."

"Were they able to resolve the dispute?"

"I am not sure. The discussion ended and they both calmed
down. I don't know what decision was reached. Even as Belasco
left, I sensed there was tension between the men."

"Enough tension to cause someone to consider murder?"

"Objection," Garfield said.

The judge considered a moment. "I'll allow it."

Elena gave the jurors an unflinching look. "I have seen the
Captain kill to eliminate minor inconveniences. Because a girl
cried. Because a member of his crew was slow to perform his
duties. I know that he killed a...a—" Her voice choked. "A friend
of mine. A younger girl. Because she tried to escape. He tried to

kill me. I cannot imagine him failing to kill someone who threatened his business."

Maria changed the subject. "Elena…how do you feel today?"

"When I first washed ashore in Florida, I barely knew who I was. The police say I was babbling, repeating a lot of nonsense flowing through my brain. But the fever passed. I have rested. I am thinking clearly. And I remember what happened. Every moment of it."

"Thank you," Maria said. "No more questions."

Garfield rose slowly. Even though it was hard for Dan to show much sympathy to the woman who was trying to schedule him for a lethal injection, he felt a small amount of pity. Call it professional courtesy. He would not have wanted the task of cross-examining this witness. The potential for coming off as an unsympathetic brute was too great.

"Miss Alvarez, let me start by saying that my heart goes out to you for all that you have suffered. I'm sure everyone in this courtroom feels the same way."

Elena offered a small smile.

"You are willing to admit that when you arrived at the beach…you were not in strong shape…mentally. Correct?"

Elena nodded. "I had been swimming forever. I don't know how long. I had no way to keep track. I had suffered a serious head injury."

Garfield picked up a file. "In the hospital, you were diagnosed as suffering from exhaustion, malnutrition, and mental delusions. Correct?"

"I have not seen the report. But I assume that's correct."

"Do you doubt your doctors' ability to reach a diagnosis?"

"No."

"Then you must assume the report is accurate."

"I suppose."

"If the defense does not object, I will move that this exhibit be admitted so the jury may review it later."

Maria nodded her agreement. There was no point in objecting to a doctor's report.

"So only a few days ago," Garfield continued, "you were diagnosed as mentally incompetent. You weren't allowed to leave the hospital, much less testify in a court of law. You imagined things that were not real. You said things that made no sense."

"I was half-remembering—"

"But what you said was incoherent. Which is the definition of the delusional state of mind."

"I—I don't know what—"

"So we must wonder how much of what you said today is true, and how much is merely the product of the severe anguish you have suffered."

Elena's voice wavered. "I saw that man on the ship. Belasco. Long before I plunged into the ocean. He was there."

"I don't doubt that someone was there. But I do question whether, given your current state of mind, you're in any condition to make a positive identification, especially one of this importance."

"I saw that man on the ship," Elena said firmly.

"I know you think you did. But that was after you were visited by these defense attorneys, a meeting that no prosecutors were invited to attend. They talked to you at length, despite your delicate mental state, and when they were done, they had what they've wanted all along. An alternative theory of why George Belasco was murdered."

"I saw that man on the ship," Elena said. Her voice grew louder, making it sound thin and strained. "No one put that memory in my head."

"I'm sure that's what you believe," Garfield said, in a much quieter voice. "But you've been manipulated. Turned into a pawn in someone else's game. Only a few days ago, when you washed up on the beach, you were claiming to be..." She glanced at her notes, then read with an arched eyebrow. "The fire that never burns cold. The lover who's never been kissed."

"I was confused!" Elena's voice cracked. Tears appeared in her eyes. "I didn't know what I was saying!"

"Exactly. And you still don't. No more questions."

CHAPTER FORTY-TWO

DURING THE BREAK, DAN HUDDLED IN A CONSULTATION ROOM with Maria and Jimmy.

"How do you think it went? Do you think the jury believed Elena?"

"Elena did a good job," Jimmy said. "Amazing, really, all things considered. But Garfield made her point too. We're asking the jury to forget all the evidence pointing at you based upon the testimony of a witness who they have serious reason to suspect may not be firing on all cylinders."

"So basically," Maria added, "they have to choose between the jailhouse snitch and the kid suffering from severe post-traumatic stress."

"How do you think that will play out?"

Maria appeared to be choosing her words carefully. "I don't know. I wish I did. But I don't. The prosecution has put on more than just the snitch."

"The jury doesn't have to absolutely positively believe everything Elena said," Jimmy insisted. "But surely it's enough to create doubt. Reasonable doubt."

"In a world where jurors took those words seriously," Dan said, "I would agree with you. But they don't."

Garrett burst through the door. "I might be able to help with that."

Dan peered at him. "You need to stop with the sudden rushing into the room. You're going to give me a stroke." He paused. "Okay, what've you got?"

"A lead. Maybe. I thought about Elena's testimony. If the Captain—or anyone that nasty—wanted to take someone out, would he do it himself? No. He wouldn't take the risk. Ask one of his sailors to carry out this complex violent murder? No. He'd hire a pro."

Dan's lips parted. "A hitman? Like Warner claimed I hired?"

"If I've learned anything lately, it's that anyone with a web browser can find someone willing to do anything they want. Look what I found on the dark web."

"You know how to access the dark web?"

"I've had a lot of practice lately. Besides, it's not called 'dark' because it's hard to find. It's dark because the people who post there are nearly impossible to trace. Which is what they want. Because everything they sell is illegal. Like murder, for instance."

Dan looked at the screen. The text described the individual offering services as a "slayer" and said he had successfully completed more than two dozen executions without even being questioned, much less arrested. It provided details for contacting him and promised a reply within twenty-four hours. "I am extremely professional and will maintain all contractual terms." Elsewhere it assured potential customers, "As well as assassinations, we also offer services like cripplings, acid attacks, torture, and much more." An assassination by gun was a mere $20,000. By knife—$22,000. Poison—$40,000. Death torture—$50,000.

"What's death torture?" Jimmy asked.

"I don't want to know," Maria replied.

"And this is for real?" Dan asked. "Not some kind of joke or scam? Or maybe a government sting operation?"

"I think it's the real deal," Garrett said. "Take a good look at the pic?"

Dan leaned in again. The text was accompanied by a reverse-exposure photo with the eyes obscured to mask the identity, but it was still possible to make out the general shape of his face and features.

And he was wearing a stocking cap.

He looked at Garrett. "Are you thinking...?"

"I am. He looks like you. I mean, he's not an identical twin or anything..."

"But close enough that someone who saw him in a dark alley might later choose my pic from a photo array. Especially if it had been augmented with a stocking cap." He threw his shoulders back. He wasn't sure if he was excited to have a new lead—or terrified because he knew what they would have to do next.

Garrett showed him a second screen, related to the first but more detailed. On this one, the man wore a green hood that obscured most of his face. He held a gun pointed directly into the camera. A gold embossed seal shone in a far-right corner. "What's that? The Good Housekeeping Seal of Approval?"

"Advertising," Garrett replied. "He's trying to assure people he's an actual bona fide hitman."

Dan read more of the fine print. The hitman—who used the professional name of "Anatole"—required fifty percent up front "to protect himself against losses when people have a sudden change of heart." He preferred to receive his funds in Bitcoin, "one of the few payment options that keep the customer, the market, and me, safe."

Dan looked at his friends. "I never thought you'd hear me say this, but...we're going to have to set up a hit."

Jimmy took a step back. "That's crazy."

"It's the only way. We have to act like we're serious until Anatole agrees to meet us or gives us the means to track him down."

"And then?" Maria asked.

"If he was hired to off Belasco, we might convince him to testify."

"Are you joking? We get a professional hitman to admit he was hired by sex traffickers to take out the district attorney? Good luck with that."

"It's a long shot," Garrett said. "But Elena's testimony wasn't enough. If there's any chance we can fill in more of the story, we should do it."

"I'll make the contact," Dan said. "This is my problem. I'm the one who should take the risks."

"You're already on trial for murder," Maria said. "Imagine what would happen if the cops found out you were trying to hire a hitman."

"Nonetheless, if someone has to take a risk, it should be me."

"No, I'll do it," Maria said. "At least then I can claim I was acting as a lawyer to help your case."

"I can't let you take that risk."

Maria stepped closer, inches from him. "You don't get to decide what I do, buddy. You're the client. Your job is to be quiet. My job is to find a way to win the case."

"I'm sorry, but I can't allow—"

Garrett stepped between them. "Stop. Both of you. This discussion is completely moot."

"Don't try to talk me out of it," Maria said. "Dan is not doing this."

"Neither of you is doing this."

"Really? Then—"

Garrett clicked to a different tab on his web browser. "I've already done it."

CHAPTER FORTY-THREE

GARRETT SAT AT A SMALL TABLE IN THE BACK CORNER OF Beachcombers staring at the man who had finally, wordlessly, taken the chair on the opposite side. He was almost twenty minutes late. He suspected the man had spent that time casing the bar, watching for guards or accomplices, making sure he wasn't walking into trouble.

Which he was. But they had taken care to make sure it wasn't apparent.

The man appeared slender but strong. He was about Dan's size and height and had the same color hair. Though they were hardly doppelgangers, he could see how this man could be mistaken for Dan, especially with a stocking cap on his head in back-alley lighting.

"You're Anatole?" Garrett asked. Did he sound nervous? He didn't want to sound nervous. He didn't want to do anything that might make the man suspicious. But he suspected that all of Anatole's potential clients were nervous. Who wouldn't be when they were speaking to a hitman?

"You can use that name." His voice was surprisingly high-pitched, reminding Garrett that this was a real person, not a shadowy character from a John Wick movie. In real life, villains didn't always come from Central Casting. He didn't have a scraggly beard or tattoos. He had an eerie calm about him. "What is it you want?"

"Isn't it obvious?"

"Nothing is obvious. Are you a cop?"

That surprised him. "Do I look like one?"

"You look like you could be. Desk cop. Detective maybe."

Surprisingly close. "Wrong."

"I need a yes-or-no answer. Are you a cop?"

"No. I am not a cop."

"Is this a scheme you've concocted for the purpose of entrapping me?"

"No." Not in the way that he meant. But since he wasn't a cop, he could say any damn thing he wanted. "I need a job done. And I hear you can do it." He paused. "I knew George Belasco."

Anatole stiffened a bit. "I never worked for him."

"But you...took care of him."

"That doesn't matter."

Garrett hoped to get at least a hint of a confession out of Anatole. He needed some leverage if the plan was going to work. This situation was incredibly tense, much more so than he'd expected. His stomach was churning. If this lasted much longer, he would probably start heaving.

Anatole flagged a passing waitress. He grinned at her as if he planned to take her home with him. Maybe he did. "Bourbon. Neat." He glanced across the table. "You want anything?"

He thought he should probably order. "Scotch and soda. Glenfiddich."

Anatole pushed a twenty into the waitress's shirt pocket. He noticed the man's fingers lingered longer than was necessary. "You keep the rest for yourself, sweetheart."

The waitress blew him a kiss. "Thanks, sugar. Back in a flash. I'll make sure yours has a little extra."

Garrett stared at her. That worked? Seriously?

"What is it you want done?" Anatole asked.

Garrett drew in his breath. "A hit."

"Crippling? Torture? Or the Full Monty?"

He hesitated to employ hip killer slang he might not fully understand. "I need her dead."

"Who's *she?*"

"Beverly Garfield. She works at the DA's office."

"Again?" Anatole leaned back and stretched. "Do I have to kill them all?"

He tried not to appear too anxious. "What do you mean?"

The question seemed to trigger something inside Anatole's head. "Does this have something to do with that trial? That lawyer?"

"Maybe. Why?"

"I don't need to get in deeper than I already am." He looked behind him, as if searching for his drink.

Anatole wasn't going to volunteer anything. Maybe the smart approach was to act as if he already knew. "Look, I hated Belasco. That's why I went looking for you."

The corner of Anatole's lips tugged upward. "You weren't the only one who hated him."

"You too?"

"I didn't know anything about him. I don't work where I play, if you know what I mean. But my client..." He shook his head. "Belasco couldn't be dead enough to make that client happy."

"So you took care of it?"

"I did my job. Look, if you want me to go back to the same stomping ground, there's risk. I'm increasing my fee."

"I can handle that. It's worth it." Okay, that was more or less a confession. But could he get more?

"Give me an address on this Garfield woman. Let's get it done, quick and clean. I need fifty percent up front."

"Do you take PayPal?"

Anatole stared at him.

"That was a joke. I brought cash. Hard to get it, though. I'm not as liquid as your last client was."

Anatole's eyes narrowed. "You keep bringing that up. Why?"

"No reason. Just curious."

The light dawned all at once. "Damn." Anatole stood suddenly and shoved the chair behind him. He turned and took two steps—

And found himself face to face with Dan. "Going somewhere?"

Anatole ducked and raced toward the front door. He barreled between tables, knocking over a waitress and sending a barstool spinning.

Screams broke out. People ducked and jumped out of the way.

Anatole kept running. He almost made it to the front door—

Two men stepped in front of him, blocking the path.

"Freeze," one said. "You're under arrest."

Anatole whipped around and headed toward the kitchen. He hadn't moved five feet before he found that pathway blocked as well. Two more men. One with his gun extended.

"This will be a lot simpler if you surrender."

Anatole started to swerve around again, but too slowly. One of the men from the front door reached under his shoulders and wrapped him in a headlock. The other man snapped cuffs around his wrists.

"You have the right to remain silent. Anything you say can and will be used against you..."

Garrett watched from a discreet distance. "Think we got enough?"

"I hope so." A woman sitting at the bar swiveled around. Jazlyn Prentice. Wearing an almost invisible headset. "He said more than enough to bring charges. And we got it all."

"Another audio confession," Garrett muttered. "What are you going to charge him with?"

"Everything possible," Jazlyn replied. "He was going to kill one of my prosecutors."

"Think he'll agree to testify?"

"I'm almost certain of it." Jazlyn turned to face Dan, seated at the barstool beside her. "I'm afraid I haven't been much use to you during this nightmare. I felt I had to keep my distance. Avoid any possible accusation of partiality. But that's over now." She smiled. "I'm going to make Anatole an offer he can't refuse."

CHAPTER FORTY-FOUR

DAN REMINDED HIMSELF, NOT FOR THE FIRST TIME SINCE THIS ordeal began, of the value of having good friends. Jazlyn had managed to swing yet another short continuance while they worked on the man who called himself Anatole, though as it turned out, his real name was Marvin Elliot. Dan could see why he used a professional alias. Marvin wasn't a name that struck terror.

By the time afternoon rolled around, they had a deal in place, signed and executed by all parties. Marvin would testify in exchange for a reduction in sentencing options. Basically, the death penalty was off the table, though Dan suspected he would be behind bars for the rest of his life. Which did not bother Dan in the slightest. The more they learned about Anatole, the more frightening he became. The whole story was like something out of pulp fiction.

According to Anatole, there was a thriving assassination marketplace on the dark web, though also many scams, people who would take your money and deliver nothing. The gold seal on his webpage was intended to convince people that he delivered what he said he would and had on many occasions. He couldn't make a list of successful hits—that would be too dangerous—and he couldn't have endorsements from satisfied customers—who would agree to provide one? So instead, he posted enough brutally professional detail to convince people that he did what he claimed.

Anatole said that in 2013 someone created the first assassination market, but it was largely distrusted and unused until people realized that Bitcoin could be used to make virtually untraceable payments. In 2018, a user-friendly protocol called Augur made it possible to set up blockchain markets. The assassination business exploded. His greatest problem now was not finding clients but avoiding white-hat hackers. The FBI was little threat. They were always slow to grasp the latest tech. But there were independent cybercrime researchers who spent their spare time roaming the dark web and forwarding what they found to the proper authorities. That was why Anatole started meeting people in person. He believed he could spot a federal agent a mile away. "There are some things you cannot fake. And if people won't meet me, they're either not that serious about it, or they're cops."

Garrett did some research. Turned out, the first proven case of dark-web assassination came to light on March 19, 2019, when two teenagers were arrested for murdering a Moscow investigator. Nine others have been charged in connection with commissioning murders—including a Minnesota man who, after paying $6000 in Bitcoin for a murder that was never delivered, resorted to killing his wife himself. The police caught him because the Bitcoin signature of the payment matched a key the cops found on the hard drive of his home computer.

Many people used the dark web to generate an extra income stream. Talk about a gig economy. It was one thing for people to drive an Uber in their spare time. Assassination-for-hire was a much darker reflection of the financial squeeze some people felt. Anatole thought this was their way of getting back at the world that had been so cruel to them.

Dan could barely believe what he heard. That was twisted justice indeed.

After Jazlyn played the taped Beachcombers recording, Marvin admitted that he shot Belasco, then dragged his body to the back alley and pinned it to the fence, as directed by his client. But he would not identify his client, beyond saying it wasn't Daniel Pike.

"That will have to do," Dan grimaced. "Surely identifying the hitman who committed the crime will be enough to get me off the hook."

Jazlyn looked at him earnestly. "I hope you're right. Because I think that's all we're going to get. He may not know the client's name."

Dan stared out the window toward the ocean. "I can't ditch the feeling that I'm missing something. Something that's right before my eyes."

Jazlyn checked her watch. "I hope it comes to you soon. Judge Hembeck has been extremely patient, but we've pushed her to the limit. You need to get this man on the witness stand. And hope the jury believes him."

DAN DIDN'T WANT TO STARE AT THE JURORS WHILE MARVIN testified, but it was impossible not to look at all, so he tried to be discreet. Didn't matter. The jurors had their attention focused on the witness.

Maria did a fantastic job of leading Marvin through his incredible testimony, especially given how little time she had to prepare. She had complained about not liking to speak in the courtroom and not being quick on her feet, but her performance today proved that she sold herself short. Garfield interrupted five times in the first five minutes, but her objections were all overruled and eventually she stopped. He thought he knew why. She'd seen the jurors' faces. They were mesmerized by this bizarre tale.

Maria established that the witness had been offered a deal, a potential sentencing reduction in exchange for a guilty plea and substantial assistance, including his testimony today. They played the audio recording in court, which left little doubt that Marvin was a hitman who killed for cash. Eventually, Maria reached the punchline.

"Did you kill George Belasco?"

Marvin did not hesitate. "Yes."

"How?"

"I shot him, six times, while he was headed toward his car. Following the instructions provided to me, I collected some of his blood and moved the body to the alley behind Beachcombers. I stuck him to the fence, using the metal handlebar left there for me. It did the trick. I splashed some of the blood around, then I went home. His death was verified by the media the next day. Afterward, I was able to collect my fee. Twenty thousand dollars in Bitcoin."

Dan wondered if Maria would push it any further. She did.

"Sir, who hired you to kill George Belasco?"

"I can't tell you that."

"Can't? Or won't?"

"Both. I never asked for a name. Names are irrelevant. All I needed was to be assured of payment, and to receive clear instructions about who the target is and what precisely should be done to them."

"Do you have any other information about your client?"

The witness thought a moment before answering. "I know my client hated Belasco."

"I think we can assume—"

"No, seriously *hated*. I could track his movements online

through the stroke history on my webpage. The client first considered buying a maiming. Then crippling. Ultimately settled on murder, but insisting that it had to be violent. There could be no chance of it being mistaken for a suicide."

What?

Something triggered inside Dan's brain, something that had been tickling the surface but refusing to declare itself.

Suicide. Violence. Hatred.

He let the wheels spin while Maria continued to ask questions. "Poison was not an option?"

"No. That's why I shot the target so many times. A person could conceivably shoot themselves once. But not six times."

Six shots. Grudge match. Never enough. He was never satisfied. Particularly cruel.

"Was that the reason for the crucifixion?"

"The target couldn't possibly string himself up on the fence. Especially after he was dead."

Crucifixion. Religion. Adultery.

No, that wasn't it. Dan thought harder.

Torn jeans. Bitter fruit. Computer skills.

No, no. What was it?

"And the kitesurfing handlebar was planted to frame my client?" Maria asked.

"I guess. And to guarantee this would look like a violent murder. Like a weird insurance policy to prevent misinterpretation."

Insurance policy. Sister. No time. Never any time.

That was it. Dan rose to his feet.

"But still," Maria continued, "you claim you don't know who hired you to commit the murder?"

"I don't," Marvin replied.

"That's okay," Dan said, loud enough to be heard throughout the courtroom. "Because I do."

The gallery erupted. Everyone spoke at once. There was so much babble he could barely hear himself think.

The judge pounded her gavel. "Mr. Pike, sit down. You're interrupting the testimony."

"I'm sorry, your honor. But this is important."

"I don't care. This is not your time to be heard."

He heard Maria muttering. "Dan...what are you doing?"

Dan stepped toward the center of the courtroom. "Isn't the point of this proceeding to determine who killed George Belasco?"

"Yes, but that doesn't give you the right to interrupt—"

"Could we, maybe, press the Pause button? For a moment." The judge looked completely at a loss. He took her failure to respond as an opening to continue. "This witness doesn't know who hired him. But I do. And I know why. And here's the best part. The person who hired this man to kill George Belasco is in the courtroom."

The tumult grew even louder than before. The judge pounded her gavel without effect. Several people in the gallery rose to their feet.

"Your honor," Dan continued, "may I ask that the bailiffs seal the doors and prevent anyone from leaving? Till I've had my say?"

Judge Hembeck drew in her breath. "This is completely irregular." She clearly didn't like it and wasn't even sure what was happening. But she grudgingly pointed at the back doors. "Bailiffs. No one leaves till Mr. Pike finishes his Hercule Poirot routine."

"Thank you." Everyone sat down. He had a captive audience. Which he liked much better than having a room full of people convinced he was a cold-blooded killer. "You know what has bothered me about this case all along?"

"The fact that you were accused of murder?" Garfield mumbled.

"No. The fact that anyone could think I was the murderer, despite the violent nature of the crime. Are we really surprised that a professional killer was involved? Good grief—Belasco was shot six times, the last shot to the head. He was pinned to a fence for no apparent reason. Except, as I kept telling myself, there must be a reason. I just couldn't figure out what it was."

"But now you have?" the judge asked, drumming her fingertips.

He continued. "A lot of people in this room had reasons to want Belasco dead. This tall drink of water with the blue hair to my left had been...um...counselling him for years. She knew his secrets. And I suspect he knew some of hers. The cutie-pie sitting beside her knew Belasco was into something dirty. She also knew he'd had financial setbacks and might cut her loose, which would probably mean she'd lose her apartment and... have trouble building her nest egg."

The judge did not look happy. "As entertaining as this is, Mr. Pike...get to the point."

"I will. Because Marvin here has forced me to focus on what has bothered me from the start. Why now? Why was Belasco killed now? And why was it so important that the crime not be misinterpreted as a suicide?"

"Vengeance?" Garfield guessed.

"No. Insurance. Marvin said the magic word—in the wrong context. You usually can't collect on a life insurance policy if the decedent is a suicide. And who do I know who had a life insurance policy on Belasco?"

Maria's eyes widened. "His widow. Evelyn Belasco."

He turned to face the front row of the gallery on the prosecution side.

Evelyn rose. "I don't know what you're playing at, shyster. But I did not kill my husband."

"Why should you? He wasn't in your way. You were having it on with your masseuse and he didn't interfere. But there was someone else who wasn't so complacent about what was happening in the family..."

Evelyn's lips parted. "Are you saying..."

"I am."

She peered down at her son. "CJ? You did this?"

Her son stumbled to his feet. He seemed wobbly. And scared. "That's...stupid. I would never kill my own dad."

"Not on your own, no," Dan said. "You don't have the guts. But hiring a hitman on the internet? Any loser could do that."

"I didn't!" CJ shouted.

"You hated your father. Resented him, especially how he treated the mother you adore. You tried to hide it when Maria and Garrett spoke to you, but you couldn't. Your father constantly criticized you, belittled you, and made you feel like the scum of the earth. Your mother said he was particularly cruel to you. And fair or not, you blamed him for your sister's death."

"He could've stopped Annabel from driving that night. Instead he threw her out of the house. Even though he knew she was messed up. She was killed and it was his fault!"

"Your father had squandered most of the family money, which is why he got involved with the trafficking ring. But you had a better idea. That million-dollar insurance policy would take care of your mother. And you would get even with your cruel dad, for yourself and your sister. It would all work perfectly—as long as it was clear his death wasn't a suicide."

"You're lying." CJ's eyes looked wide, desperate. "None of this is true. None of it!"

"All of it is true, and if I hadn't been so worried about myself I would've seen it sooner. You hired Marvin to take out your dad."

"CJ," Evelyn said quietly. "Is this true?"

"Would you care if it was?" the boy screamed. He pushed away from her. "You wanted him dead, too. You know you did.

So you could be alone with your disgusting boytoy. I found a way for you to get what you wanted and have enough money to take care of yourself."

Evelyn covered her face. "Oh, CJ...no..."

"Everyone hated that son-of-a-bitch. Everyone wanted him dead. I made it happen." CJ's voice rose. *"But you all wanted it!"*

CJ pushed away and started to run. He saw the bailiffs posted at the back door, then whirled around and started for the door behind the judge's bench.

He didn't get far. Garfield tackled him like a linebacker.

CJ tumbled to the floor. A second later, the bailiffs had him surrounded. One of them snapped cuffs around his wrists.

Garfield pushed herself to her feet, smoothing out her dress and brushing her hands. "Mr. Pike," she said slowly, "it appears...I may have been mistaken about your guilt."

He smiled. "No hard feelings. You came around in the end."

"In a manner of speaking." Garfield looked at Maria. "Ms. Morales, the prosecution will withdraw the charges against your client. With our...sincere apologies for all he has been put through."

"You were doing your job," Dan said. "I hope next time we meet in the courtroom, I'm the lawyer. Not the client."

Garfield almost smiled. "Keep talking like that and I'll find something else to charge you with."

CHAPTER FORTY-FIVE

DAN PULLED HIS PANKO-CRUSTED TEMPEH OUT OF THE OVEN. HE knew this was one of Maria's favorites. He thought she'd earned it.

For that matter—so had he. He'd barely been able to cook lately. Too distressed to focus. Okay, he had managed the brownies, but that wasn't hard and, after all, brownies are comfort food.

Camila hugged him around the waist, avoiding the hot pan. "I'm going to have to come by more often. Do you always cook like this?"

"Not often enough," Jimmy shouted from the kitchen table.

"We're celebrating Maria's courtroom victory," Dan explained.

Maria made a scoffing noise. "You had way more to do with getting the charges dismissed than I did. Garrett and Jimmy's investigating had more to do with it. I was just along for the ride."

"Hardly." Dan scooped the entrée onto individual plates, then added some grilled asparagus as an accent, plus homemade bread. "Needless to say, I also made dessert. Homemade ice cream. Recipe I stole from Salt & Straw. So save room."

"This looks spectacular," Maria gushed.

"Least I can do for my fearless vegan defense attorney."

"Oh, stop already."

Camila took her plate. "Any word on what's going to happen to the kid? CJ?"

"I called an old prosecutor friend," Garrett answered. "CJ Belasco is in custody and not likely to get out any time soon. Once they've got their ducks in a row, they'll charge him. Given his virtual confession in front of about a hundred people, I doubt it will take long."

"And Evelyn had no idea what her son did?" Camila asked.

Dan looked at her but said nothing.

"If Evelyn had a hint, she didn't share it," Garrett answered. "She says she didn't know, and I tend to believe her."

"She'd have tried to stop him," Maria said. "If only for her son's sake. She may have had a hate-on for her hubby, but she wouldn't kill him, and she wouldn't let her son arrange his murder."

"The whole thing is sad," Jimmy said. He took his first bite. "But on the brighter side, dinner is delightful."

Dan smiled. "Does it compensate for the damage to your action figures?"

"Don't be—" Jimmy stopped short. "You're the one."

Dan looked wide-eyed and innocent. "The one who what?"

"The one who found identical action figures—still wrapped in plastic—and had them delivered to me anonymously."

"I have no idea what you're talking about."

"Yeah. But thanks just the same. I didn't think they could be replaced. Count on a superhero to prove me wrong about superheroes." Jimmy took another bite. "What is tempeh, again?"

"No one knows," Maria answered. "But it isn't meat."

"That's all that matters." Jimmy took another bite. "Now that this is over, Dan, any idea what you're going to do next?"

He thought a moment before answering. "I'm going to ask Mr. K for some time off. I've been haunted by my father's conviction for so long—but I really haven't done that much about it. It's time for me to get serious. Find out what happened. Expose the true murderer."

"I'm sure Mr. K will agree. You deserve it," Garrett said.

"You know, you were right, Garrett. I've been obsessed with my father's case, and Sweeney, and it's clouded my judgment. I thought Sweeney was behind Belasco's murder. But I was wrong. I think he may have had plans regarding Belasco, but CJ beat him to the punch. And I think he may have been involved in my father's case, but—" He shook his head. "Anyway, I need to figure it out. Resolve this once and for all." He glanced at Garrett. "So I can stop ranting like a lunatic and causing scenes at the office."

Garrett smiled.

"That makes good sense," Maria said. "And you know that, as always…your team supports you. One hundred percent."

"Thank you. Jimmy, I'll still drop by periodically to cook dinner."

"Thank goodness for that," Jimmy said. "But all that really matters is that our Aquaman has been restored to us."

AFTER DINNER, DAN INVITED CAMILA TO JOIN HIM ON THE BACK porch. They sat in matched lawn chairs, gazing at the setting sun.

"Must be a relief to have those charges dropped," Camila said.

"Indeed."

"I remember how I felt after I was charged. I thought my life was over. As it turns out, it was just beginning. Thanks to you."

He did not reply. Instead, he picked up his backpack and pulled out a file.

"I still can't believe it was the kid," Camila said. "I mean, I disliked Belasco too. But I never would've guessed that kid would resort to murder."

"He didn't really," Dan said. "He hired someone. Like the petulant brat he is."

"Even that took courage. And knowhow. Finding Anatole on the dark web. Arranging for payment in Bitcoin. Seems beyond his resources."

Dan drew in his breath, then said quietly, "It was."

Camila turned toward him slowly. "What do you mean?"

"The kid had help."

"I know. Marvin committed the actual murder."

"More than that. Someone helped CJ make all the arrangements. Encouraged him. Helped him bring it off."

Camila waited a long time before replying. "How do you figure that?"

"I read the report Maria made after she interviewed Evelyn and CJ. One thing Evelyn mentioned was that her son was computer illiterate. Couldn't even handle email competently. So how would that kid find a killer on the dark web? Answer: He couldn't. Not without help."

"What are you saying? Dan?"

"When you said this crime seemed beyond CJ's resources—you were fishing. Trying to find out how much I knew." He closed his eyes. "Camila...I know it was you."

"I don't know what you're talking about."

"Of course you do. I've been suspicious for some time, but I kept telling myself it couldn't be true. Because you...cared about me." His head fell. "But eventually I had to face facts. You used me. Then you threw me to the wolves."

Camila pressed her hand against her chest. "Dan...sweetheart..."

"Oh, stop. You're making it worse." He stood, then took a few tentative steps toward the sun. "You used CJ as a pawn. You knew he hated his father. You knew he blamed his dad for his sister's death. You knew Belasco had blown a fortune but had a life-insurance policy. I doubt the kid was too hard to persuade. You, my resourceful mayor, have proven time and again that you can accomplish anything."

She looked stricken but didn't speak.

He continued. "You told CJ how to find Anatole. You told him how to create a Bitcoin account."

"I don't have that kind of money."

"CJ found the money. You provided the means."

Her head shook. "You don't know this. You're guessing."

"It was your idea to create the crucifixion. Not only to make it clear this wasn't a suicide. That was already apparent. And not simply to frame me, though you clearly intended that. You wanted a big dramatic tableau that would attract media attention. You wanted the world to believe your enemies had once again tried to lay you low, so you could triumph later. You knew when Marvin was going to strike, so you made sure you had plenty of alibi witnesses. You became a heroic figure and your approval ratings soared, just as you knew they would. You went from being a long shot to the frontrunner overnight. Just as you planned."

She stared at him, lips tight.

"I tried to pretend Sweeney taped our conversation, but it was you. You were on the boat, so planting a recording device was easy. You probably used a phone app. You initiated that conversation about taking Belasco out, knowing full well his days were numbered. You sent it to the cops, knowing your alibi would free you. It was easy for you to snag pieces of scalp from my pillow or comb to be planted at the crime scene. You knew I'd be accused." His voice took on an edge. "That was what you wanted."

"You...don't know what I wanted," she said quietly. "I needed..."

"A patsy? The whole time we were making love, you were planning to set me up to take the fall for your murder."

All at once, words flew from her lips. "I had no choice!"

"Everyone has a choice. And you chose. Poorly."

"I had to eliminate Belasco. He...knew things about me. Threatened to expose me. I had come so far. I couldn't let him destroy everything."

"What did he know?"

She looked down at her hands. "I'd...prefer not to say."

He whirled. "And that may be what makes me maddest of all. Did you think I was so damn fickle I'd care that you turned a few tricks when you were young?"

She stared at him, mouth gaping. "How—" She stopped. "Of course. Your gift."

"More like a curse." He hovered over her. "I know you grew up poor. On the Southside. No family to speak of. No money. But somehow went to college. Made connections. Got into politics." He reached into his backpack. "You know, all holding-cell conversations are recorded, except for attorney conversations. Jazlyn liberated this for me." He handed her the document. "It's a transcript of a conversation you had during your brief stay behind bars. With some prostitutes. They were from a different world. But you didn't distance yourself. In fact, you offered them advise. At one point, you said, 'I know exactly how you feel.'"

Her eyes were watery. "I didn't do it often. Only...when I needed money. More money than I could make flipping burgers. It was a mistake, but I knew so little about the world. Some pimp offered me a chance to make some quick cash, more than I could make in a year at a legit job. So I did it. And I've regretted it ever since."

"Evelyn Belasco told Maria that George had known you a long time. Knew secrets about you."

"And like the loser he was, he threatened to expose me. I think Sweeney was leaning on him. They both wanted me out of the picture. I had to defend myself."

"You didn't have to hire a hitman."

"I thought I did."

His voice dropped. "And you didn't have to throw me into the fire."

She did not reply. She wiped her eyes with the back of her hand. A few moments later, she said, "I suppose you're going to...tell someone?"

He just looked at her.

"Could I persuade you to remain quiet?"

"About murder?"

She gave him a broken smile. "We make a great team."

"Yeah, we did. Till you stabbed me in the heart."

She turned away. "That's fine. I deserved that. Could I... Could I have an hour? To get my things together. Before you call Jake? Or Jazlyn?"

"You won't try to run?"

"I promise."

"At the moment, your promises aren't worth much."

"Where would I go? I would be recognized everywhere."

She had a point. "One hour."

"Thank you." She hesitated, then turned quickly and kissed him on the cheek. "I wasn't faking...everything."

"Just go."

She left through the patio door. A few minutes later, he heard her car drive away.

He threw himself down in a lawn chair. And cried.

And cried and then cried some more, until finally he had no more tears left.

I've survived the worst threat I've ever encountered, he thought. *And now I have nothing left.*

EPILOGUE

More than an hour passed before Maria came through the back patio door. "Mind if I join you?"

Dan barely looked up. "Suit yourself. I doubt I'll be good company."

"That's okay. I'm largely self-sufficient."

He smiled a little. But not nearly enough.

They remained silent for a few minutes. At last, Maria spoke. "I saw Camila leave. Alone. I waited awhile before I came out here."

He nodded.

"She did not look happy. And neither do you. Did...something happen?"

He almost wanted to cry all over again. He supposed there was no reason to keep secrets. It would all come out soon enough. "Yes. Something definitely happened."

"You won't be seeing Camila anymore?"

"I will not."

She raised her chin. "Well, I know this must make you sad, and I'm not pleased about that. But I think you're better off without her."

"Do you now."

"Yes. I never trusted her. Not for one minute."

He chuckled softly, sadly. "It's true. You never did. I assumed that was..." He trailed off.

"Yes?"

"Never mind. Turns out you were wise to have reservations."

"I hope you weren't about to say what I think you were about to say. Because that would be incredibly sexist."

"No. I...forget it."

"I just think you deserve better. Let me be more specific. I think you deserve the best. I know I was a little skeptical about you when we first met, but you've proved what you're made of. Time and time again."

"Thanks."

"There's absolutely no reason for you to be wasting your life away on some woman who only cares about herself. Camila was using you."

He raised an eyebrow. "Oh?"

"You're like the smartest guy on earth, except where it matters. In the courtroom, you're king. In real life, you need a keeper."

"Do I now?"

"You do." She fidgeted, obviously uncomfortable. "You really really do."

"And...have you got any nominations for this position?"

"In fact, I do." Before he even understood what was happening, she slid into his lap and pressed her lips against his.

She wrapped her arms around him and hugged tight. "You'll always have me."

PREVIEW OF JUDGE AND JURY (BOOK 5 OF THE DANIEL PIKE SERIES)

Dan watched as the 500-TEU container ship slowly eased into port, knowing full well that every member of its crew would kill him on sight—if they knew who he was. But he put that thought out of his head. Because he had to meet them. He had no choice.

His father was counting on him. Even though his father had been dead for more than twenty years.

The cargo boat was surprisingly maneuverable. The wind was low and the waves were negligible, so it had no trouble easing into the dock. It didn't need a tug. Its crew was experienced. The boat had already passed through the port authorities and delivered the official cargo listed in its bill of lading about three miles north. But he was convinced there was more on board. He'd spent the last four months collecting information and it had all brought him here. He was certain he was right.

He had to be right.

A few minutes later a middle-aged Hispanic man emerged on the bottom deck and lowered the gangplank. Huge beard. Tattoo of a heart squeezing a dagger. Solid black clothes. This was the man Dan knew they called The Captain. He'd been supervising smuggling operations for a South American cartel for more than a decade. Which was far too long.

Three other men appeared behind The Captain. Large men, burly, tough. Protection, no doubt. Men who had flouted the law so long they only recognized one authority—profit. They made their own law. They killed without thinking about it. They knew how unlikely it was that they would be arrested, and even if they were, they'd be bailed out instantly. Once free, they would disappear, never to appear at trial.

Given that Dan had spent his entire adult life in service to the law, this was a hard reality for him to acknowledge. These men were beyond the law's grasp. And he wanted information from them.

The Captain strolled down the gangplank, maintaining a watchful eye. He found a midpoint on the dock and stopped. The three men positioned themselves around him, forming a vague semicircle. Dan could tell they carried handguns, probably Sig Sauers, beneath their jackets.

He drew in his breath. Now or never. All the chips on the table.

The Captain was waiting.

He emerged from behind one of several small shacks used as offices during operating hours. "You The Captain?"

Even the smile had a swagger. "You the Bank?"

"I am." He nodded toward the black metal briefcase he held, indicating that it contained money, which it did. Damn it—were his knees shaking? He couldn't afford a tell, not now. He needed to look like a cool experienced professional. The Captain would be flattered to know how badly he terrified others, but Dan wasn't interested in delivering that kind of ego-boost.

The Captain strolled closer, his entourage close at hand. He spoke with a thick Spanish accent. "A few questions. Are you a cop?"

"Do I look like a cop?" He wore a black shirt and jeans, with a ballcap pulled down low, several days' stubble, and a pair of eyeglasses he didn't need. He didn't flatter himself that he was world-famous, but it was just possible someone might recognize him. A few months before, he had put a witness on the stand who was smuggled into the country by a human-trafficking cartel, and The Captain had been in charge of that operation too.

"You will please to answer the question."

"I am absolutely not a police officer."

"Are you wearing a wire? Any kind of recording device?"

"I am not."

"Do you have the money?"

"I do."

"Show it to me."

Dan laid the briefcase flat across both arms. He didn't like how that immobilized his arms, made it impossible to defend himself. But he suspected there was not much he could do against these brutes anyway. He was in good shape, exercised regularly, but that was not the same as being an experienced, cold-blooded killer.

He popped open the briefcase. The bound bills fluttered a bit in the breeze. "It's all there."

"Very good. I will take it now."

Dan took a step back. "After you've shown me the goods."

The Captain smirked. "Do you not trust me?"

He did not answer the question. "After you've shown me the goods."

The Captain waved his hand vaguely and pivoted, returning the way he had come. Dan assumed he thought that was sufficient to indicate that he should follow. One of The Captain's bodyguards hung back to make sure he followed. When he didn't walk fast enough, the man, who was at least a foot taller, gave him a shove. "Move."

"Keep your filthy hands off me."

The man's fists clenched.

"Stay cool, Frankenstein. Your boss doesn't want this deal to go sour."

The man growled—actually growled—like a rabid dog. Probably not smart to provoke a monster. But then again, he was playing the role of a professional black-market organ dealer, and he suspected you wouldn't get far in that business if you allowed yourself to be pushed around.

He followed The Captain up the gangplank—but the bodyguard slapped him hard on the back of the head as he passed. Just to make sure he understood the man had his eyes on him.

As if he didn't know that already. They all had their eyes on him. And they were all ready to take him out at the first sign of trouble.

They stepped inside the lower cabin and took a flight of stairs to the fore balcony railing. Why? He didn't see anything here. No carriers, no cases.

The Captain cleared his throat. "Invoice."

One of his associates handed him a crumpled piece of paper. "For delivery upon receipt of payment: sixteen kidneys, eight livers, sixteen corneas and numerous unfertilized eggs. Correct?" He handed the paper to Dan.

He barely glanced at it. "Correct. I want to see the merchandise. I assume you've used a hypothermic solution. How have you stored it? Dry ice? Liquid nitrogen?"

"We use a different kind of container," The Captain said. He pressed what appeared to be a silver bolt on the side of the railing. Dan heard a clicking sound. The hull of the boat vibrated a bit.

A secret hold. He wasn't surprised. This was a smuggling boat, after all. It probably had a dozen hidden nooks and crannies.

The Captain placed his fingers on the edge of a compartment door. It was dark inside—but he heard movement.

"As you can see, a different kind of container. The original container." One of his men shone a flashlight inside the compartment.

Dan's lips parted.

Eight young women were bound and gagged inside what appeared to be a refrigerated box. They were chained to the walls, barely dressed, wrapped in blankets, sitting in filth. Their eyes were wide and frightened. Terrified. They looked as if they hadn't eaten for days.

Dan rubbed his sweaty hands on the sides of his jeans. *Keep your head together,* he told himself. *Bottle it up.* Even though his heart was pounding so hard it threatened to explode, he couldn't let that show. If he revealed his feelings, they'd know he was not the real buyer.

"You will have to develop your own means to remove the organs from their containers," The Captain said, chuckling. "But I'm sure you will think of something. A scalpel, perhaps."

"This was not our arrangement," Dan said, clenching his teeth.

"It was necessary. We could not be certain when we would make port and did not have the resources for long-term storage. We leave the extraction to you."

"This—was not—our arrangement."

The Captain shrugged. "I will make it easier for you. We will kill them now. Then your people can take all the organs you want. Everything on the invoice and more. I understand there is a market for every part imaginable these days. Even for the bones." He glanced toward the largest of his three bodyguards, the one who had hassled Dan. "Kill them."

Dan drew in his breath, crouched, and whispered. "Move. Now."

Four men appeared against the skyline, silhouetted on the rooftops of the onshore office buildings. They were dressed in black but clearly armed. Someone spoke through a bullhorn.

"This is Jacob Kakazu of the SPPD. You are all under arrest. Drop your weapons and prepare to be boarded."

The three bodyguards pulled their guns out and started firing at the shadows. Dan did a drop and roll, then took off down the side of the boat. Gunfire sounded all around him, thudding into the boat and ricocheting off metal railings. One whizzed past his head, far too close. He had to get out of here—

Something grabbed his ankle, yanking him to the floor. He fell with a clatter, banging his chin.

The Captain had him. "You lied to me."

"About being a cop? No. About wearing a wire? Yes." He kicked hard, pushing his captor back.

The Captain lunged. He threw himself on top of Dan, wrestling him down to prevent him from escaping. Behind them, the goons kept firing and dodging, but that wouldn't last forever. They were massively outnumbered.

He needed to do something fast. He wasn't much of a match for The Captain. He certainly wasn't a match for all four of them.

He heard someone running down on the dock below. If he could just stay alive another minute or two…

The Captain grabbed him by the throat. "You think you can cheat me? You think you can steal from me?"

Dan grabbed his wrist, trying to yank the arm away. "You—kidnap women and sell them for parts."

"Worthless whores. If they save a life, it will be their greatest achievement." His fingers tightened. "Killing you will be mine."

"I—don't—think so." He managed to bring a knee up, right between The Captain's legs. The man winced and loosened his grip. Dan seized the opportunity. He threw The Captain off and scrambled to his feet.

Another bullet whizzed by. The bodyguard who had harassed him appeared at his boss's side. "There are too many of them," he reported.

"Have they called the Coast Guard?" The Captain asked.

"The waters are clear."

"Then we must go. I'll start the engines."

"What about him?" He jerked a thumb toward Dan.

The Captain opened a door to the control cabin. He paused only briefly. "Cut him up. Slowly. Then feed him to the sharks." He slammed the door behind him. Barely a second later, he heard the engines engaging.

The bodyguard pressed his gun toward Dan's head.

Dan raised his hands. "You're going to be caught. The FBI and the local police are already here."

"Still time to kill you."

"Why? So you can do time for kidnapping *and* murder."

"Because it will give me pleasure."

Three dark-clad FBI agents emerged from the stairwell. "Freeze."

The bodyguard fired anyway, but Dan had already moved out of the way. An officer tackled the guard amidst a hail of bullets.

"There are two others," Dan said.

The man in the lead disagreed. "They're already down."

"The Captain is inside. He's started the engines."

"He's not going anywhere." The door flew open. The Captain was shoved out the door—by Jake Kakazu, senior detective for the St. Petersburg police department.

Dan collapsed, leaning against the bulkhead. "Jake, this may be the first time I've actually been glad to see you."

"I won't take that personally." He pulled The Captain's wrists back and snapped cuffs on them. "Thank you for your help. That was a gutsy move."

"You promised you'd let me talk to him."

Jake glanced at the frowning FBI agent in charge. "We will honor our agreement. You have one minute."

One minute? Well, he wasn't going to waste it. Dan crouched down and rolled The Captain over. "Do you know who I am?"

"A liar. A weasel. And soon, a dead man."

"No. I'm Daniel Pike. My father was Ethan Pike."

A slow smile spread across The Captain's face. "I have heard of you."

"And I bet you know Conrad Sweeney too."

The Captain didn't take the bait. "I could tell you much about your father."

"Like what?"

"I want a deal. Immunity?"

The FBI agent made a snorting sound. "For giving this lawyer info about his dead dad? I don't think so. Now if you give us information about the cartel-—"

"That will never happen." He turned back to Dan. "But I could help you. There are many important details you do not know."

"Like who framed my father? Who really committed the murder?"

The Captain only smiled.

The FBI agent glanced at his watch. "Okay. Minute's up."

"But I'm not done. I—"

Two more agents hauled The Captain to his feet. "You're under arrest."

"I'll be out before sunset."

"I don't think so." They hauled him toward the stairwell, but he turned and gave Dan one last look. "It seems I need a lawyer. Can you help me?"

Dan's answer was succinct. "Never."

"There is much I could tell you. But you must give me something in return."

"Never."

"Come talk to me later. Perhaps we can reach an...accommodation."

Dan hoped they could get some information out of this man, but it wasn't going to happen tonight. "Someone should release the women. They must be terrified. And get this scumbag out of my sight."

The agents tugged on The Captain's arm, but he remained in place, staring straight into Dan's eyes. "Let me give you a taste of how much I know that you do not, Mr. Pike." He smiled, but it looked more like he was baring his teeth. "You have a sister."

DAN'S RECIPES

Thank goodness Dan got off the hook so he could get back to the kitchen. Want to try his recipe for panko-crusted tempeh? Only takes about 30 minutes to make. Fabulous.

Ingredients (for two servings):
    tempeh (4 oz)
    soba noodles (4 oz)
    panko breadcrumbs (1/3 cup)
    yeast flakes (2 tbsp)
    cornstarch (1/4 cup)
    1 chile pepper
    1 avocado
    1 zucchini or yellow squash
    1 lemon
    tahini (2 tbsp)
    tamari (1 tbsp)
    sesame oil (2 tsp)
    olive oil (1 tbsp)
    vegetable oil (3 tbsp)

Instructions:

1) PREP: Bring a saucepan of salted water to a boil. Halve the lemon. In a bowl, mix half the lemon juice, tamari, agave, tahini, and sesame oil, then add olive oil and 1 tbsp warm water to make a sauce. Whisk until smooth. Add salt to taste.

2) MORE PREP: Peel the zucchini (or squash) into ribbons. Split the avocado and thinly slice the flesh. Thinly slice the pepper. Cut the tempeh into thin triangles. In a bowl or on your cutting board, toss the ribbons with the remaining lemon juice and a dash of salt.

3) COOK: Add the noddles to the boiling water. Cook al dente (4-6 minutes). Drain and run under cool water. Stir in the tahini sauce.

4) COAT: In a bowl, add the cornstarch and 1/4 cup of cold water. Whisk until smooth. Combine the breadcrumbs, 1 tbsp of yeast, and a pinch of salt on a large platter. Dip the tempeh triangles into the cornstarch, then press them into the breadcrumbs to coat both sides.

5) CRISP: Put a nonstick skillet on medium-high heat with 3 tbsp vegetable oil. Add the coated tempeh and cook until golden and crispy, 2-3 minutes on each side. Add salt to taste.

6) SERVE: Put the noodles in bowls. Add the zucchini, avacado, and chile (to taste—it's spicy) and the tempeh. Drizzle with the tamari sauce. Sprinkle with yeast. Enjoy.

ABOUT THE AUTHOR

William Bernhardt is the author of over fifty books, including *The Last Chance Lawyer (#1 Amazon Bestseller)*, the historical novels *Challengers of the Dust* and *Nemesis*, two books of poetry, and the Red Sneaker books on fiction writing. In addition, Bernhardt founded the Red Sneaker Writers Center to mentor aspiring authors. The Center hosts an annual conference (WriterCon), small-group seminars, a newsletter, and a bi-weekly podcast. He is also the owner of Balkan Press, which publishes poetry and fiction as well as the literary journal *Conclave*.

Bernhardt has received the Southern Writers Guild's Gold Medal Award, the Royden B. Davis Distinguished Author Award (University of Pennsylvania) and the H. Louise Cobb Distinguished Author Award (Oklahoma State), which is given "in recognition of an outstanding body of work that has profoundly influenced the way in which we understand ourselves and American society at large." In 2019, he received the Arrell Gibson Lifetime Achievement Award from the Oklahoma Center for the Book.

In addition Bernhardt has written plays, a musical (book and score), humor, children stories, biography, and puzzles. He has edited two anthologies (*Legal Briefs* and *Natural Suspect*) as fundraisers for The Nature Conservancy and the Children's Legal Defense Fund. In his spare time, he has enjoyed surfing, digging for dinosaurs, trekking through the Himalayas, paragliding, scuba diving, caving, zip-lining over the canopy of the Costa Rican rain forest, and jumping out of an airplane at 10,000 feet.

In 2017, when Bernhardt delivered the keynote address at the San Francisco Writers Conference, chairman Michael Larsen noted that in addition to penning novels, Bernhardt can "write a sonnet, play a sonata, plant a garden, try a lawsuit, teach a class, cook a gourmet meal, beat you at Scrabble, and work the *New York Times* crossword in under five minutes."

ALSO BY WILLIAM BERNHARDT

The Daniel Pike Novels

The Last Chance Lawyer

Court of Killers

Trial by Blood

Twisted Justice

Judge and Jury

Final Verdict

The Ben Kincaid Novels

Primary Justice

Blind Justice

Deadly Justice

Perfect Justice

Cruel Justice

Naked Justice

Extreme Justice

Dark Justice

Silent Justice

Murder One

Criminal Intent

Death Row

Hate Crime

Capitol Murder

Capitol Threat

Capitol Conspiracy

Capitol Offense

Capitol Betrayal

Justice Returns

Other Novels

Challengers of the Dust

The Game Master

Nemesis: The Final Case of Eliot Ness

Dark Eye

Strip Search

Double Jeopardy

The Midnight Before Christmas

Final Round

The Code of Buddyhood

The Red Sneaker Series on Writing

Story Structure: The Key to Successful Fiction

Creating Character: Bringing Your Story to Life

Perfecting Plot: Charting the Hero's Journey

Dynamic Dialogue: Letting Your Story Speak

Sizzling Style: Every Word Matters

Powerful Premise: Writing the Irresistible

Excellent Editing: The Writing Process

Thinking Theme: The Heart of the Matter

What Writers Need to Know: Essential Topics

Dazzling Description: Painting the Perfect Picture

The Fundamentals of Fiction (video series)

Poetry

The White Bird

The Ocean's Edge

For Young Readers

Shine

Princess Alice and the Dreadful Dragon

Equal Justice: The Courage of Ada Sipuel

The Black Sentry

Edited by William Bernhardt

Legal Briefs: Short Stories by Today's Best Thriller Writers

Natural Suspect: A Collaborative Novel of Suspense

Made in the USA
Coppell, TX
07 August 2021

60101575R00194